THE
BOOK OF
MOTHER

A Novel

VIOLAINE HUISMAN

Translated from the French by
Leslie Camhi

SCRIBNER

New York   London   Toronto   Sydney   New Delhi

Scribner

An Imprint of Simon & Schuster, Inc.

1230 Avenue of the Americas

New York, NY 10020

Originally published in France in 2018 by Éditions Gallimard as *Fugitive parce que reine*

Excerpt of "Sickly Autumn" from *Alcools: Poems by Guillaume Apollinaire*, English translation © 1995 by Donald Revell. Published by Wesleyan University Press and reprinted with permission.

First Scribner hardcover edition October 2021

SCRIBNER and design are registered trademarks of The Gale Group, Inc., used under license by Simon & Schuster, Inc., the publisher of this work.

For information about special discounts for bulk purchases, please contact Simon & Schuster Special Sales at 1-866-506-1949 or business@simonandschuster.com.

The Simon & Schuster Speakers Bureau can bring authors to your live event. For more information, or to book an event, contact the Simon & Schuster Speakers Bureau at 1-866-248-3049 or visit our website at www.simonspeakers.com.

Interior design by Wendy Blum

Printed in Italy

1 3 5 7 9 10 8 6 4 2

Library of Congress Cataloging-in-Publication Data has been applied for.

ISBN 978-1-9821-0878-6
ISBN 978-1-9821-0880-9 (ebook)

For my sister

PART I

ON THE DAY THE BERLIN WALL came down, I was ten; television screens all over the world glowed with images of people cheering and chanting, swarms of men and women dancing and crying and raising victory signs in front of crumbling stones and debris and clouds of dust; in France, we attended this historic event via the evening news, with fadeouts to the somber face of the anchorman, whom we'd invited to sit down to dinner with us—at least those among us who *were* sitting down to dinner, who still followed that family ritual and for whom the eight o'clock news had replaced the saying of grace as a sort of prayer for the Republic. I could tell, by the way the pitch of the anchorman's voice fell, that something serious was going on, yet despite his explanations, the geopolitical significance of all this chaos was entirely lost on me. I had no idea of the issues at stake. Still, I was transfixed by the footage, riveted to our television set, in which I discerned—past the glare of the screen, among the ruins, the debris, the rubble—traces of my mother: her mangled face, her scattered body parts, her ashes. Up to that point, I'd admired my mother blindly, rapturously. But now a shadow had fallen over her image. Maman had sunk into a depression so severe that she had been hospitalized by force, for months. After having been lied to regarding the reasons for her sudden disappearance, I was informed that Maman was manic-depressive. The words all ran together— your-mother-is-manic-depressive—a sentence pronounced by one

1

adult or another, one of those useless grown-up sentences that only added to my distress. I rolled the words around on my tongue; they became the leitmotif of my torment. Manic-depressive. It didn't mean anything. Except Maman had disappeared from one day to the next. My memories of the events preceding her flight are probably too fragmentary and disjointed to weave into a coherent narrative, but the explanations offered by the adults around me were both implausible and unacceptable. In the end, no one knows my childhood better than I do, apart from my sister, who is two years older and recalls slightly different episodes from the epic of our youth. Only one point continues to elude us: the precise moment of our mother's collapse. The definitive incident, if indeed there was one, seems to have slipped away from both of us, leaving behind only a vague and ominous sense that whatever precipitated her fall almost took us with her. In the absence of any specific catalyst, this memory will have to do: a car crash on the way to or from school, with my sister up front in the death seat and me in back, not wearing a seat belt (as usual), and Maman, stopped at a red light where the avenue George V meets the Champs-Élysées, suddenly accelerating into the intersection as tires screeched and people screamed. It's impossible to tell now how many cars smashed into us in the pileup but there were enough to total our little green Opel.

We were used to Maman's sporty driving habits. She was constantly running late, and she sometimes climbed onto the sidewalks when the roads were backed up, a time-tested method for avoiding traffic jams. Cigarette dangling from her left hand, she'd scream at pedestrians: Get out of my way! We're late! If she hesitated before taking the emergency shoulder lane on the highway, it was only when she suspected cops were around—Look out!—and if the cops did pull us over while she was driving on the sidewalk, or heading the wrong way down a one-way street, or running several red lights and stop signs, all the while insulting numerous drivers, cyclists, and other assholes, my sister and I had been instructed to pretend that we were deathly ill. She would then claim that her two daughters— or one of us, in which case the other one had to assume a worried expression—required urgent medical attention, we were on our way to the hospital, it was a matter of life and death. This strategy worked sometimes, but mostly because of the charm offensive that accompanied it, in which my mother's beauty played a starring role. Maman was one of the most beautiful women to have ever walked the face of the Earth, swore all those who knew her at the height of her splendor, and her beauty was almost as fatal to Maman herself as to the men and women who fell under its sway. It was no surprise that Maman drove like a madwoman, the rules of the road were purely theoretical to her, and pointlessly annoying, although she would, if she saw a truck bearing down on us as we swerved into the wrong lane, retreat: Oh well, he's rather big, that one! But the day she hurled us into the Champs-Élysées she betrayed no interest in self-preservation. I still don't know by what miracle we survived.

WITH MAMAN IN THE HOSPITAL, we landed first at the home of friends. Our parents had been separated for a number of years by then—something to do with my father chasing a piece of ass, our mother had told us—and my mother had remarried; later on she would explain that it was the disastrous breakup of that new marriage that had triggered her collapse. Our father was not exactly thrilled with the idea of having sole custody of his daughters, so every other option had to be exhausted before arriving at the inevitable conclusion that we couldn't continue to be tossed from one home to the next. My sister and I were happy to be staying with our classmates—or at least, we weren't unhappy with that particular aspect of our fate; on the whole, we were desperate. Our friends were then, are now, and always will be our chosen family, a family we built for ourselves. At twelve and ten, my sister and I suddenly had to manage on our own, without Maman, and our makeshift families would prove to be our greatest support.

Oh fuck off! was one of my mother's refrains, as was ordering us to go fuck ourselves or to fucking leave her alone, to stop fucking around, to understand that she didn't give a fuck about our little moral dilemmas or the concerns of a couple of spoiled brats. Oh will you please fuck off! Who gives a shit about your stupid problems! Maman's diatribes didn't build to that climax—that was their starting point. My sister and I were so often subject to her harangues that from the opening notes, we'd avoid looking each other in the eye; we'd look at our feet instead. Let her have her say, above all, don't look up—that was our rule. And no laughing, not even when her tirades became extravagant to the point of hilarity, to the point where we had to pinch ourselves to keep from giggling. We'd try to appear contrite, repentant, even when she'd hit us with the clincher, the craziest line of all: You do realize, don't you, that I wiped your asses for years! That sentence, a classic in her repertoire, amounted to proof positive that the woman was nuts. How could we take such a declaration seriously? We hadn't asked for any of this, above all, we hadn't asked to be born to such a lunatic! The expression served to remind us that, in fact, we weren't responsible for all of her suffering. These speeches, always delivered with the same feverish indignation, all began more or less the same way:

4

You self-righteous little shit, if only you knew how much I've done for you! You ingrate! You can't even begin to suspect the number of sacrifices I've made for you and your sister. Who are you to judge me for my lapses? Do you know anyone who's perfect? Who? Just who do you think you are, you sanctimonious little cunt? You do realize, don't you, that I wiped your asses for years? No, obviously not. Well, I couldn't care less about your stupid drama. Deal with your own shit, for once. And we'll see who comes crying for help after you've finally managed to do me in. I do what I can, get it, I do the best I can, and if that's not enough for you, have a look around to see if you can find a better mother. In the meantime, Maman does what she can, Maman is sick and tired, Maman has had it up to here, and Maman is a human being, by the way, and Maman says: Fuck off!

In fact, at the time we didn't realize that for Maman to have changed our diapers, to have wiped our asses, wasn't something to be taken for granted. For Maman, being a good-enough mother didn't come naturally. Given the course of her life, her illnesses, her past, when faced with an infant's incessant demands, with the mind-numbing work and emotional upheavals of motherhood, with the identity crisis that becoming a mother had entailed for her, she could only respond violently, unpredictably, and destructively, but also with all the love that was missing from her own childhood and that she dreamed of giving and receiving in return. That insane love, that almost intolerable passion for and from two brats who were annoying at almost every age; that boundless love that would outlast everything, transcend everything, forgive everything; the love that led her to call us (when we weren't little shits, or bitches, or cunts) my adored darlings whom I love madly—that love kept her going for as long as she could.

5

My sister and I had a formula for this love, an expression that functioned like a spell: Darling Maman, I love you like crazy for my whole life and for all eternity. That sentence, if we managed to answer one of her tirades with it, had the power to dissolve her anger and transform her mood. Suddenly she'd calm down, be reassured, knowing that we loved her enough to respond to her attacks with an outpouring of affection. The antidote to her rage wasn't sobriety—it was veneration. We loved her more than anything, and that proof of adoration was sufficient to pacify her and soften her tone. Yes, we loved her and she loved us. The storm would pass with a gentle caress on the back, a kiss on the neck, a shower of kisses, more and more kisses.

Finally, inevitably, we landed at Papa's house. This was after a brief stopover at Grandma and Grandpa's—Maman's mother and stepfather—who couldn't very well drive us every morning from the suburb of Montreuil to our school at the far end of the 15th arrondissement, because Grandma and Grandpa worked! And they were not taxi drivers! They explained to Papa that if he wished to send his chauffeur for us—Papa had a company car at his disposal—then he should go right ahead. That the question of who should house us was a source of conflict was not lost on me. During our stay at Papa's place, I locked myself in the bathroom and wept. How can you be such a crybaby, Maman had scolded me throughout my childhood, when she found me sniveling. Stop crying, for fuck's sake! What, you don't know why you're crying? Want me to smack you, so you'll have a real reason to cry? Of course, Maman was a hypocrite. She herself would cry at the drop of a hat, not all the time, of course, but when the season of tears arrived, it was a veritable monsoon. It's from Maman that I've inherited the annoying habit of leaving a trail of tissues behind me wherever I go, and when she was in one of her weepy phases, her tissues would leave damp marks on the furniture, the couches, the beds, and the pockets of her jeans, the disgusting jeans that she no longer bothered to wash and that she never changed out of, because she no longer had the strength to decide what to wear.

WITH MY MOTHER GONE, I lost all sense of time, the minutes and hours seemed too long in themselves to imagine them adding up to days, weeks, or months. Someone explained to us that Maman was ill—so there was something worse than manic-depressive after all, there was ill, your mother is ill. The adjective, in this context, had nothing to do with a temporary indisposition, the type of routine childhood illness we might have experienced in the past. Rather, this ill seemed definitive, final, ringed with darkness. It no longer served to describe a transitory state, with specific symptoms; it drew a line around her whole being. It was probably, I thought, a euphemism— probably they weren't telling me the truth, they were continuing to lie to me to obscure the fact that Maman was gone for good. If I've doubted my memory at times, if I've worried, with the distance of years, about exaggerating the despair I felt then, I have proof of my desperation in the form of a poem that I wrote to my mother when I was ten, and whose first lines read: *Maman, maman / You who love me so / Why, without telling me, would you go?*

It was during that very autumn of my mother's disappearance that I discovered Apollinaire:

How much I love o season your clamor
The apples falling to earth

7

The wind and forest weeping
Their tears in autumn leaf by leaf
The leaves
Trampled
A train
Passing
Life
Disposed of

The transience of being, the sense of slipping from existence, the meter that captures that fleetingness, embodies, in verse, life's inexorable passing; that poem, in my memory, merges with a walk in the woods near my grandmother's country house, when a friend of Maman's—the first one to dare—tried to explain to us what had happened to her. It was November, the light was pale, at our feet were strips of gold the chestnuts had set down along our path. In the intermingling of poetry, conversation, and branches, a timid autumn sun broke through the canopy, tearing a hole in my heart.

That Christmas, like every other Christmas, my sister and I were buried in presents, snowed under with packages wrapped in brightly colored paper and encircled with ribbons, all of it laid out under a fir tree decorated—by whom? Who knows. How could the adults in our life—and Papa above all—have had the audacity to prepare such a holiday for us? We wanted Maman for Christmas, was that so hard to understand? We didn't want any presents when we couldn't have the only one that counted—Maman. Where was Maman? And when would she return?

Christmas was always a calvary for us, but that year, we were obliged to proceed through all the Stations of the Cross, and at the

8

time I couldn't believe—and I still can't believe—that we were forced into pretending that we loved our presents, that they were sufficient, so as not to hurt Papa's feelings. It was all meant to please him, and we mustn't upset him, he was the only one we had left. We weren't prepared to be orphans, so we did our best to play along, to smile and say thank you, and to go into raptures as much as possible, so that Papa wouldn't throw us out in a fit of rage. We couldn't let our ingratitude betray us—not the ingratitude Maman had regularly accused us of, but the eternal ingratitude of children (because as everyone knows, children are always ungrateful, their lack of appreciation for the many sacrifices their parents have made for them is an established fact). We celebrated Christmas even though Papa was a bit Jewish around the edges, as Maman said. He said he was an atheist.

The defining event of my father's life was the Second World War. The son of a Cabinet member and former Vice President of the Republic, from a young age Papa had grown up in the Élysée Palace and, later on, in official residences of comparable luxury, but when the war broke out, the Judaism of his ancestors had nearly cost him his life. His father, dismissed from his post and banished, found himself penniless. Papa recalled that one day in the middle of the war, when they were hiding out under an assumed name in Marseille, his father informed him that if by the end of the month he couldn't find the money to support his wife and children, they'd all go throw themselves off the dock of the Old Port. I had noted, in my father's personality, the ravages of this psychic wound, the extent to which he remained scarred by the unspeakable experience of fearing he would be killed because of his religion, of losing everything from one day to the next. Between the difficulty of our respective childhoods there could be no competition. The disappearance of

Maman, for my sister and me, could not compare with the war's horror for my father.

Maman finally returned, but returned unable to sleep or eat, returned in a semi-comatose state, shaky and haggard, in a fog of antipsychotics. She said they'd put so many needles in her ass at the Sainte-Anne psychiatric ward that she had to sleep sideways. She told us over and over about the barbaric treatments to which she'd been subjected, offering details that were both disturbingly realistic—the smells, the pains—and unimaginable. The scenes she described belonged to a theater of cruelty, whose naturalistic elements served only to confuse her audience: a glassy-eyed witch smashing her cigarette butts into the pot of a crimson plant; the nurses, their faces overly made-up, lurching around with giant syringes; a ghost floating over a sea of piss. The courage and willpower she'd needed to free herself from that prison, that pharmaceutical straitjacket, we had no idea! She had fought the sons of bitches in their white coats—fought with her bare hands!—she had forced herself to take cold showers and hide pills up her sleeves or under her mattress. She had gone along with their absurd rules, she'd done violence to herself in letting herself be treated like a doormat, turning herself into a human dish towel, to show them that she was very cooperative and calm, entirely calm and docile. In her heart of hearts, she knew that her rebellion would be more likely to succeed if she could hide the traces of it. So she lay low. She bartered with other patients on the sly to make calls at the pay phone because she didn't have a dime, not even to buy herself some smokes, and there was no one, no one around to help her! She called all her most trusted friends in Paris—*all* meaning the two or three she hadn't alienated or outraged—trying to at least get herself transferred to the capital, because she had been hospitalized at first in

Tulle, the town that was closest to the little village in Corrèze where she had taken refuge, before being hauled off, bound in a straitjacket, et cetera. Maman had bought a house in Corrèze with money that she had stolen from Papa. It had taken her some time to get the cash together. While they were still married, little by little she had swiped bills in small denominations from the giant bundles of banknotes that he kept in his safe and never counted—money was only worthwhile for the pleasure one had in spending it, and never to be hoarded— until at last she had amassed the sum needed for a security deposit on the house of her dreams. It was a ruin with a wonderful slate roof full of holes, on a hilltop overlooking a microscopic village in the Massif Central, one of the most rural areas of France, the middle of the country, far away from everything except a couple of extinct volcanoes and the national center of porcelain manufacturing. She had asked Papa to buy it with her, for her, but he'd told her that she couldn't be serious, that she was nuts, that he'd never set foot in such a dump, in Nowheresville, no way, what a crazy idea!

That house in Corrèze, which she had restored with boundless passion—and by withdrawing still more bundles of bills from the safe—was her paradise, a haven surrounded by a granite wall, which she had helped the masons to build, stone by stone, and along which she had planted ivy that she waited impatiently to see throw itself over the other side of the enclosure. That house, which she called the house of happiness, whose uneven stones were like a projection of her gap-toothed smile—that house was her fortress. There she felt protected not only from outside attack but also from self-destruction. She felt invincible there, unshakable. So it was only logical that, when she felt herself hunted down by the men in white coats, threatened by demons who had pursued her since early childhood, she took off for Corrèze to save herself. She'd borrowed a friend's car so as not to be spotted, so they'd lose track of her—them! her enemies!—and she drove all night, arriving at dawn in Puypertus, the village where the house was situated. There, she sought shelter at the home of some neighboring farmers. I was astonished that Papa had thought to go looking for her there, I was astonished because doing so demanded not only considerable presence of mind on his part, but also a deep understanding of her psychology. I understood later, piecing together fragmentary stories told to me by Papa, Maman, and others, that it had been Maman's last husband who had told Papa that she must have been hiding out there but that neither her husband nor Grandma wanted to go searching for her—they were both afraid of being physically attacked, and perhaps rightly so. Papa shared their anxiety, but somebody had to intervene. To get Grandma to sign the form authorizing Maman's involuntary hospitalization, Papa had sworn to high heaven that Maman would never know a thing about it—his mother-in-law's fear of her daughter's vengeance was that great. You must be kidding, Maman had said when Papa—acting out of sadism? or duplicity? or just curious to see her reaction?—told her about her mother's fear. Really! It's comical. You'd think they were dealing with a war criminal. Why not Hitler, while we're at it? When Papa finally arrived at the farmer's house—other neighbors having informed him as to her whereabouts—Maman emerged with a hunting rifle aimed at the van. Well, how could I have known that it was loaded? What a moron I am, I should have pulled the trigger! I would have been better off shooting at those assholes, I would have made out better in the end. For one thing, I would have had a trial—the presumption of innocence, apparently that was beyond them, never heard of it, presum-what? I declare the accused guilty as charged! They put me on trial behind my back, it's so much easier to slander someone when the accused isn't around to defend herself. Go directly to jail, do not pass Go! I'm telling you, I wouldn't have been any worse off in prison, I might have at least made some friends, whereas in the loony bin, I was fucked.

When Maman came back to us, her mind still hazy and dark, she confessed that she was the one who had forbidden us to visit her in the hospital. She justified it by saying that she feared that seeing her there would traumatize us. In the midst of total collapse, she had held on to her position, her role as mother, her dignity and authority. Whatever else happened, she had to remain a mother, she couldn't let go of that. I pictured the hospital—the hospital, not the clinic, an important distinction—as it had appeared to me on-screen a short time after her departure (when her diagnosis was repeated to me at every turn, your mother is ill, your mother is manic-depressive, your mother is ill, mentally ill) in *One Flew over the Cuckoo's Nest*, which happened to be on television just then. That the parents of the friend with whom I was staying at the time allowed me to watch this film, dazed and numb with fear as I was, no longer surprised me. Clearly, the adults surrounding us were either scatterbrained and irresponsible, or blind, or overwhelmed. A bunch of morons! Maman might have said. Her descriptions of psychiatric treatment matched in every detail the treatment Jack Nicholson received, at least as I recall it. I have never watched that film again.

ONCE HOME, MAMAN WOULD frequently ask us to forgive her for having yet again almost set fire to the kitchen by allowing the strange stew that was supposed to be our dinner burn. It was the fault of those damn antipsychotics, she said, she couldn't get over them, they'd leached her brain, it was all scrambled inside, there was too much static on the line. We told her it didn't matter, don't worry, above all don't beat yourself up over such a small thing, we couldn't care less about dinner. It's no big deal, Maman. Don't cry, Maman, it's no big deal! She burst into tears, sobbing that she couldn't take it anymore, it was too difficult, too hard, she'd never manage. Don't worry, Maman, we know you can do it! Look, everything's fine, you're doing really well, it's just a casserole, it's nothing! We tried hard to convince her, we exhausted ourselves trying to restore her confidence in herself and in the future. But we weren't sure about anything; we weren't even sure we'd find her alive the next morning. So our bedtime ritual took hours to unfold, a prelude to the nightmares that never failed to visit us in our sleep.

The apartment we moved into the following fall, just before school started, had three bedrooms along a hallway: my sister's room, my room, and Maman's room. At bedtime, Maman would first go kiss my sister, and then me, and that configuration—my bedroom right between theirs—would come to define my entire adolescence. Maman began by saying good night to my sister, and I'd overhear them talking, faintly—though in fact, I'm not entirely sure that I really heard what they were saying, I remember only that I tried to listen in on them, and that the ritual went on for ages, centuries, light-years. I would count the minutes as they passed or rather, as they dragged on, huddled under my comforter, imagining that I was counting schools of multicolored fish, pausing to describe their hues in vocabulary that I hoped was fancy—opaline, cyan blue, vermilion. When I finally heard Maman's footsteps coming down the hallway, I knew I had to tough it out awhile longer. Because as soon as Maman had one foot out the door of my sister's room, my sister called her back. Maman! One more kiss! Maman, wait! I've still got something to tell you! Maman, I swear, it's superimportant! Maman, come back! And when at last Maman went out, leaving the door slightly ajar, just the right amount—no, that's too closed, yes, just like that, that's good—when the last kiss had been bestowed, and then the very last kiss, and then the very very last, the chorus of See-you-tomorrow-Mamans took over. This chorus was repeated at least a hundred times with some slight variations—See you tomorrow morning, Maman!—to which Maman had to respond Yes, sweetheart! in a tone that was at once clear, open, and decisive, otherwise they'd have to start again from zero. I've never asked my sister if there was a magic figure, if she counted the number of times she repeated that sentence. I don't believe she did. I think the figure must have corresponded to a certain emotional temperature, and measured by that thermometer, the fever was always running dangerously high. When at last it was my turn and Maman had finally crossed the threshold of my bedroom to come tuck me in, more often than not she would have to return to the side of her elder daughter, who still had a little something to tell her, something superimportant, absolutely essential. She wanted to let Maman know, using the coded language they had developed between them for these occasions, that on waking, she expected Maman to be there. With the puny means at her disposal, my sister was trying her hardest to make Maman swear that she would survive the night.

But you promised me! Before the hospital, that's how we would have chided Maman if she tried to get out of finishing a story she'd started telling us a few days earlier. There would be serious consequences if Maman didn't finish the story tomorrow! It was the game of a child who mimics the authority of the parent, because the parent in question, having broken her word, finds her status temporarily diminished; after the hospital, we didn't play that game anymore. We were no longer certain of the rules, we would no longer play around with our mother's place in our lives. Maman had collapsed, was languishing on a corner of the couch, a defeated mess; we saw her struggling to get out of bed, or limply pretending to have dinner, or passed out in the hallway. Very early on, without having taken a single first aid course, we learned how to revive her. We knew a few simple techniques that she herself had taught us: have her sniff some vinegar, wipe her face with a damp washcloth, slap her, lift her eyelids, shout her name, shout it louder, ask if she can hear us, and when she wakes, ask if she can understand us, ask what day it is—no, too difficult—ask if she knows who we are. Maman, do you recognize me? Say my name! Who am I? You're my daughter, you're my darling daughters. What happened to me? You fainted, Maman. It'll be okay, don't worry, it'll be okay. When we couldn't manage to wake her, we'd call the fire department; the firemen, with their impressive uniforms and their EMT kit, always arrived very quickly. They'd put an oxygen mask on her, and watching her regain consciousness, we ourselves began to breathe again, we exhaled a deep sigh, midway between relief and exasperation. Maman bawled us out for having called the fire department for no reason, it was nothing at all, everything was fine, look, everything's fine! She'd give us a dirty look and, with a knowing air, explain to them that she'd stupidly skipped lunch, her blood pressure had just dropped a little, it was nothing, really, no reason at all to bother them. She'd gather herself up and adopt a serious look, the one she used for officials or our teachers, chin up, radiating maternal authority. Girls, don't you have homework to do? Come on, come on, get to work! But if the firemen insisted, as a precaution, on taking her to the hospital, Maman would start to scream:

Not the hospital! Don't take me back to the hospital! I don't want to go to the hospital! No, not the hospital! Then my sister and I would say calmly to the worried firemen, Please, leave her be. She doesn't want to go to the hospital. The question that inevitably arose—what would become of us if they took Maman away?—always resolved things in her favor. Is there another adult living here? these great big guys would ask us gently. Well, no. There was just us. Maman and the two of us, now thirteen and eleven years old.

Papa didn't live with us, but he stopped by every night. That is, Papa visited us behind the bars of our cage, us, his adorable little girls and his still-beautiful ex-wife. (I so hoped to discover, on waking, that this separation was just a bad dream. I fell asleep praying to the half-worn-away Hello Kitty decals on the railing of my bunk bed that Papa would stay, that Papa would come back to live with us.) When we were younger, he usually arrived precisely on time to tuck us in and kiss us good night—unless his schedule didn't allow for it. After Maman had come back from the hospital, he'd stop by during the hour between homework and dinner, when we'd managed to finish our assignments and Maman had miraculously prepared something to eat. Papa, too, loved us madly and for all eternity, and he told us so frequently, both he and Maman regarded their offspring rapturously and with delight. We were stupefyingly beautiful and intelligent, we were perfection incarnate. Thinking to please Maman, he would declare emphatically: Our girls have their father's intelligence and their mother's beauty! It always surprised him that she was offended by this. He never understood what, in that sentence, could possibly displease her. The moment Papa arrived, we were under orders to put down our pens as at the end of an exam, to hang up the phone, to close our books and notebooks, to get out of the bathtub or immediately stop whatever we were doing and fix our hair to make ourselves presentable. He had honored us with his presence; we must bow before him. If he was the absolute monarch of Maman's heart, we were his courtiers, his faithful vassals. The moment he stepped over the threshold of our apartment we bent ourselves to his wishes, we made sure that he felt at home, that he was made comfortable. Seated at his feet, we listened to the stories about his day or about his past with which he entertained us, we listened without interruption, even when we might have been hungry or tired, even when we might have been sick of listening to Papa tell and retell us his stories. Our desires and needs were of no concern to Maman and Papa in this ritual. It was about them; we were pawns in their game.

Even though she had remarried after their separation, Maman had never stopped loving our father—adoring him, adulating him, idolizing him—to the point where this passion dominated her daily life. She was utterly dedicated to it and made sure to communicate it to her daughters so that, if need be, they could act as her replacements. So we, her daughters, *their* daughters, had to somehow explain to ourselves their disastrous exchanges, explain them away, keeping their relationship strong in our minds, and strong it certainly was. There usually came a moment during the hour Papa spent at our home when Maman said she needed to speak with him privately. They locked themselves in the living room, which was separated from the entry foyer by a double door with glazed glass panes which reverberated with their voices, so that from our rooms on the other side of the apartment we could hear most of their secret conversation. In general, they argued about money, it was a matter of big bucks, Papa would say, because your mother spends sums that are astronomical, gargantuan, completely insane and without reason, and utterly inconsistent, so that nobody understands what the money buys or to whom it goes. At this rate, it's tantamount to a magic trick—a disappearing act! Papa paid our rent and all bills related to our housing, and the butcher, and the grocer, and the pharmacist, with whom Maman kept a running tab. And even with all that, she found a way to burn through her monthly alimony—a tidy sum—in less than a week! The truth was that our father couldn't care less about money. He was no better at arithmetic than she was, he owned a company that generated a lot of capital as if by miracle, and he never imposed any limits on his own lavish spending. Papa would never even have realized that Maman had stolen many tens of thousands of francs from him if she herself hadn't told him in a fit of rage. For Papa, calculating whether he could afford something meant seeing if his accountant criticized him for it, and he found it tiresome to be continually reprimanded by his own staff because of his ex-wife's extravagance. Maman was constantly overdrawn at the bank, threatened with bankruptcy. And here we go again. For fuck's sake, what a pain in the ass, really, these damn problems with cash and the bank, it's like the driver's license, once you've been blacklisted, it's a nightmare! Afterward you spend years lugging around the file, it follows you like the plague, and you have to work like a dog to be put back in good standing. Papa and Maman argued a lot. I often had the impression that the main reason Papa came by was to get Maman all wound up, like a clock. He slammed the door as he left, triggering, like a spring, the emergence of the cuckoo. Cuckoo! Maman never fainted during Papa's visits; she always waited until he had left to collapse in our arms. The vaudevillian nature of these marital rows—between two people who were no longer even married—could turn hysterical at times, they were so outsize, so grotesque. They tore each other's hair out, they threatened to tear each other's eyes out, he warned that he was about to die of a heart attack, she threatened to end things once and for all, and then he'd come out with the clincher, which might have seemed conclusive, had we not heard it so many times before: You're a living Hell! It was really something to hear his tortured moan, his tormented squealing. The next day, he'd come back to visit Hell, again.

During all this time, we went to school like other children our age. We were conscientious and hardworking. We didn't mention anything to anyone, we hid the difficulties of our home life as much as possible, fearing that Maman might be carted off again. She had lost custody of us during her stay at the Sainte-Anne psychiatric ward. I never really understood what our custody had to do with it, but Maman claimed that Papa had used her spell in the loony bin as an excuse to get custody of us so that he could deduct us from his taxes, but above all, above all, above all, so that he could use it as a means of blackmailing her. Well yes, you see, he grants me the favor of raising my own daughters! He very generously allows me the right to raise my daughters under my own roof, because you see, he has that piece of paper, he just has to raise his little finger and off you go, move along, there's nothing more to see! I'm entitled to nothing. Zilch. It's his charity alone that gives me the right to exercise my role as mother, it's by the grace of his immense mercy, his incomparable generosity! He's entitled to everything: he's got the money, the connections, the social standing, the power, and custody of you. Bravo. He's got it all wrapped up. As for me, all I'm entitled to is to shut up, to crawl like a worm and shed tears of gratitude for his largesse. Thank you, O my great ex-husband, for allowing me to raise our daughters! You asshole!

In fact, we did well at school. We weren't interested in excelling for our own sakes, it was a matter of Maman's survival, it was about her proving to that bastard, that swine, that god, that king, that we were the best possible daughters and she the best possible mother in the world. It was a matter of survival for all three of us that we were the most beautiful, the most intelligent, the most devoted, the funniest, the most discreet, the most independent, the most reasonable, the most receptive of girls, the most perfect in every way, and that we intuited, that we anticipated at all times, the desires of Papa and Maman. Getting good grades wasn't the hard part, except for the fact that we had so little time to read and do our homework. Our house was a mess. Between Papa's visits, Maman's conflagrations in the kitchen, the firemen, and the parade of lovers—men, women, young people and old, junkies, drunks, the longtime friend, the newest encounter, the recent recruit—just finding the time and space to study for a history test or prepare our Latin translations was something of an achievement. We lived in a fine apartment in the 7th arrondissement of Paris. We belonged to the *grande bourgeoisie*, we were upper-crust. Often we'd find neighborhood bums having a drink in our living room when we got home from school, but even so we were wealthy and well turned out. My sister and I attended the top high schools in Paris: Louis-le-Grand and Henri IV, respectively. We'd ask to stay in school after classes were over in order to work in peace. We'd pretend to Maman that we had a group presentation to prepare so that we could go study for exams at our friends' houses. One year, Papa was being named an Officer of the Legion of Honor—the acting President of the Republic, François Mitterrand himself, would be awarding him his medal, pinning it on his chest. We had very humbly asked Maman for permission *not* to attend the ceremony, because it was taking place during finals week and we preferred to study. Maman let us skip the spectacle; why should her daughters prostrate themselves before such trifles? It was an error for which she never forgave herself, and only half-forgave us. We should have gone, so that at least we could have been photographed, so that our presence there would have been recorded, so that we would figure in the historical documents pertaining to this family to which Maman herself had never really belonged. She had never been accepted by them, let alone respected by them, even as a married woman, even with two children. Yet though she'd been erased, she certainly had no intention of letting her daughters be forgotten. Her daughters would have a place of note in this family. Mark my words! With my daughters things will be different!

A faint odor of death lingered on Maman's lips when she came to tuck me in at night. There were flecks of foam at the corners of her mouth; her breath had a musty smell. Her complexion had been blanched by sadness, her eyes clouded by doubt, rage, anguish, and more doubt again; her dirty blond hair hung limp; her sharp cheekbones pressed into my still-round cheeks. Once she'd left my room, the odor of her breath, laced with alcohol and pills, clung to my sheets. Her signature scents, Fidji by Guy Laroche, First by Van Cleef & Arpels, languished in the back of a closet. In the medicine cabinet, the various eaux de toilette that, before her hospital stay, she'd worn with haughty coquetry, had been relegated to last place on the shelves. Everywhere there were bottles of pills. The *Physician's Desk Reference* had always been a kind of bible at our house, but as for looking up the properties of these drugs, I didn't dare. I so loved discovering new words in the big Larousse dictionary that sat in our library, but I forbade myself from looking up the ingredients or the side effects of Rohypnol, Lexomil, Théralène, Voltarène, Di-Antalvic, Prontalgine, Stilnox, Haldol, Fluanxol, Spasfon, Débridat, Augmentin, Sevredol, Tranxene, Teralithe . . . There were many others. We had the right to a little Xanax when we were a bit anxious, or half a Stilnox when we couldn't fall asleep, or a vigorous round of antibiotics when we had a cold. The tiniest little sniffle and Maman would declare it wise not to let that cold drag on for weeks, I don't see the point of postponing the inevitable, you may as well get it over with, she would explain when I began to question her regarding the drugs she had me take. She and Papa were regulars at several Parisian pharmacies, but just in case their status as longtime clients wasn't enough to convince the pharmacist, they had the habit of swiping prescription pads during visits to the doctor—as soon as the doctor's back was turned they'd steal one, which they'd then fill out themselves, depending on what was bothering them or their children. There was the vial of Totapen, with its fine pastel powder that you had to dilute with water to obtain a coral-pink liquid, which was then poured into a square-shaped plastic spoon, about the size of a doll's shovel. Starting from when we were very little, we were entitled to a gulp of Théralène syrup, with its chemical strawberry taste, in order to get a good night's sleep. Maman had a rare tolerance for physical pain—and probably psychological pain as well, though that was harder to judge. We'd seen her cut her finger to the bone, imperturbable, or walk on a violet ankle, as swollen as a beehive, as if it were nothing, or brush away with the back of her hand a wasp that had just stung her. She nursed us with the same ferocity that had allowed her to survive a terrible childhood malady, her mother's cruelty, the horror of her own history. The drugs she self-prescribed were enough to kill a horse, or so said the horrified nurses when, at the entrance to a hospital or clinic, they had to draw up a list of the medicines she routinely took. Maman was a force of nature and her patience for the whining of wimpy little brats was very limited. You had to get hold of yourself, you had to grit your teeth or tighten your ass, either way, there was no question of whimpering about a little nothing booboo. She disinfected our cuts and scrapes with 90 percent alcohol—Neosporin was for spoiled children, apparently. And then there was ether, which came in a flask of cerulean, a blue like that of the evening sky, the same blue as the blue of the methyl alcohol that she swabbed the backs of our mouths with whenever we had a sore throat. That was her color, that blue, that midnight blue, glowing through the glass of the Gifrer bottle with its suffocating odor of chloroform, with which, in the country, we put the butterflies we'd caught in our nets to sleep. Ether left white powder-like marks on the skin, similar to the traces of drugs on Maman's chapped lips; I imagined her face covered with a cotton gauze soaked in that vaporous liquid, and pictured her vanishing into the place where conscience surrenders to darkness.

Maman often fainted due to the cocktail of medications that she combined with alcohol. She hid her whiskey under her mattress, in the back of kitchen cupboards that she imagined were secret, in glasses of Coca-Cola that she forbade us from tasting, Coca-Cola which we usually drank directly from the same family-size bottle, just as the three of us dried ourselves with the same bath towel. The fact that we possessed plenty of towels didn't make a difference—No one around here has scabies as far as I know! Confronting her directly could be dangerous; inebriation made her volatile. My sister, always bolder than I was, received some serious beatings. Maman couldn't stand how we spied on her, how we questioned her authority; how we forced her to reckon with her own fragility. My sister held her head high; I lowered my eyes. My sister ignored her own fear, or rather the fear of being hit paled beside the far more pressing fears regarding what Maman did with her days, what schemes she was cooking up with the latest sleazy guy, how many of those white pills she'd swallowed, what she'd had to drink, if she'd eaten, whom she'd just hung up on in haste as if she had something to hide, whose business card that was in her purse, how long had she been seeing that psychic who answered the phone when my sister pressed call back, was she one of the charlatans who'd stolen all Maman's money, because where did all that alimony and child support go?

As for me, I kept a low profile around Maman. I wouldn't have been able to take as much as my sister did, so I kept quiet, I stayed out of the way. But my sister couldn't help herself, the impulse was stronger than she was. She had to make our mother face her contradictions, her aberrant behavior, the precariousness of her condition. Maman had to prove to my sister that she wasn't insane, that she knew what she was doing. But in fact, Maman was completely out of it, everything around her was swaying, she herself had to hold on to the walls so that she didn't collapse. She was far from able to reassure her daughter, but she wasn't ready to admit defeat, so rather than pretending to be stable in an attempt to recover some semblance of maternal authority, she put all her effort into showing her daughter who was boss. She threatened to kick her out, to hit her, and then she did hit her. She dragged her daughter—my sister, sitting in a rolling desk chair—across the apartment by her hair because the girl had once again spied on her, or rummaged through her things, or demanded an explanation about something that was none of her business. Maman pulled her by her braids out onto the landing, crammed her into the elevator, and took her all the way down to the building's lobby. I raced down the stairs from the third to the ground floor, thinking to intervene—I was always hoping to find the courage to come between them. Maman must have kicked my sister over onto the ground: my sister, hanging on to the arms of the chair, was now using it as a shield. Get out of my house! Maman screamed. I won't have a snitch under my roof! If you want to play at being a cop, go direct traffic outside. Get out! I waited it out, huddled by the emergency staircase. In the end I was too afraid to interfere, I was afraid of being hit, and I couldn't figure out how not to take sides. In general my sister and I were united, we were on the same team no matter what. I should have defended her, but during the worst conflicts Maman needed me to remain neutral, so that she could have a witness who would help her recover from her guilt, the guilt that would suffocate her when she became once again more or less lucid. She needed to be forgiven. I had to tell her that my sister also forgave her. Late at night she'd stick her head in the doorways of our rooms to see if we were sleeping. When she saw that my eyes were open, she'd come in. Are you still mad at me, you, too? I'm so mad at myself, if only you knew. Do you still love me? I love you, my love, I adore you. I love you madly, both of you, I'm so sorry, sweetheart.

Maman and my sister loved each other like wild things, they would have killed each other in order to prove it. Neither of them would ever have ceded an inch in the fight, never would they have wavered. Often, when Maman came near my sister, my sister reflexively raised her arm, she was protecting herself from the slap that she was always expecting. Maman would then cry out, in a snide tone: No, really! You'd think she was an abused child! On top of everything else, she mocked us. She mocked our fear. Drunk, she ridiculed her crimes; she forgot how much being cruel cost her, and the depth of the remorse that would come for her afterward. In her alcoholic delusion, she found the terrified faces of her children funny. She said we were a pair of pathetic little spoiled-rotten brats. If only we knew an eighth of what she'd suffered, if only we knew what suffering was, real suffering, not the preposterous problems of a couple of jerks. If only we could get it into our heads that certain things were none of our business, that it wasn't our place to judge her, that she wasn't taking orders from anyone, and certainly not from a pair of twelve- and fourteen-year-old girls, no, but you must be dreaming! Just where do you think we are, exactly? At the zoo? You're not going to shut me away under my own roof, is that clear? I'm not some animal you can put in a cage! I'm a human being, can't you see? I do what I can. And if that's not good enough for you it's all the same to me. Can you get it through your heads once and for all that all I've done is for your sakes, everything I've done with my life is for you? I've sacrificed everything, my whole life, everything revolves around you, and even so, it's never enough for you, you always need more, and more, and more! But I can't do any more than I've already done! Do you understand that I've reached my limit? You don't need to spy on me. I'm a mother first and foremost, and that should be pretty clear, with all the sacrifices I've made for you, I'm a mother but I'm also a woman, and my life as a woman is none of your business.

We would have liked nothing better than to be kept apart from her life as a woman, for there to be boundaries discreetly maintained. But she couldn't help making a display of her life as a woman, the same way she was always going around naked at home and pissing with the bathroom door wide open. The shape of her vulva intrigued me from an early age, and years later I learned that my sister had also wondered if it were normal for a woman's genitals to stick out like that, or if that was something peculiar to Maman, who was so hairless that she barely had any bush and so it was possible to see, very clearly, her clitoris coming up out of her vulva. It looked like an upside-down cock's comb. As neither my sister nor I knew what was normal, I asked my boyfriend—who had nicknamed my pussy (with his charming American accent) his *poussin* (French for baby chick)—if he thought I had reason to worry that sooner or later my vulva might come to resemble the head of a rooster. He found this question very amusing, he imitated the whole barnyard, clucking and squawking, the bed became a chicken coop, with feathers flying over the shaking of the comforter. When I insisted on getting an answer, he told me that I was so cute, so adorable, that even if I ended up with a cock's comb between my thighs, he would still love me—perhaps. He also said I tasted like peach, which interacted distressingly with my memory of our parents comparing our little private parts to apricots, another pink-fleshed summer fruit.

Maman hid neither her body nor her lovers from us. There was the girl who suffered from constant tics, the boy whose bulging eyes were accentuated by his sunken cheeks and the purplish shadows under his eyes, and who, one night, attempted suicide in Maman's bed; there was a series of visually impaired people coming from the National Institute for Blind Youth, which was just across the street from us. Maman, who had one leg shorter than the other because of a childhood malady; Maman, who had hidden her handicap with extraordinary bravura, was nevertheless subject to falls, and with her bum leg she was often getting her foot caught in and stumbling over their white canes. To apologize for making a scene in the street (a scene in itself absurdly funny), she'd invite the young blind person to come for tea at our house. Relationships developed, which occasionally veered into brief love affairs. We weren't supposed to ask questions, but we wouldn't have in any case; we didn't want to know anything about things we couldn't help knowing about. Sometimes Maman wasn't home when we got back from school, and if it was getting late and we sensed Papa's visit approaching, I'd go out looking for her. Maman enjoyed spending time with the local shopkeepers; she felt entirely at home sitting and schmoozing behind the counter with the pharmacist, the butcher, the grocer. She was a woman of the people, she'd grown up working class, and even while dressed head to toe in Saint Laurent, in this neighborhood of old snobs, she felt much more at ease with the shopkeeper on the corner. I often found her in the back of the shop; she'd hide there to drink a Coke, one I wasn't allowed to taste. One evening, when I'd made the rounds of her usual hideouts and was beginning to worry—Maman had recently spent the night at the police station after attacking a police officer who had stopped her for a reason that she considered unjust—I went to have a last look behind the storefront of the butcher shop, where the door didn't appear to be entirely closed. I went in quietly. I should have immediately made my presence known, and I blamed myself afterward for having snuck into this shop where the lights were off and the counters of washed butcher block suddenly looked oddly ominous. I saw, looming by the light of a naked bulb in the back room, Maman bending over a block, and behind her, a disgusting fat guy whose face, convulsed in ecstasy, it took me only a moment to recognize. I left immediately and on returning home I told my sister that Maman was helping the butcher to close up shop. My sister shot me a sidelong glance, a suspicious look that she had a particular talent for, and I opened my eyes wide as if to say: Do you want me to draw you a picture or can we just let my explanation stand? She hesitated; I knew from the frenetic movement of her gaze and the twisting of her lips that she was wondering if she should find Maman and intervene somehow; then our eyes met and we—surprising ourselves—burst out laughing, a laughter at once raucous and pathetic, freighted with unspoken grief.

Hey, you little jerks, are you done making fun of me? Maman, blissfully happy, would ask us with an almost sensual delight when she saw her darling daughters laughing together. Even if she wasn't always in on our jokes, she loved participating in our games. She had suffered so much from being an only child that our affection for each other moved her deeply. My sister was a talented comic, and on good days, days when she knew that she could provoke in Maman not just a smile, but real laughter, that she could make Maman double over and howl that her jaw hurt, that she'd pee her pants if my sister continued, on those days my sister would launch into her clown act. She'd juggle with fruit or cheeses or cartons of milk, she'd juggle with eggs that would splatter all over the kitchen floor, which left Maman thoroughly unperturbed—excess was always welcome in our household. When we were little, during bathtime, Maman would often end up climbing into the tub with us. My sister would spend hours playing with Maman's flimsy locks of hair, transforming her into Goldorak or the Gerber baby. Her hair was so fine that once she'd dunked her head in the water she appeared almost bald. My sister nicknamed her Kojak or Mr. Spock, the latter because of her pointy ears. They were too funny, her ears! Especially when we pulled down on them from the top of the cartilage, one of us on either side of her, our pudgy little fingers mauling her until she cried out: But you're hurting me, dammit! Haven't you had enough of torturing your poor old mother? Then she'd start a water fight to get back at us for our pranks, just a little splash at first, a little flick of her forefinger, and pretty soon we were outdoing one another, the bathroom became a water park, with me getting out of the tub just in time to avoid drowning and leaping into the hallway, which was soon flooded. I played cheerleader, and I always rooted for my sister's team, Go on, *chouchou*! You're winning! Okay, well, you guys totally won, Maman would say when at last she was ready to admit defeat, and you've made a hell of a mess!

My sister would come up with ideas that were as crazy as our mother's. She'd put on some background music—preferably Tchaikovsky, the *grand pas* from *Swan Lake*—and she'd push the living room furniture around, calling on me to help move the couch, the tables, the chairs, until we'd transformed the room into a stage. Maman, despite her handicap, had studied ballet for many years, pushed by her own mother, who had been frustrated in her ambition to become a ballerina. In fact, with one leg nearly an inch and a half shorter than the other, Maman could never have made a career of it, but she could execute a series of *fouetté* turns so perfectly that one could be forgiven for thinking she might have. She'd passed the technical aptitude test to be certified as a ballet teacher by adapting variations in the competitive exam to her good leg. My sister was the conductor, with a half baguette as a baton, swaying her arms with boundless enthusiasm and belief in her mother's talent: Maman, it's your cue! she'd say, solemnly. Maman would complain that she hadn't warmed up, that she was going to break a leg, or pull a muscle, so then the two of us would beg her with one voice: Maman, please! She'd set herself up in the middle of the Persian carpet, she'd do a few *pliés* to warm up, a little stretching in fourth position, left and right, she'd wiggle her ass like a cat about to pounce, plant her feet firmly on the floor, and then: Okay, let's go, are you ready? Wait, Maman, I'm going to restart the music! Go! From the first notes, Maman took off like a shot: Like a runner from the starting line, she threw herself into a manège of *tours piqués*, following up with a circle of *grands jetés*; brushing against the furniture, skimming the walls, she reinvented Nureyev's celebrated choreography, performing the steps of both male and female dancers, the turning jumps, the *pirouettes en arabesque*, the *pirouettes en attitude*, and then the famous thirty-two *fouettés*: her arms in second position, majestic as a bird of prey, her right leg folded against her left knee before being unfolded perpendicularly in the air as she turned, her arms parallel to her legs in perfect synchronicity, folding the better to unfold in dazzling turns, one turn, two, three, four turns, she was stunning, astounding. Sitting cross-legged on the carpet, I admired my mother and sister, and I applauded them, slapping my hands on my inner thighs to the rhythm of the music: Bra-vo bra-vo bra-vo! Maman completed her thirty-two turns, easy-peasy, and if she fell flat on her face at the end, it was only to lend a comic turn to her performance, a pratfall controlled with all the expertise of a seasoned actress. She was sublime, she was divine. Poor Maman, she could spin like a top on the tips of her toes without ever losing her balance, but she couldn't put one foot in front of the other without stumbling in the dance of daily life.

Maman's feet had always fascinated me, her dancer's feet, with their thick calluses, their leathery skin along the arches, their heels and metatarsals the color of rosin. The curve of her instep resembled the Arc de Triomphe, as seen from the far end of the avenue in the apartment where we had been born, a typical Parisian apartment in the style designed by Baron Haussmann and situated above a little square at the corner of the rue Balzac. A gigantic statue of the writer had pride of place. This image of Honoré de Balzac, pensive and in his dressing gown—a dressing gown like the one Papa wore—created a bridge, in my childhood imagination, with our subsequent apartment. When Maman remarried, we moved to the rue de Varenne, near the Rodin Museum, which housed an even more imposing bronze statue of the author of *The Human Comedy*. Our parents had chosen literary names for my sister and me, which I liked to think were inspired by poems or plays, but Maman swore that she had *not* called me Violaine because of Paul Claudel, that bastard who'd had his sister locked up, when of the two of them she was the real genius, because he was jealous of her talent, just as Rodin was, that asshole! We went to see *Camille Claudel*, the film starring Isabelle Adjani and Gérard Depardieu, which came out a few months before Maman was hospitalized, and that version of the artist's life, as vivid as only film can be, entered my imagination; the resemblance between the main character and my mother became only more marked for me when my mother returned home from the psychiatric ward obsessed with sculpture, the only art therapy workshop at the hospital that had interested her. Her first attempts were in clay; later, she began to work in marble. A foot carved in stone with remarkable verisimilitude is the work I'd like to associate with my mother as a sculptor, but I become quite sure it's not hers when the memory returns of the gifts we received that year for Christmas—from your mother for Christmas, said whoever it was that handed them to us—that abominable Christmas which we so would have wished to strike from the calendar of 1989. They were figurines in cut metal, among them a small cat painted over in an iridescent blue-gray, a pitiful object whose absurdity wasn't lost on a ten-year-old, evidence of Maman's alarming regression. During the Second World War Giacometti only sculpted figurines that could fit into a matchbox. In a book of interviews, Christian Boltanski, speaking about the foundations of his artistic practice, describes his first creations: little, wadded-up balls of bread, resembling rabbit or hamster turds, sculptures—if they can be called sculptures—that in their very banality express life's sorrow and anguish, the scourge of war, the endless calamities in the face of which humans can only feel themselves to be tiny little shits. Perhaps because she was typecast as Camille Claudel, or perhaps because people said she'd gone into a downward spiral after shooting that film, or that she'd always had a screw loose, that she was crazy and thus excelled at playing crazies, Isabelle Adjani became my idol. *One Deadly Summer* was my favorite film, and I watched it over and over on our television set (we owned a VHS cassette of it, the tape rewound hundreds of times), sobbing silently from beginning to end. During that same period, my sister and I shared a passion for another film which, while not exactly a tragedy, spoke to us of our mother's situation, though I was careful to avoid mentioning that idea to anyone, above all my sister, who would have made fun of it, or worse, would have worried about me. The film was *Splash*, with Tom Hanks and Daryl Hannah, the story of a mermaid who lands in Manhattan, knowing neither who she is, nor where she comes from, nor how to live in this world, and frankly I was astonished to be the only person to recognize Maman in this absurd and fantastical character, the woman–fish. Maman, whose feet were covered with a tough, leathery carapace, as hard and roughened as a shell, Maman who had trouble breathing the same air as the rest of us.

We knew that Maman forced herself to vomit because we heard her in the hallway bathroom, and even though she ran the faucet to hide the sounds, the cloudy water in the toilet bowl gave her away. I don't know where she picked up that habit. When she lived with our father, she tried to sit down to dinner with us before going out to restaurants or dinner parties with him every night, which meant that she would go from one meal to the next, and in order to keep up her appetite—Papa liked people to have a good appetite—she got into the habit of emptying her stomach in between, so that she'd still fit into her

Saint Laurent pantsuits and Dior sheath dresses. Dancers are known for being anorexic or bulimic, but that explanation seems insufficient to me, and in any case Maman wasn't someone you could generalize about easily. The labels or pathologies one might apply to Maman were not in short supply: alcoholism, schizophrenia, mythomania, kleptomania, and by turns neurasthenia or hysteria. She could become overexcited or crushed, she could eat like a bear or like a bird, she was excessive in everything. For the most part, however, these labels were of no use to us; none of them seemed right, none of them were helpful. Maman often ate at night, sugar cookies dunked in café au lait made with very little coffee and a lot of milk, that vile Nescafé which she was so fond of. I think it was the only meal she kept down. The feeling of her fingers at the back of my throat when she'd force me to vomit because I complained of a stomachache—It's for your own good, you'll feel better afterward!—came back to me with a jolt one night, when my mouth was around the penis of a boy I loved, feeling it push against my vocal cords. I'd hesitate to call my lovers men. Not out of ambivalence regarding my sexual orientation—I like rough skin, strong smells, being sized up, dealing with bodies that take up more space than mine and can find a place inside me, hands restraining mine—but because men belonged to Maman. Though some of her lovers were in fact closer in age to me, my lovers always remained boys. With this linguistic infantilization I set up a barrier in words. I placed limits where we were so lacking in them, rules where there were never any.

NOT SO OFTEN THAT IT became a weekly tradition, but often, with the pocket money Papa had given me, I bought Maman flowers. White roses were her favorites. The only flowers she could bear

to see cut were white, virginal. Red flowers made her furious, re-
minding her of the giant bouquets that her ex-husband would send
her, during their marriage, as apologies for his absences, his infidelities, his being a cad, an incurable cad. She'd toss them out the
window, his shitty red roses, he could kiss her ass with his clichéd
bouquet, did he know where he could shove it? I'd imagine Papa
stunned, petrified, just as we remained paralyzed when she screamed
that we all took her for a fucking cunt, that she was fed up, that
we were all the same, the whole lot of us, we were a bunch of
bastards. What she was asking didn't seem so extraordinary to her,
some might even say it was owed to her, that minimum degree of
respect which she had to beg for like a pauper, even a leper would
have been awarded more consideration than she was. How disgusting. Who does he think I am? I may have dumb bitch written all
over my face, but whore isn't stamped on my ass. But go ahead, my
poor darling, go ahead, dry your tears, pick up the mess, as always,
pretend nothing happened, go on, go on, it's all fine, everything's
fine. Monsieur has every right, he can have his cake and eat it too,
and also enjoy the baker's wife.

As for me, when I gave Maman flowers—always white flowers,
never anything but white flowers, roses, lilies, freesia, tulips, lisianthuses,
ranunculus, lilacs, jasmine, hyacinth, hydrangea, or my favorite, lily of
the valley, which (when it was in season) required transforming a small
mustard pot into a vase—it wasn't that I had something for which I
needed to apologize. I gave her flowers to brighten up our daily life,
to mask the rancid odor of her smoking, to give expression to the innocence of my love. She was always moved to tears by this gesture, she
never tired of this attention, just as she was never blasé about our passionate declarations of love or our frantic hugs and kisses. She would

never have turned away our caresses, we could cuddle all night long with her when we felt like joining her in her bed, her arms were always wide open, ready to embrace us with all their strength and for all time. My mouth was still full of baby teeth when we began competing to see whose mouth was bigger. Mouth to mouth, I opened mine as wide as possible, until I almost dislocated my jaw; winning proved that your love was the strongest. It wasn't fair, I should have won, I was sure that I loved her more than she loved me. As an adolescent, I was reluctant to dole out all the kisses she demanded. But I've already given you plenty! I'd try to get out of kissing her for the umpteenth time. Yes, but you didn't do it properly, you didn't mean it. With an exasperated sigh, I'd grant her a last little kiss, on the cheek, not on the lips. For fuck's sake, with both arms! she'd cry. Kisses had to be delivered with both arms wrapped around each other, chest to chest, because we love each other madly and for all eternity, dammit!

Maman's tragedy, the one she never recovered from, the scratch on the record that caused her to repeat herself, endlessly, was the emotional neglect she had suffered in her own childhood. Her mother, of course, was the one to blame. She had opened a hole in her daughter's heart by giving birth to her, and had left it gaping. Faced with her mother, Maman was an abandoned child all over again, choking up at the very sight of her. She said she felt something rising in her throat as we approached Grandma's house, she felt a lump—as if the stifled sobs of her childhood had congealed there. In front of her mother, she became an overgrown teenager, perpetually angry, puerile. Grandma responded to her daughter's tirades or effusive tenderness with the same paralyzing coldness, powerless before Maman's excesses. That Grandma was icily beautiful didn't help matters. Her features, exceedingly fine, possessed an in-

37

timidating symmetry. Her habitual expression was a kind of pout, midway between weariness and annoyance, her pinched lips, her narrow nose turned up with disdain. Her face resembled a Venetian mask, brandished against the steel blue of an arctic sky. Her jet-black hair, always pulled back into an impossibly tight chignon, called to mind the black swan from the famous ballet. That hairdo, it's just too much! Maman would say, making fun of the hairstyle her mother had adopted after opening her dance school in Montreuil. Maman's birth had been neither planned nor desired, and on top of the accident of her birth, there had been her childhood illness, and then her mental illness. Grandma had done what she could: pregnant at twenty, married to a nightmare of a man, giving birth to a puny little baby girl, anorexic, sickly, and soon gravely ill. Maman said that from eighteen months until she was five years old, she lived at Necker, the famous children's hospital, in the immediate aftermath of the war. Grandma was vague about the dates. Maman said that Grandma never came to see her in the hospital, even though visits were allowed, she knew that because Granny, her grandmother, came regularly! Maman remembered the name of the great professor who directed the wing of the hospital in which she'd grown up, she recalled the hospital beds around her emptying, she knew very well what that meant, that the children were not cured, that they were not coming back. She said that if she got out of there alive it was thanks to a nurse on her floor who became fond of her. Psychologists have studied the effects of separation on young children, orphans or seriously ill children. Without the constant presence of a stable, affectionate figure to whom they can become attached when they are young, some children will waste away and die, others will never learn to walk or to speak, all will suffer serious behavioral problems. Human contact is required to create a human being: bodily warmth, a comforting smell, a calming breath, the fluctuations of a beloved voice, a loving touch, the brush of someone's lips. Maman understood this intuitively, and maybe a nurse did save her life. In the same way my sister was sure that she owed her own good health to my birth, twenty-two months after her own. The permanence of my presence, the simple fact of my existence had evidently rescued her. Maman, however, was an only child, and her own mother would probably have aborted Maman if she could have done so.

According to Maman, Grandma was so vain, so afraid of getting old, that when Maman was a teenager, she made her dress like her twin, in order to pass Maman off as her sister. Oh, is that your sister? people in the street would say . . . It's my sister, yeah, right, some sister. She didn't have a maternal bone in her body, not one, she was mean, cruel! She'd pinch my thighs to bring out the cellulite; look at this orange peel, look how ugly it is! I was skinny as a stick but she was jealous, that nasty witch, she made me pay for the fact that boys liked me, she couldn't stand being in my shadow. She'd beat me endlessly, she'd pull my hair so hard that I'd find handfuls of it on my pillowcase, it fell out whenever I ran my fingers through it. Be that as it may, she's not a bad grandmother, but I'll tell you something, that's another way for her to get back at me, by showing me everything I never had!

Maman threw herself into these never-ending diatribes against Grandma, repeating them ad infinitum. There existed no serpent, no monster more odious, no brush was wide enough to paint the portrait of such a subject, a woman incapable of the least tenderness, bitter, pernicious. Yes, Grandma was a harpy, a rotten swine, pure venom; she was toxic, and a fraud. But Maman often left us for the weekend with

Grandma and Grandpa—Maman's stepfather, the man who raised her, our grandfather. We used to spend half of our summer vacations with them at seaside resorts, where they would rent a room in a modest boardinghouse or a furnished one-bedroom where you could do your own cooking; there would be a little balcony overlooking the parking lot; Grandpa and Grandma would sleep on the sofa bed in the living room so that we could have the bedroom; these were the corny vacations that Maman and Papa made fun of, and that my sister and I soon made fun of as well, with an innate snobbery, the thoughtless flippancy of children of the wealthy. Our grandparents owned their apartment and the dance studio underneath it, on the ground floor, where Grandma had started the school that would become her empire. Grandpa, a traveling salesman, added his savings to their common property and they were later able to buy a suburban bungalow in Normandy, and still later, a two-bedroom in one of the Three Rivers apartment blocks in the suburbs of Cannes. In contrast, Papa had never owned anything, because hoarding, investing in real estate, that was for hicks, he was above all that, his money was inexhaustible. Maman would leave us with our grandparents for the weekend or the month, and she would come to pick us up at the end of our stay. It was better that way. When she stayed for lunch, it became a battle, and if unfortunately it happened that she spent a few days with us there, the battle became a war. Our grandparents were nice to us, as long as the subject of Maman didn't come up. Merely pronouncing her name would bring forth a string of invectives: crazy, liar, thief, spendthrift, irresponsible, out of control, unreliable, violent, pretentious, nasty, bossy—always problems, with your mother there are always problems. At Grandpa and Grandma's house, we always knew where things stood, there were never any surprises, everything was in order, the chaos Maman created when she stopped by was the only thing to trouble the daily routine of this most conventional, petit-bourgeois, humdrum couple, who always ate the same cheese, a Pont-l'Evêque, after the main course, the same quarter of an avocado as an appetizer, or half an artichoke cut lengthwise. Grandpa, what would you prefer this evening, an avocado or an artichoke? Your choice, Grandma! Everything was always Grandma's choice. In summer there were tomatoes with hard-boiled eggs sliced with a slicing machine that worked less than half the time and that really annoyed Grandma, who complained that the gadget was another rip-off, it got on her nerves, Grandpa had been scammed yet again, like an imbecile, into buying the lousy thing. The vinaigrette was always prepared ahead of time in an old pickle jar and poured over hearts of lettuce, a week's supply of which had been washed and placed between sheets of paper towels in Tupperware containers. Saturday afternoons, Grandma cooked roast beef, Saturday evenings two cornish hens, Sunday afternoons a leg of lamb that Grandpa sliced off the bone with the electric carving knife that Grandma had allowed herself to be persuaded to buy for him as a gift only when she saw it on sale on the Home Shopping Network. The rest of the week, Grandma used up the leftovers. When we'd ask Grandpa what there was to eat, to make us laugh he'd say, Shabbage! And what's shabbage? It's shit with cabbage! Would you stop clowning around! Grandma would cry. You think you're funny, teaching them to swear, don't you think they get enough of that from their mother? Only one time did Grandma dare raise her voice with Maman, to attack her directly. As a rule she held her tongue, coward that she was. Oh boy, she really didn't hold back that day! Maman would tell anyone who'd listen, which usually meant us, even though we'd witnessed the scene ourselves. I even got to smack her one! That slap, I'll tell you, she had it coming to her. That, that was just a little bit of payback for all the beatings she'd handed out to me, that bitch. Nobody made a peep afterward; no more disagreements after that incident. Radio silence. Over and out.

Our childhood pets shared one principal purpose: to prepare us for grief. Grandma and Grandpa alone had dogs that didn't disappear suddenly, two or three generations of miniature poodles who each lived a dozen or so years, in contrast to our cats and dogs, who never survived until adulthood. In chronological order, they were a dog killed by the neighbors, a cat who fell to its death from the fourth-floor window, another cat lost in the jungle of the city, a dog abandoned by the side of the highway. There was the dog we left in someone's care and never picked up; the subsequent dog run over by a motorbike and given a shot to end his suffering; and finally the puppy whom Maman, just before her hospitalization, told me that Grandma had thrown into the Seine after fitting it with a collar weighted down with bricks. I looked at Maman incredulously, shuddering with sobs, because it was too horrible, too cruel, how could Grandma be such an ogre! Grandma, who averted her eyes at the sight of blood; Grandma, who cried as much as I did at the death of Bambi's mother when we watched the Disney film together; Grandma, whose eyes welled up at particularly beautiful moments of figure skating . . . Just go ask Grandma, if you don't believe me! So I called Grandma, stammering, stuttering, tearful: Gra-ha-mah! Why did you drown my dog in the Seine? Even more confused than I was, she responded that she was not aware that my dog had disappeared, but that I had to forgive my mother for lying to me, that Maman was ill. Your mother is ill, my darling little girl, I'm so sorry, you mustn't be angry with Maman, that's the way she is, she doesn't do it on purpose, you know your mother is very ill. I didn't know. Later, much later, when Maman was insisting that I tell her about the book I was trying, with difficulty, to read, I described the chapter I'd just finished, the opening of *Moravagine*. The main character disembowels his dog, his faithful companion, who had been up until then his only friend. Darling, I have something I must confess to you . . . No, please don't. By then, the age of looking for explanations was behind me. Really, I preferred not to know. But Maman insisted. No, Maman, I swear, I don't want to know. It was too late, the confession had already begun. That little puppy—she was the one who had killed it, with a kitchen knife. You've got to understand, I had to kill someone, and it was either him, that swine, or his whore, or the dog. I was in so much pain, you've got to understand. But I wasn't entirely crazy, I knew that if I killed that bastard I'd end up in prison, and I couldn't do that to you, my daughters. So yes, the dog had to go, and it was unfair, and it was hard for you, because you were very attached to that little dog, but somebody had to go, there was no helping it.

THAT GUY, I HAD WARNED her that he was bad news. When I was five years old, and she asked for my opinion, I had told her I really didn't like the look of him, not one bit. She told me that we were going to live with him, and I told her no thanks, no thank you, but she'd already made up her mind. The three of us were going to leave Papa to move in with *Ducon*—that's what she called him afterward, Mr. Asshole, after the episode with the little dog.

Ducon had two children, a boy and a girl the same age as my sister and me. Maman had met him during pickup at the school we all attended. He was the very image of a family man, but had recently divorced a hysterical woman, at least according to Maman. And it was

Maman who had helped him obtain custody of the children, and now Maman had gotten it into her head that she wanted a large family, that she was going to raise all four of us together. She was absolutely against the idea of shared custody, which she considered senseless and destabilizing to everyone. She had mounted a rock-solid case, with the help of the best lawyer specializing in family law in Paris (a friend of Papa's), asserting that the father was the responsible parent of the couple—especially given his new partner, our mother. Maman at that time could pass for an irreproachable mother, or nearly so: there was her hair-raising driving as she took us to school in the morning and then ferried us afterward between tennis lessons, horseback riding, dance classes, and piano lessons; she was plastered the whole time. There was the cigarette smoke with which she suffocated us, but there was nothing extraordinary about that, all the children of our generation complained about it. There were the slaps she doled out to us, but there too, there was nothing so crazy about that, children of all generations have moaned about that, and I believe Ducon, too, raised his hand against us when we disobeyed, in contrast to Papa. Papa screamed like a madman but he never hit us. Yes, Maman was in those days a nearly perfect mother, and she presided over entire groups of kids—the four of us, plus the friends, both boys and girls, whom she looked after in addition to us, because she was always the first one to volunteer as a chaperone for field trips, always ready to make fourteen different detours on the way back to get everyone home. My guess is that her social disjointedness, her eccentricity, her serious touch of madness, went unnoticed behind the façade of a perfectly turned out school mother. If clothes don't make the man, they do signal membership in a certain tribe or club, and Maman, styled from head to toe with all the accoutrements of an upper-class housewife of the 7th arrondissement, blended perfectly into the crowd at pickup at our snobbish little school.

Our ground-floor apartment, on the rue de Varenne and near several government buildings, was shadowed by policemen. I saw them keeping watch on the street corner from my bunk bed in our big bedroom, which had been divided in four, with each of our four beds perched over a desk and an armoire, constituting the entirety of our private space. We had our favorite stuffed animals to sleep with, but we kept the rest of our toys in a giant trunk. Until I was five years old, my sister was in the habit of holding my hand in order to fall asleep at night. She'd asked our parents if my crib could be placed in her room, and later on she'd insisted that our twin beds be right next to each other. The worst part of this move for her was being deprived of the comfort of feeling her sister's hand in hers as she fell asleep. Every evening, when the lights were off—I said lights out! Maman would cry if she saw, through the half-open door, that a bedside lamp was turned on—when the breathing of the boy and girl became heavier and they began to snore peacefully, my sister whispered, *Chouchou*, are you asleep? I wasn't asleep, but even if I had been asleep, she would have come over and climbed the ladder of my bed to whisper the question in my ear, lifting my eyelids with her index finger: *Chouchou*, are you asleep? She had to get back to her bed before Maman found her. What are you thinking about? my sister would ask me. I wasn't thinking about anything in particular, sometimes I was looking at the policemen, by the light of the streetlamp I observed the details of their clothing, the cap, the uniform, the buttons, the badges, behind the curtain through which a ray of light filtered in at an angle, between the rod and the windowpane, with my pillow wedged directly in line with it. It was a corner apartment and there was also a traffic light, which I watched changing color. I noticed that the red light lasted longer than the green, and the green longer than the yellow, the yellow barely a few seconds, seconds that Maman always ignored, for

Maman a yellow light meant step on the gas before it turns red, that shade of yellow resembled the color of the streetlamp, and if I blinked, if I forced my vision to become blurry by squinting, the halos of the two lights would almost meet and become one. I had to think before responding to my sister, who always worried. I pretended that I was thinking about tomorrow, that I was thinking about my classes, that I was thinking about recess, that I was thinking about the weather, or the clothing I'd choose in the morning. Sometimes I would tell her that I was trying to count how many seconds the light stayed green during the whole day, but I was having trouble calculating the number of seconds in twenty-four hours, so she'd help me with multiplication. We learned to love the other children like a brother and sister, even though they hadn't previously been our friends, we hadn't chosen them among our classmates to play with, they were simply other children at our school, but soon we were having dinner together, we carried the same lunches in our lunch boxes, had the same after-school activities, learned to ski together.

Maman, though her mismatched legs rendered any sport in which one had to slide unthinkable; Maman, who hated the cold perhaps even more than she hated beating about the bush; Maman took all four of us skiing in the Alps, and after getting us into our leggings, crew-neck sweaters, ski suits, parkas, extra socks, shoes, mittens, hats, goggles; after applying fluorescent ChapStick to our lips, she dragged us, she towed us in single file, with a courage and an altruism that bordered on saintliness, up the mountain to drop us off at ski school while her husband—yes, that guy—stayed behind to work in Paris. He promised to come join us very soon, but there were so many hurdles to clear, he kept running into problems at work, and it really was the worst luck because he loved to ski! If I wasn't a fan of these ski trips, it wasn't just because I suffered from vertigo—merely riding the chairlift made me want to die, no need to wait for me to kill myself skiing—but also because, like Maman, I hated the cold, and I would have preferred to have uneven legs myself if it meant I didn't have to mount those instruments of torture in boots that were too tight for me, which numbed my ankles and made my freezing feet swell; I would have gladly surrendered all my toys not to have to go up and down the slopes from morning to night and, at the end of the day, put my two skis together and search in vain for a spot to store them on the premises, a test of skill and endurance similar to the final level of Tetris, a game the others excelled at, and which we played on the Nintendo we'd brought in our luggage, a game that once again allowed me to make a spectacle of my ineptitude, just as I was inept at this absurd sport which consisted of slipping and tumbling on sheets of ice without breaking anything—For God's sake, on top of everything else, don't bust your arm!—so that we wouldn't have to complicate our stay with an emergency room visit. How unhappy Maman looked behind her enormous sunglasses, sitting on the terrace of the chalet at the top of the ski slopes, bundled in the marmot fur Papa had given her. At the French Ski School, the other kids managed to get stars in bronze, silver, or gold, distinguished merit badges, and I'd get, as a token of participation, a medal in the shape of a snowflake. I was finally granted a star, mainly because the instructor took pity on my sister, his best pupil, the most gifted, the bravest on the slopes, when he saw that she was in despair over my failures. As a consolation prize, there was the summer in Corrèze.

The house in Corrèze became the headquarters of our blended family, my memories of the four of us children together are centered on this fairy-tale palace, Maman's quixotic castle in the air, in which she had invested all her faith in life and in the future. There was nothing to do there; from time to time we would go trout fishing in the river, an activity that allowed for peaceful contemplation, long periods of silence interrupted only by sighs from the more ambitious members of our group, those who were frustrated that the fish weren't biting. I'd pick wildflowers for Maman, who swore to me that the only flowers she liked in the countryside were tall stalks of wild grass and daisies, a white lie that I understood much later was meant to keep me from pulling up the neighbors' flower beds. The six of us would leave Paris by car, Maman sharing the driving at night with her new husband, because it was a long way and they preferred to stay up all night rather than deal with our racket and incessant whining: I need to pee, I need to throw up, I feel dizzy, hungry, thirsty, I can't fall asleep, tell me a story, are we there yet? What does *almost* mean? They'd bought a full-size Volvo station wagon and they'd put the backseat down to make it into a camper, and we four children slept there, lined up in a row or head to toe. By daybreak we were in Corrèze. The pure country air dispelled the smell of stale tobacco that we'd been steeped in since Paris, waking us gently. I glimpsed the dawn from behind my sister's naked arm in her short-sleeved pajamas, which the bumpy road had randomly set down between my forehead and my shoulder. One by one we rubbed our eyes, and though scarcely awake we opened them wide, so as not to miss a single detail of the idyllic landscape. We got on our knees in the back, our chins resting on the seat that separated us from the drivers, and we took turns chirping, Are we almost there? Yes, we're almost there! came the response from the parents, as relieved as we were. We were throbbing with enthusiasm, we were arriving for a whole month in the house of happiness, we passed the old, abandoned train station at the foot of the hill you had to climb to get to the village. That's it, we're almost, almost there! we cried out in unison. When our car entered the little winding road that wound up, up, up to the very, very top, Maman put on music, always the same music, the *Spring* movement from Vivaldi's *Four Seasons*, joy turned to sound, and we piped up in the back, laughing and singing, first in a chorus, and then as a round: We're almost there, we're almost there, we're almost there . . . We made it! We whooped with joy, anticipating the pleasures awaiting us on this vacation: so many friends would come to see us that the children's bedroom would be turned into a dormitory, the mattresses lined up end to end along two walls to form a kind of sleeping bank, so that the number of available beds would never be a problem, at worst they'll just pile in together, Maman would say, there's always room, if there's room for four, there's room for twelve, or sixteen, or more.

Our house stood proudly at the top of a tiny village where the neighbors to the right of us kept chickens and two sheep, and the neighbors to the left had cows they'd let us milk. Their barn contained a tractor with manure stuck to its wheels, and feral cats who birthed their litters in the straw. Their home smelled of hearty soups and oilcloth, and behind the house there were rabbits of different colors, whom we fed with carrots, sticking them through the bars of their cages. On the other side, at the far end of a meadow, there was a pigsty whose foul emanations and ear-splitting grunts awakened the dulled senses of the little city dwellers. In the evening, Maman served feasts on an immense wooden table, a find, she said, from one of the local secondhand shops, a massive oak monastery table with church pews on either side of it. We all ate together, adults and children, and no one made a fuss, whether or not they liked salmon trout, grilled, marinated, or in escabeche—menus had to be invented to accommodate the sometimes miraculous catch of the day—and there were also wood-fire potatoes, covered in ash and roasted in the embers of the fireplace. Don't tell me you don't like potatoes! Maman would bellow to anyone who made a face over their plate. She cooked with her fingers, she mixed noodle salads using both hands, she tasted sauces and vinaigrettes by dipping the tip of her fingernail into the pot or bowl, with a mixture of hunger and pleasure that bordered on lust. There was something orgiastic about our parties, bacchanalian revels with dances choreographed by Maman, our costumes made from clothing we borrowed from each other or artisanal creations: athletic socks with holes in them transformed into white opera-length gloves, scarves worn as saris, dish towels as turbans or flounced skirts, garbage bags became evening gowns, crumpled tinfoil for accessories. Maman knew something about theater, she'd performed onstage and from the wings, and in the long attic corridor that she'd made into a dressing room, she helped us prepare to meet our public. Maman was beside herself with joy, but the ecstasy couldn't last. One had to come down to earth eventually, and Maman didn't know how to come down gently.

An alley ran between the house and an orchard with hundred-year-old apple trees, a plot several acres in size with a little path that ran alongside it and that seemed to belong to no one in particular; at the far end of the path stood a hazelnut tree. The month of August required patience, resignation, even: walnuts were not yet in season, nor were hazelnuts, nor apples, nor pears. We had to wait until the very last moment, the final hours before our departure, to forage for wild mushrooms, hidden under the ferns that kept the earth humid and cool even in the dog days of summer, a moment which we prepared for by cautiously studying the different varieties of edible mushrooms—be careful, our farmer neighbors told us, having known more than one person who had poisoned himself. Maman made a fricassee of them in runny omelettes, and the strange, spongy, and slimy vegetables resembled slugs that had been sliced and sautéed in butter. The orchard's sole boundary markers were, on one side, a hedge with holes in it, and on the other, a tiny stream which we played let's-step-over-the-river with, so that the whole area seemed to belong to everyone; as long as the apples hadn't ripened—otherwise we would have filled baskets with them, or eaten them off the branch—the danger we incurred of being run off as trespassers was minimal. Eventually Maman managed to acquire this plot of land to add to the tiny garden that came with her village house. Up to that point all she possessed was a small patch of lawn, scarcely big enough for the trestle table, which had to be constantly refolded and stored in the basement because it got in the way of our comings and goings. At lunchtime, we'd picnic on big tablecloths, and in the evening we dined indoors; it was freezing at night. Maman got it into her head to buy the orchard at any price, and the exorbitant sum that the owner was asking for it did nothing to discourage her. Ducon would take out a loan, he could well afford it, she paid for so many things with her ex-husband's money, and they'd put a pool and a tennis court among the trees. There was a twisted old apple tree under whose branches I had dreamed up a fabulously romantic life for my favorite doll. One year when we were there for our fall vacation I had secretly tasted the apples of this tree, and no fruit would ever again compare. Maman told me that my apple tree was in the way of the tennis court, there was no helping it, I'm sorry, sweetheart, I know how much you love this tree, but we're going to have to cut it down. I wept about it for weeks. Maman, noticing that my sadness persisted, told me that perhaps it would be possible to replant the tree a little distance away. I believed her. Work began the following spring. Maman went on her own to supervise the construction site. When she came back, I asked if she had replanted my tree. She had told me she would, and I clung to that hope with all my might, but I never saw my apple tree again.

It was off to a bad start, this expansion project. I wasn't the only one to think so. The neighbors who up until then had been fond of the kids whose mother, the beautiful eccentric, had restored the ruin at the top of the village suddenly forbade us from feeding their chickens, and barred us from their barn. Only the old couple whose shack at the edge of town marked the entrance to our domain still welcomed us happily, and gave us violet-flavored candies when we stopped by. They took care of the house in our absence, and Maman had assigned them the honorary role of surrogate general contractor, which meant that they were in charge of dressing down any workers who were slacking off while the boss was in Paris. The pool and tennis court were constructed in record time, and in the meantime Maman got married to Ducon for real, ensuring that they were co-owners of the land. The leisurely rhythm of vacations formerly devoted to aimless wandering suddenly became regimented, athletic; we had to take advantage of all the work that had been done on the new part of the property. We had to organize tennis tournaments, swimming races, diving competitions, soccer games, water volleyball, and those vacationers who the year before had whined that there was nothing to do in this dump were now overjoyed. I tried in vain to come up with objective reasons for getting out of these games; I moped around in silence. I would have preferred that everyone continue to be bored stiff—everyone but me with my pastoral spirit, with what I considered my superior sensibilities. My suffering lasted two consecutive summers. If I had known what awaited me at the end of this ordeal, I would undoubtedly have been more tolerant of the shambles these changes had made of my idyllic vacations and my little routines. It was precisely in the barn adjacent to the pool, which had been converted into a party room, a bathroom suite, a dressing room, a playroom for Ping-Pong, billiards, et cetera, that Maman found her new husband fucking his secretary, whom Maman—too nice, too dumb—had invited to be our guest, along with her fiancé. Heavily pregnant as the woman was, Maman could never have imagined such a thing . . . Well, you had to be really perverse, really, she had to have landed on an incredible pervert, her bad luck was unbelievable, how was it even possible to get things so wrong? And with her and her husband's breakup Maman began to break down, and tear apart stone by stone all they'd built as a couple, all they'd given each other in good faith and which was henceforth worthless, less than worthless. The two of them began to tear each other to pieces, figuratively and literally: back in Paris, in our beds, the covers pulled up over our heads, their cries reminded us of the pigs in Corrèze, except that these cries numbed us with fear. Maman, in a rage, broke a windowpane one day and with a piece of broken glass she gashed the face of her husband, who, despite what he had done, was still the father of our friends, the children we had lived and grown up with for four and a half years. We didn't know what to think but we took sides, perhaps in spite of ourselves. The policemen whom I had admired as they kept watch under our windows were now coming regularly to our door; the neighbors complained that we were disturbing the peace; in this neighborhood one didn't raise hell.

Drastic measures was one of Maman's favorite turns of phrase. Drastic measures were often needed in order to achieve her objectives: driving on the sidewalk, knocking down a door, having her husband followed, denouncing him to the government tax office; all available means must be deployed, and the more drastic the better. Likewise,

Maman always said that the bigger the lie, the more plausible it was, that the most fantastic tales would be treated as more credible than cli- chéd stories that anyone could have invented. Reality is always stranger than fiction, she used to say. And then: What's that got to do with the price of tea in China? And: People are morons!—a statement she deployed whenever my sister and I let slip that *people* were saying unkind things about her, or about anyone else for that matter—Well, people are morons! And: The richer people are, the cheaper they are. And quotes she borrowed from Papa, along with Oh, for fuck's sake, what a motherfucking piece of shit! This time Maman's drastic measures involved calling the Duluc Detective Agency and having her husband followed so that she could then deliver a detailed report of his activities during working hours to his employers. Maman had certainly married an asshole, and she had good reason to nickname him Ducon after the Duluc investigation, which concluded that adultery had been the least of his crimes, and that the latter included embezzlement, fraud, and abuse of power, among other things. His tax returns were either nonexistent or fraudulent. However, Maman didn't realize that sinking Ducon would also cause her own downfall. She reported him to his employers and to the authorities, and Ducon was indeed left high and dry; but guess who got screwed yet again? Ha, *her*. Always her! It was fucked up, it was downright disgusting, but she was married to the son of a bitch and responsible for his debts, even though she was one of his victims. The asshole declared himself bankrupt, she said, in order to leave her hard up, bearing the burden alone. He was undoubtedly insolvent, fired for a serious offense, pros- ecuted for tax evasion, et cetera, at this point, well, bravo, bingo, per- fect, she'd won the lottery once again, she'd definitely hit the jackpot with this one. What was to be done? Call Papa. Papa would get her out of this mess, Papa would rescue her, Papa her savior.

Papa came by every evening without exception, meaning that Papa also came by while we were living with Ducon. Papa said that Maman shouldn't be surprised if her new husband went looking elsewhere, when she forbade him access to his own home so that her ex could come by to see her and their children in peace. Those two, they're two of a kind, Maman used to say. The most urgent matter facing us when Maman finally decided to pack up and leave—first throwing all Ducon's things into the Seine; it wasn't the little dog, but *the suits* that she'd drowned—the most pressing problem was the question of our housing. Where were we to live? Her best option, she decided, was to return to the apartment where we children had spent our earliest years, that apartment in the handsome Haussmannian building, which Papa's new wife hated and which, following her wishes, they'd moved out of, but which he continued to rent and had partially converted into offices. Maman was returning to the scene of the original crime, which was now defined by two crimes. Adultery had led her to leave the father of her children and now adultery had led her back to his apartment, where she foundered, where she collapsed, with no more mooring than her two powerless daughters, who were forced to watch her drown, weighed down with her garbage bags full of glad rags and heels, her head full of blown fuses; she sank to the very bottom of the river. We were only there for a short time before she was carted off in a straitjacket.

AT THE START OF THE next school year, when she returned from the hospital, she managed to find a new apartment for the three of us, the apartment in which we would remain until my sister and I left home; she decided that we would move to a building across the street from the National Institute for Blind Youth, at number 1, rue Necker—right by the children's hospital where she had spent the longest and most painful years of her childhood. She refused to set foot there, not even if we had to have our tonsils out or our appendix removed; she preferred to go across Paris, she would have gone to the other side of the world, rather than risk reviving the traumas that haunted those corridors. Yet she had chosen to live near this memory palace, a building that loomed so large in her personal mythology. It towered over us like a ghost when we left our apartment house; she stumbled in its shadow. It was a sign of the inescapability of her past, both the past she had lived and the past she had invented. That she had chosen to live near the edifice of this past, just next door to it, was an indication of how much she needed to make visible, to make material, a cause, an origin story, for the disaster that was her life.

And tell the story of her life she did, continuously, ad nauseam, an unbearable monologue. She was like Winnie in Beckett's *Happy Days*, hectoring us, calling upon us as witnesses, her two darling, adored daughters, whom she loved for all eternity. During the years that followed her hospitalization at Sainte-Anne, she worked day and night on the writing of a story she called *Saxifrage*, for the flower that grows in rock. It was published by Éditions Séguier. Or rather, it was published at the author's own expense, but with her incomparable powers of persuasion, she succeeded in convincing the publishing house to print it for her. This text demanded more than three years of indefatigable labor; she wanted to do everything herself, including the layout, which involved little bits of paper cut out and pasted onto sheets that she folded into a booklet. She presented her autobiography in the form of calligrams made of rhyming expressions she sometimes made up, all ending with -ing: *Babbling/Floundering//Deporting/Hospitaling//Abandoning/Dead-bed-emptying//Trauma-ing* . . .

The story ended with her being locked up, her need to pull through for her daughters' sake. As evidence of her daughters' need for her, she chose to publish poems which my sister and I had written for her. She wrote that she had received them while still in the hospital, that the poems had cut through the fog of antipsychotics, had cleared her head with a force far more powerful than the electroshocks the orderlies were administering. My poem was a talisman. This was all invented for the sake of the narrative she was shaping in her book, but I had really written that poem, and it was soon impossible for me to untangle the truth from the story she was weaving. She had me write out a fair copy of my poem on graph paper, and that's the way it appeared in the book, in a color photocopy. I recognized my childish handwriting, I recognized the blue and pink tints of the lines in the Clairefontaine notebook. She had had me write the date, and my name and my grade in the upper-left-hand corner, like a piece of homework I'd handed in to my teacher. This element of realism tore a hole through the memory. That date was probably a falsehood, but I was no longer certain of that. I caught myself believing her literary invention. Yes, after all, perhaps she had received my poem in the hospital? Perhaps my verses had given her faith in the future. Perhaps poetry can help a person live a little longer.

The last time we went to Corrèze, it was after her collapse, just before the house was to be auctioned off, for next to nothing. Maman had begged in vain for Papa to buy it, she'd implored him, she'd wept and wept. That house was her very flesh, it was more important to her than anything, it was as important as her own daughters, upon whose heads she was always swearing—but usually lying, which somehow had the effect of making my sister and me wildly superstitious, a superstition that compelled us to avoid touching the white lines of the crosswalk, that had us counting our steps, making sure that no matter what, we arrived at the other side of the street on an even number, a superstition that caused us to suppress certain words from our vocabulary—God, for example—otherwise we'd end up in Hell. We, who had only seen that house flooded with friends, filled with laughter, we now arrived at the foot of the village in silence, and in the car that ascended the winding road, the weight of absences stifled us. Our brother and sister were no longer there, we would never see them again. No friends had been invited for this last visit. To close the coffin, there were only the three of us. The echo of our footsteps in the empty hallways sounded the death knell of our childhood. For the first time, Maman saw the red ivy—for it was early November—covering both sides of the stone wall that with her own two hands she had helped the masons build. We dined in the kitchen, seated on the extra stools that used to be for company. Now, in the dormitory for happy children, the beds were too big for our two forlorn bodies, and we knew that Maman wasn't sleeping, we heard her pacing up and down; we didn't ask to sleep in her bed, we remained where we were, which had the advantage at least of allowing my sister to take my hand as we tried to fall asleep. We left the house choked with sadness and with fear. Seeing Maman turn the key in the gate for the last time, I felt like the happiest moments of our youth were being locked away. Now it was time to grow up, to grow up quickly, and we did. We became unfailingly vigilant, we were very mature girls, entirely understanding of adult problems, or so Maman would tell us, a compliment that we accepted reluctantly. The hospitalization, the disappearance of the new husband's children, the loss of the house in Corrèze, the little dog's death, it all happened at the same time, the year the Berlin Wall fell.

MAMAN'S CIGARETTE PACKS, her red Rothmans, were left lying around everywhere in our subsequent apartments. She bought cartons exclusively—a pack scarcely lasted her half a day. At the time, children could be sent out to buy them for their parents without the tobacconist asking any questions. Maman would double-park, hand us the money, and one of us would run out and buy her a carton. She smoked like a chimney, and the expression suited her, I thought, because she was also our hearth. Maman had lovely, chic cigarette lighters that Papa had given her, lighters by Dupont and Cartier in silver or solid gold, but most of the time she lit one cigarette from the next. She left the discarded cigarettes, still burning, in different rooms of the apartment. They burned like incense, she forgot about them, she'd take another from an open pack lying on the sideboard in the living room, on her bedside table, on the kitchen counter, in her pocket, in her purse. In the car, we complained that the smoke was suffocating us and making our eyes burn; she'd tell us off, as she always did when we got in the way of her doing as she pleased. When you get your license and wheels of your own, then you can decide that you don't want people smoking in your car, but for now you're in my car, and I'll smoke whether you like it or not! Disgusted, indignant, we'd roll down the window in the back. We'd scarcely have time to breathe in a mouthful of the comparatively pure air, no matter that it was full of car exhaust, before she'd scream that it was cold as Hell: Roll that window back up right now! Is something wrong with you?

It's freezing, for fuck's sake! The ashtrays had to be emptied regularly, because she hated disgusting ashtrays overflowing with butts. Empty that disgusting old ashtray, would you please, sweetheart. Be a good girl, go empty it into the garbage can. We poured mountains of ash on top of food scraps, so that our household garbage didn't smell, or rather, it smelled like the furniture, curtains, carpet—it smelled of cigarettes. I started smoking at a relatively young age, stealing cigarettes from Maman's packs. Unlike my friends, I didn't need to hide it, Maman would generously offer me her smokes, inviting me to take one from her open pack—Take one, sweetheart, they're for everyone. My friends who were smokers were entitled to the same treatment and often left our house with a whole pack Maman had given them: Take, take, don't worry, my pet, I have plenty more! She smoked in bed with her café au lait, and her sheets were shot through with charred circles, so that her pillowcase resembled a target riddled with bullet holes.

On school forms or administrative documents, in response to the question of my mother's profession, I would write homemaker. She had taught ballet at the conservatory, and she had briefly been the owner of a school in Marseille, where she had lived with her first husband, whom we'd never met, and then Papa had helped her to finance the opening of a school in the posh suburb of Boulogne. The place had burned down under shady circumstances—it was quite possible that she had set fire to the premises herself, thinking perhaps that the insurance would cover the cost of damage, but it didn't—and Papa refused to act as guarantor for the loans she needed to restore it. Grandma, who had spent her whole life scrimping and saving down to the last cent in order to open her own dance school in her working-class suburb of Montreuil on the eastern edge of

Paris, was horrified by the idea that Maman might attempt to get involved in her school. For Maman to work with her mother was out of the question: it would have meant endless screaming matches, they would have ended up bludgeoning each other with toe shoes, strangling each other with ribbons. Not a good look for a ballet school! Maman roared, she couldn't help making a mess of things wherever she went. But Grandma was the opposite, Grandma was fanatically tidy, everything had to be dusted, spotless, there was scarcely time to finish what was on your plate before it had to be rinsed and put in the dishwasher, and don't leave any crumbs under the table, they'll attract bugs. Everything was perfectly in order, a place for everything and everything in its place. She scrubbed everything herself because if you want something done right, do it yourself, and even Grandpa, her assistant—whom she had attempted to mold to her specifications— found himself getting an earful all the time. Girls, look at all the cookie crumbs you've let fall on the floor! Quick, quick, pick up your feet so I can sweep under them before Grandma comes to scold us! Otherwise she'll chew me out again, just look at this mess! At Maman's place, household chores were scarcely a priority, ironing or cleaning the toilet weren't really her thing. Other women, often immigrants, from underprivileged backgrounds, took care of these sanitary rites for her. Maman quickly befriended these women, she would never have been able to refer to any one of them as the maid, as did Papa, who had grown up with servants. Maman invited them to have lunch, to chat, to have a smoke in the living room. She called them all honey or my darling and Grandma said it was crazy to be intimate like that with just anyone, and Papa found it entirely unsuitable for his ex-wife to be tenderly embracing the maid, but Maman said, Screw you, every single one of you, with your stupid bourgeois principles!

The devil finds work for idle hands, Papa would say, to explain or condemn Maman's collapses, the waves of lethargy that came over her, broken by sudden outbursts of wrath. Maman should make something of her life, Maman should keep busy. Keep busy! Me, who started working at seventeen, who set up a dance school on my own in Marseille, without anyone's help, who got a two-page spread in the city's newspapers with the shows I produced, alone, entirely on my own, by working my ass off without ever asking for help, without ever receiving even the tiniest bit of support from anyone—certainly not from my mother, my stupid bitch of a mother, who cared only about herself, who always managed to take credit for my successes, that slut. I could have set up my own dance company and might have become a great choreographer if only I hadn't met the bastard, the asshole who has the gall now to tell me that I need to keep busy! Well, I was doing very well before I met him, everything was fine until Monsieur decided to transform the life of the poor little dancer from Marseille! And I'm busy, guess what, asshole, I'm busy raising your daughters, in case you haven't noticed, even though I don't even have custody of them, even though I have to beg for the privilege of having them under my roof! You want to know how I spend my days, is that it? Want me to give you the rundown minute by minute? Well, even prisoners have a certain degree of freedom, times when nobody checks on them! I don't owe you any explanations, not you and not anyone else, do you hear me? I won't respond to your interrogations, I won't tolerate this harassment. I do as I please, is that clear? I'm big enough to look after myself and I say screw you, every single one of you! I swear one day I won't take it anymore. The day I finally go to the dogs, you're going to ask yourselves how is it possible, why'd she do it? Why? Because I'm human, that's why. Can you get that through your heads once and for all? I'm a miserable human being, like everyone else, I have faults, weaknesses, and yes, sometimes I even have desires, and right now what I really, truly desire is for you to fuck off!

Maman always said that her biggest mistake had been to leave her first husband, who was—at least in retrospect—a wonderful man. Afterward, her life was turned upside down, and the idea of a professional future lost all meaning: her work would have been nothing more than a pastime; the hobby of a kept woman. Maman had her pride, and she preferred to wreck her health, to spend her days ruminating, moaning, despairing, rather than settle into some pointless occupation. She'd rather die.

Maman didn't get very far in school; she was not a particularly gifted student and she certainly was not encouraged to study. I'm quite sure she didn't make it through high school. Much later on, when I was an adult, I let on that I knew this, and seeing her eyes fill with tears, those endless tears, I understood the extent to which her academic failure was more than shameful to her, it was tragic. So she'd been no good at school, big deal! We all knew she wasn't one for following rules. I didn't think it was so terrible, but for Maman every defeat took on epic proportions, any particular failure opened onto that giant failure that was, in her mind, her life. Since she'd failed to obtain them herself, Maman boasted of our good grades all the more, and her smile widened in proportion to the complexity of the poetry we recited by heart, or the multiplicity of unknowns in the equations we solved, or the erudition we (supposedly) displayed as we translated Virgil, the impressive Latin-French dictionary lying open on one of our desks.

Papa, on the other hand, was an intellectual, and on school forms, in the blank beside father's profession, I wrote, alternatively, philosopher, writer, or CEO, an acronym whose meaning was lost on me, nor was I certain what Papa did in his office on the Champs-Élysées—one block from Fouquet's, where he took his lunch for years—the office where he spent his life on the phone, seated behind a magnificent desk in the French Empire style inherited from his maternal grandfather. Behind him was a portrait of his father seated in an identical position, like a mise en abyme, the only difference being the gilt decorations, captured in the painting, of the Ministry of Culture on the rue de Valois, where my grandfather worked. During the six years prior to the Nazi invasion of France, Papa's father had signed, at his own desk, numerous letters addressed to the greatest artists, writers, playwrights, film directors, and architects of the interwar period. As the managing director in charge of fine arts, he also founded an international film festival on the French Riviera, to compete with the Venice Film Festival. The very first Cannes Film Festival opened with great fanfare on the beach of the Carlton Hotel, attended by the giants of Hollywood, on September 1, 1939, two days before France declared war on Germany. The poster by Jean-Gabriel Domergue, the illustrator who claimed to have invented the pinup, promised Parisian-style glamour. The Americans were crazy about it, they needed no convincing to return in 1946, when the festival began in earnest, the brilliance of French culture an indication that France would again be a world power, a paragon of democracy. Papa's father died twenty-two years before I was born; Papa was eighteen years older than Maman; fifty years separated Papa and me. I formed a mental picture of my paternal grandfather—that ancestor from another century, born the year of the Paris World's Fair, as the Eiffel Tower was going up—through his portraits, the one of him seated at his desk, and then another one, life-size and painted by a family friend, which showed him standing in an art gallery, elegantly dressed in a steel-gray, pin-striped three-piece suit, the medal of a Commander of the Legion of Honor at his buttonhole, looking thoughtfully into the distance, a Gitanes hanging from his lips beneath a graying, well-combed mustache, his hair slicked back, showcasing an inveterate seducer's grin. Papa, following the example of his father, had read every book and would become indignant at his daughters' appalling lack of culture, when, say, we failed to immediately recognize a line from one of Corneille's plays which he had quoted. Ahem, excuse me, *Le Cid*? Ever heard of it? Really, they go to school, these girls?

Maman was always asking us to look over her administrative correspondence to correct her numerous spelling errors. Her syntax was all the stranger for the way she combined her uncertain grammar with her attempted imitation of Papa's eloquence. She wanted to be worthy of his world, to speak in the formal language of his peers, but she also livened up this respectable French with working-class references, popular sayings, slang, and the obscenities that she couldn't help adding to her sentences the way other people might add salt to their meals. She learned catchphrases, courteous expressions that she repeated perfectly. She wrote out respectfully yours and thank you in advance for your consideration at the ends of her letters with the punctiliousness and attention to detail of the good student she never was. Because with Papa—or rather for Papa—Maman had wanted to learn. She had been fascinated by his endless travelogues through the humanities, from ancient Greece to German Romanticism, from the France of Rabelais to Shakespearean England. She gazed in wonder at the shelves of his library. That he'd read everything there—she was one of those people who asked if he'd really read all those books, thus unwittingly betraying her lack of education—amazed her; it seemed inconceivable to her that someone could be so learned, have access to so much knowledge. Papa organized his books neither alphabetically nor by theme, nor by author nor genre, but by their size and color. The books had to look lovely lined up on the shelves, and he collected them avidly, he bought cases of them wholesale, because they went well together, because they harmonized elegantly, like the entirety of the Soleil collection, those gorgeous hardcover volumes bound in solid-colored canvas, and about which Gallimard, in their promotional leaflet, says: as the sun is the pride of the planets, the books in this collection, all in octavo format, will be the pride of your home library. Papa had been pals with Michel Foucault during his second year of the preparatory course for the École normale supérieure; he had passed (and failed!) the *agrégation* (the high-level, competitive exam for teachers) with some of the greatest French philosophers of his times, whose names meant nothing to Maman. When she found herself at dinner with these celebrated members of the Parisian intelligentsia, she repeated names that she'd heard Papa pronounce indiscriminately, without distinguishing between the merely famous and the great. Between Kojève and Hegel, she couldn't say who was the more important philosopher, the intellectual significance of the works of French writers entirely escaped her, for her it was a universe as hermetically sealed off as the cans of beluga caviar my father encouraged her to sample. Maman had been born in the Upper Marais, at a time when the neighborhood was far from the boho wonderland that it's since become. Papa was born in Auteuil, a neighborhood that hasn't changed in a hundred years—timeless chic. Papa was the very incarnation of a champagne socialist. He rode around in a chauffeured Jaguar with a phone in it, fastened to the dashboard, the enormous receiver just an inch or two from the windshield, so that Papa howled every time he answered the phone, having hit his hand against the window in picking it up. He wasn't registered as a member of the Socialists—the atmosphere of trade-union meetings gave him hives—but he'd never voted for another party. He believed in democracy, in Diderot, in the triumph of reason. He admired Maman's will to rise above her social class; his admiration was tinged with condescension, but nevertheless, admire her he did. He was proud, she used to tell us, of her progress, when after having been corrected for the umpteenth time, she no longer made the syntactical mistakes that betrayed her lowly background. However it also happened that she sometimes told him he could go fuck himself with his shitty lessons, and she might spell it out for him, without any mistakes. Her grammar was impeccable when she cursed him.

DO AS YOU LIKE, my darlings, precisely as you like, all I ask is that you don't follow along with the masses like sheep. If your little friends throw themselves off a bridge, will you jump too? I should hope not. Make up your own minds, make your own choices. I couldn't care less what people have told you—people are morons! Despite her shame about her own lack of education, Maman considered mere book smarts to be the lowest form of intelligence. Anybody could read books and quote from them like a moron at every opportunity. The important thing was not to merely accumulate knowledge, but to do something with it, to nourish oneself with it in order to better understand the world, to come away from it with greater empathy for the human species, a bird's-eye view, to broaden one's consciousness, one's horizons. In our teenage years, Maman let us cut classes. That is, she let *me* cut classes, because my sister had no desire to skip school and found it scandalous that a girl of fifteen should be wandering around Paris or hanging around in cafés with her communist friends, would-be hippies who spent their days smoking hash. Well really, Maman, don't you think you should be keeping more of an eye on your daughter? My sister was aghast, and she let our mother know it, she asked her if she thought my coming home at odd hours, long after the school day had ended, and without anyone knowing what I'd been up to, was normal. Maman told my sister to shut her trap, to mind her own business, to worry about her own homework, and the people *she* hung around with: Are you ever going to stop acting like the police? Haven't you done enough snooping on me, now you're going to start with your sister? You drive me crazy! You're fucking impossible—cover your own ass! Go play with your rich friends, and leave your sister the fuck alone, would you? My sister's friends would go on to become bankers or lawyers, mostly. My friends didn't want to become anything in particular and even in adulthood their occupations were often unclear: who can say how cultural workers spend their time, exactly? Maman appreciated the idealism of my companions. My closest friends spent hours in our kitchen, smoking cigarettes and listening to Maman's rambling analyses of the unemployment crisis or the migrant crisis or the dismantling of the Soviet bloc or the war in Iraq or the Israeli-Palestinian conflict—she lay claim to her Jewish heritage but had no sympathy for Israel. One day she cut the hair of my best friend, just like that, because my friend had said she wanted a new look, a pixie cut, which my friend thought was just gorgeous! Maman let me play hooky because in exchange I brought her eccentrics who idolized her, young girls who feared nothing, who thought she was fantastic, who would have gladly listened to her all night long, she was their favorite, their adoptive mother. Maman answered questions that other mothers sidestepped, she gave us sex education classes richer in detail than any anatomy textbook, that is, she instructed my friends in these matters while I attempted to stop up my ears or else I left the room. I was sympathetic to my friends' curiosity but frankly I would have preferred that they refrain from asking these questions, I didn't really want to hear my mother talking about fellatio, sodomy, about cunnilingus and erogenous zones. I already knew far too much about her sexual preferences, not to mention those of my father.

When we reached puberty, Maman had impressed upon her daughters the need to take care not to be deflowered by the first asshole who came along. She encouraged us to preserve our virginity not because of any moral principle but, on the contrary, because she hoped to facilitate the pleasure that we might one day take in sex, and to prevent our first experience from becoming a torture session that would traumatize us for years to come. She strongly recommended that we choose a boy a bit older than us—the more experienced, the better—and strongly advised against doing it with a virgin: He won't know what he's doing, he could mangle you, my poor darling! It has to hurt a little bit, but your feelings will get you through the pain and if the boy knows what to do with his dick that can help, too. I wasn't in such a big rush to find this nice boy with a certain degree of experience who would only partially butcher me. If I was something of a late bloomer, perhaps it was because Maman's excesses left me a bit scalded or frozen, one or the other. In any case, my sister and I were wary of her omnipresent, ostentatious sexuality. And then there was the question of our grandfather, her father.

As teenagers, my sister and I never spoke about Maman, or rather, about what was wrong with Maman. It was only later, much later, that we discussed those childhood incidents that had most deeply marked us. Among the more sordid recollections haunting our memory, we were in agreement that Maman's father, her biological father, was the most nightmarish figure of all. Maman had hidden his existence from us until her divorce from Ducon, when our daily life had become such a disaster that perhaps adding one more grotesque story didn't seem to matter much. To tell the truth, we'd never noticed that Maman had a name that was different from Grandma and Grandpa's, and her maiden name had never seemed a mystery until she revealed its secret to us. When we were born, she said, she had promised Grandpa that he would be our only grandfather, and indeed she had never explained to us that Grandpa was Grandma's second husband, Maman's adoptive father, though he had never legally adopted her, which was another source of rage and frustration for her. She revealed the existence of her *real* father by telling us the story of his deportation and death: her real father had been Jewish, and he had died in the Holocaust.

But Maman was born in 1947, after the war; her father was indeed Jewish, however, since she'd been conceived two years after the Liberation, he couldn't have died in the camps. He hadn't even been deported. When Maman first told us this story, we didn't yet know these dates, so the narrative's implausibility didn't occur to us. Maman's father hid himself during the war, like my father and his brothers, and somehow, with great difficulty, he survived, as many did, by trafficking in all sorts of goods on the black market. Maman lay claim to her Jewishness, when she claimed it, in order not to find herself alone, to assert that she belonged to a people, a tribe; she rewove her past on the loom of History to give it meaning, give it weight.

This father, whose existence and whose death in the gas chambers we learned about simultaneously, appeared one day on our doorstep soon after Maman's stay at the psychiatric ward. Girls, this is my father. Her father? A phantom, a ghost? Nothing fit together, the presence of this man in her life, in our lives, made no sense at all. She called him Papa, and he bore her name. But who was this guy? No masculine incursion into our lives ever distressed us more than this one.

Her father entered our household just as we were taking our first tentative steps in the realm of sexuality. Whatever possibility of joy or exploration might have existed for us, whatever environment of support, was destroyed by him. His very presence, his gestures, his way of looking at his daughter and speaking to her, of putting his arm around her waist, was unmistakably disturbing. To describe him as lecherous doesn't do justice to the perversity of his character: everything about him seemed threatening and seedy. For several months, or perhaps a whole year, he dined with us on Mondays. In those days, as the end of the weekend approached, I experienced acute anxiety about the coming week—a week in which we wouldn't know, during the long hours that we spent in class, whether Maman would be there when we got back, and whether this man, her father, would be there with her or in her stead. I don't know if he worked or had some private source of income. He wasn't rich—that was obvious—but he also didn't seem to want for anything, he wasn't poor. No, Maman's father was never deported, but yes, he had spent time in prison—we didn't dare question him about his incarceration, we didn't want to know anything about it, nothing at all. But he loved talking about his past even more than Maman did, if such a thing were possible. His guttural voice, his street slang, his old Parisian argot, clashed with our idea of what a father, or a decent man, should sound like. There was nothing decent about him, and if Maman had perhaps inherited her disdain for convention from him, his vulgarity was beyond measure. After a certain time, he disappeared just as he had arrived, and neither my sister nor I could subsequently recall the particular incident that was the occasion for his expulsion. I have a familiar if vague sense that something serious happened, something entirely out of line (all lines had, no doubt, been crossed numerous times), the same hazy sense that surrounds my attempt to pinpoint Maman's collapse; both my sister and I felt that, by refusing to supply certain details, our minds were protecting us. But here again, a single memory serves as the trigger, a horrible memory that probably masks far worse. I haven't sought to verify this memory with my sister, hoping instead that she has forgotten it; if I haven't been able to do so, I hope that she at least cannot recall the story Maman's father told us one evening at dinner about his return from prison. He needed pussy, any pussy would do, as long as he could get laid, and he'd told his friend to do whatever was necessary to find him a chick because after the slammer, the urge to fuck is worse than when you need to piss, it grabs you right here— he showed us with his hands—and doesn't let go, and his pal at the last minute dug up a whore for him, you don't wanna know, not a broad but a skank, a slut full of crabs, something impossible, who stank of fish, and then, when I was doing everything I could not to smell her, holding my head up high, as far away as possible, right there in the middle of fucking her all of a sudden I couldn't get hard. So she took my head in her big paws and stuck it between her thighs. I thought I'd die, I almost passed out from the smell, and I puked everything I had in my belly all over her fat gut.

From the summer when he first appeared in our lives, I recall a remark that Maman's father made to my sister after having bought us both ice cream cones at a highway rest stop, about the way she licked her ice cream. Maman had asked him to drive us from Grandma's apartment in the South of France to the hotel where Maman was waiting for us in the mountains of Haute-Savoie, near Switzerland. Who knows what Maman was doing there. Grandma had just bought a place in the perfectly tacky apartment complex where she would spend her vacations. She hadn't seen this man since their separation, forty years earlier. She said it wasn't wise to let us go with him, she told Maman this on the telephone, and we didn't understand why Grandma was crying and getting so angry. Up until then we'd only seen him once or twice, and he must have behaved more or less correctly. We understood very quickly, on the hairpin turns of mountain roads, that Grandma had simply been using common sense in recommending that her daughter not allow her granddaughters to leave with this monster. Maman said that her mother had forbidden her from seeing him, that as an adolescent she'd secretly been in touch with him. Maman said that her father had been the victim, that her mother was a harpy, that she'd gotten herself knocked up to corner him, to force him to marry her because she was so in love with him, that he was gorgeous and her mother was a slut. Her father was well into middle age when we met him for the first time, but it was obvious that he'd been a very handsome man. Grandma was no less sublime, with her liquid blue eyes, the curve of her lips as if outlined in pencil, her dancer's figure. Maman had inherited her physique from her parents. She had also inherited a poisonous history, whose truth and falsehoods were difficult to untangle.

Only by cobbling together the bits of story that Grandma and Maman let fall could I reconstruct the circumstances of my mother's birth: in tallying the dates of the marriage and pregnancy, I realized that it could only have been an accident; in listening, despite myself, to the stories of Maman's father, I understood that he'd been a crook—a pimp, among other things. I imagined Grandma's father forcing him into marrying his daughter; even being married to a Jew—Grandma's family was undoubtedly more anti-Semitic than anticrime—was better than being pregnant out of wedlock. Grandma had always seemed a bit of a prude to me, and certainly not the type to sleep with just anyone. She would not voluntarily have given her virginity to a stranger in a dark doorway.

MAMAN SPENT HER LIFE TELLING the story of her life. She also wrote compulsively, fragmentary sentences, stray thoughts, half-finished poems on Post-its, sheets of loose-leaf paper, or even torn paper napkins. With *Saxifrage*, she wanted to retrace her steps, from her birth until her breakdown, Sainte-Anne, my poem that saved her. She chose a quotation from Stefan Zweig as an epigraph: Once a man has found himself, there is nothing in this world that he can lose. And once he has understood the humanity in himself, he will understand all human beings.

Maman, whose oral performances were exhaustive, endless, tried to keep her writing brief. Such concision was unlike her, it didn't take into account the complexity of her story, its contradictions. In rereading her book, I don't find her voice in it; the sentences—the verses—seem studied, affected. She would never have allowed herself to write as she spoke, bombastically and with delight. In my opinion, this was a mistake. Her voice was so much more beautiful in its outrageousness. Restraint didn't suit her, restraint was antithetical to her personality, whether the restraint was stylistic or syntactical. In turning over my copy of *Saxifrage*, I recognize her voice finally on the back cover, and I can't help but smile as I imagine her savoring her own exaggerated jacket copy:

> *Saxifrage* is a flower of such extraordinary vitality that it can sometimes *break through rock* in order to see the light of day. . . . All on its own, this title, expressly chosen by the author, describes in a *highly symbolic* manner the trajectory of a woman whose life force was *so strong* that no obstacle could stop her.

> *Catherine CREMNITZ*, born April 1, 1947, to a Jewish father and a Catholic mother, suffered the consequences of her father's deportation and found herself confronted with the problems posed by this double identity.

> It is a scream.

(I'm quoting the jacket copy in full here; this sentence comes right after the biographical note, without transition, which is completely like her.)

> All the power of this autobiographical text resides in its search for a form of writing that embodies the paradoxes of a certain lived experience.

(I admire her ambition, her determination to use figures of speech to get as close as possible to the contradictions of her being; that, too, is like her.)

It's impossible not to be moved by this spirit, these often violent and crude outbursts of revolt . . .

(The outbursts on the page are nothing compared to the out-bursts I had experienced in person.)

which once exposed, transport the reader into a universe of extreme discretion . . .

(whatever that means)

and infinite poetry.

I often begged her to stop turning things over in her head. What I meant was for her to stop ruminating, to stop beating herself up over nothing. She replayed the loop of her misfortunes over and over again, and the wheels of the bicycle kept turning, turning, turning, a bicycle that veered off track, a bicycle that didn't have brakes, like the one in whose spokes she'd gotten her foot caught as a child, during her first ride with Grandpa, Grandma's new husband, when the foot of her shorter leg got caught in the back wheel and was skinned down to the bone of the arch. The skin of her left midfoot was smooth and fine as tissue paper, like the skin of someone who'd been burned. Maman had been skinned alive. Her whole life long she had attempted to cover that nakedness, that sense of exposure, with words and em-braces. But if there are two things in this world that one can safely say are imperfect, that inevitably fall short, they are love and language. Words—besmirched by centuries of misuse, worn out by clichés, arbitrary—are always traitors. And what can one say of love, that eter-nal inconstant, relentless in its deceit of her? Maman kept repeating her failures because it was impossible for her to arrive at a definitive version of her life. She had to tell it to us again because we hadn't understood, and not just because we were self-righteous little shits, incapable of really listening to her, but because it was incomprehensible, even to her, because all the words in all the world's dictionaries would not have been enough to explain the heaviness in her heart. So she wrote draft after draft, she created a second skin for herself with these obsessive laments, a colorful carapace, obscene, but also, yes, infinitely poetic. A fable, a fantasy.

> *Maman, Maman,*
> *You who love me so*
> *Why, without telling me, would you go?*

I did write that poem for her, never mind the date. The biographical elements that served as her history, or her mythology even, didn't need to be accurate in order to be true. They really took place in her past as she recalled it. The truth of a life is the fiction that sustains it.

In the end, Maman was not wrong to reproach us for not treating her as a human being. The hyperbolic quality of her invectives made them hard to take seriously, but when Maman screamed that we spent our time denying her humanity—I'm a human being, for fuck's sake!—she was right in part. She was our mother, in other words, both more and less than other humans, more animal and yet more mythological. She could complain and rebel but she could not liberate herself from this condition. Catherine could only be an idea for me, an abstract notion, at best an unknown. As for the woman who had existed before giving birth to me, I had no access to her. To me, Catherine could only ever be a work of fiction. So I endowed her with my fantasy of what might have been her history, her thoughts, her choices. Of course, she had told me the story of her life in great and contradictory detail, but to give shape to her I had to imagine her, interpret her. I had to become the narrator of her story in order to give her back her humanity.

PART II

CATHERINE WAS BORN IN PARIS, on April 1, 1947. April Fools' Day! So things got off to a funny start. For her birthdays, she'd put in a special order at the bakery for a cake in the shape of a fish—the April fool in French is a *poisson d'avril*, a fish who is easily caught. Catherine Jacqueline Pierrette: Catherine because it was in fashion at the time, Jacqueline because it was her mother's name, and Pierrette in honor of her uncle Pierre. Of her three given names, she finds Catherine to be the least offensive.

Catherine says that her father's family were Polish Jews. While her father didn't die in Auschwitz, his family might well have emigrated from Warsaw. Cremnitz, however, is the name of a village in Hungary, so baptized under the reign of the Hapsburgs. Cremnitz, in turn, gave its name to a specific shade of white paint manufactured there—cremnitz white—a lead-based oil paint, particularly prized by portraitists for its fibrous texture and the depth it lends to depictions of flesh. This paint is also eminently toxic, like all those lead-based house paints whose use has been banned, in recent decades, to safeguard the public's health.

For Catherine, the question of her name returns at regular intervals to complicate her life, or even jeopardize it—her mental state being so precarious that any imbalance can present a mortal danger, causing her will to live to wither suddenly. The saxifrage, that flower that pushes through hard rock to find the light, could also lay down on the stone and die.

Catherine is not the result of a planned pregnancy.

One Saturday afternoon at the start of summer, her mother, Jacqueline, meets a handsome young man at the Piscine Molitor, the celebrated Art Deco landmark in the 16th arrondissement which she visits each winter, when the open-air swimming pool turns into an ice-skating rink. That year the pool attracts international attention with the first ever presentation of the bikini. Its creator says he named it for the atoll in the Marshall Islands where a few days earlier a nuclear device had been detonated. Jacqueline is a bomb-shell. Serge notices her right away in the crowd of bathers. He's not so bad-looking himself—tall and dark, with a vaguely menacing air. He invites her to go out dancing with him, if her father will let her. Sure, she says, proud, boastful, and anyway, I do as I please. So one evening she goes out with the young man, taking her brother along as chaperone. They tell the parents they're going to eat ice cream and take a walk along the canal. Instead, Serge takes them to a bar he knows where they can dance. He holds Jacqueline firmly by the waist, she sways and wiggles her hips better than anyone, she's an expert at swing, an excellent dancer. Dance is her passion. The hit songs of 1946 talk about finding blue skies of morning forever in her eyes, and seeing *la vie en rose* while wrapped in his arms—the color palette of bruises. She loses track of her brother. Suddenly, Serge tells her they're going out for some air. She balks, she'd like to find her brother first. Forget that, he says. A half-empty bottle of beer in his hand, he pulls her out of the bar by her arm. She struggles away from his grasp, he takes hold of her hair. He drags her into an alley.

He shoves her facefirst against a wall. She screams, he tells her to shut up, smashing the bottle as she cries for help. He uses his free hand to muzzle her, his fist as a gag. She thinks she feels the shard slicing through her crotch, she feels cut in two. Now she's too frightened to cry out, but tears stream down her face. When he lets go of her, he throws her a tissue, tells her to wipe herself. She's collapsed on the ground. She cleans herself off as best she can; her torn stockings are covered in blood. She finally finds her brother again. He doesn't question her. He takes her home in silence.

She might not have gotten pregnant that night, but then there would have been no story. Obviously, back then, abortion was not an option. Jacqueline's family finds the guy who knocked up their daughter, pressures him, makes the young scoundrel face the music, marry the soon-to-be mother. Which for him was a fucking pain. He'd be sure to make the bitch pay for it. Jacqueline, who'd dreamt of becoming a gymnast, after she'd had to give up the idea of becoming a ballerina because her father forbade it—because he thought dancers were loose women, if only he'd known!—hates her deformed body. She hides her pregnancy until it shows through even the trapeze dresses and the little cloak her mother sews for her as camouflage. She gives birth in pain, which doesn't help her love for this infant born of violence and dread. As for him, well, it's hard to imagine a bigger nightmare, he's like something out of the Dark Ages, the type who beats and rapes his wife and would gladly have sold her ass for a few kopecks if she'd been a tad less hysterical. He resigns himself to haggling over the asses of other tarts whom he puts to work for him. Their home becomes a hotbed of disease. In this period of destitution, when penicillin has only just been invented, the options for treatment are limited.

Little Catherine, always sickly, falls gravely ill at eighteen months. It's not clear what's wrong with her, some kind of meningitis, and after several days of fever, her mother places a hand on her burning forehead, observes the child's sunken eyes, notices with terror that she isn't even crying anymore. There's a haggard look in her eyes, an abyssal glaze. Leaning over the crib, Jacqueline wavers: she can picture her daughter slipping into the earth. Just like that, the baby could disappear just like the birth, one immense wave of pain and it would all be over, she could leave her monstrous husband and start a new life, bear the wound inside of her in silence, bury it. Her little Catherine shivers, febrile, her little Catherine is going to die, and she remembers, in spite of herself, her baby girl's first smile, the smell of her fuzzy head, like fresh-cut grass, her beautiful blond curls now flattened against her feverish nape, her tiny teeth set far apart behind purple lips, and she picks her up, swaddled in the baby bunting she's knitted for her, she lifts the child to her face to kiss her, and she promises to help her live, my pretty baby, I love you, my angel, don't worry, Maman will make everything better, Maman will save you, my little blue baby. She takes her to the emergency room at Necker, the children's hospital. There, they look after her daughter, free of charge. The doctors make no promises, they can't tell whether she'll make it, they won't risk an opinion.

From the winter of 1948–49 until the spring of 1952, Catherine is an inpatient at Necker, fluctuating between death throes and remission, relapse and convalescence. She grows up in this boarding-house for children with tuberculosis, meningitis, polio, she grows as best she can, all crooked, one side delayed and never managing to catch up with the other; she gets used to suffering, to being strapped down for spinal taps, she gets used to losing playmates, whether they are cured or they die, she gets used to seeing them disappear, just as her mother has disappeared. How is she to understand her mother's absence? The world she knows is as chilling as her metal-frame bed. How could she guess that visits are forbidden, or imagine the woes of a battered woman? Perhaps in her child's mind, she tells herself that her mother is mad at her for being ill, and that she has to heal quickly in order to be forgiven. She leaves there miraculously cured, at five years old, lagging behind every developmental milestone, emaciated, a miniature survivor who has everything to learn, including where she comes from, who she is, and what the world is like beyond the hospital's gray walls, its smell of bleach.

Her mother had gone back to live with her parents while Catherine was at Necker. She'd left the creep, she even officially divorced him. And then she found a nice young man who wanted to marry her even though she was divorced and already had a child. She is twenty-four years old and gorgeous, and when her little daughter comes home from the hospital, she leaves her with the grandparents, so that she can set up house with her new husband.

THEY CALL HER CATHERINE, what's-her-face, little so-and-so. The grandfather is a hairdresser, they live behind the shop, near the flea market in the Marais. Catherine is anemic, she's got to learn to chow down, and fatten up, or she'll waste away. They force her to drink a tall glass filled with fresh beef blood every day at noon, followed by a spoonful of cod liver oil. It takes two people to hold her down on the chair and pinch her nose while tipping her head back to get her to swallow. She gargles it for as long as she can so as not to feel the warm, viscous liquid running down her throat, but finally there it goes, and sometimes it comes back up, too, spreading all over her lap. Fussy little girls who play at being difficult are not welcome in this house. The grandfather hits her when she throws up. Granny consoles her with caresses and candy. And then her mother, under orders from her own father, who is tired of the brat, comes to take her back. Granny cries a lot, and her little tree frog cries too, the girl's cheeks streaming with tears, her eyes puffy, snot running down to her chin. Between sobs, the sad frog promises to be a good girl with her maman, even though she doesn't recognize her. She hides behind her granny's skirts so as not to leave with the stranger.

In the new household, they have even less patience with the grumblings of this bratty little girl with no manners at all. The grandparents on that side aren't exactly thrilled to have married off their young son, just returned from his military service in Algeria, to a divorcée with a problem child, and they take it out on little what's-her-face, which is what the neighbors in Montreuil begin to call her—lower Montreuil, that is, near Croix-de-Chavaux, before the public-assisted housing projects were built, where the little Arab children remind Henri, the stepfather, of the streets of Algiers. Henri is kind, he's madly in love with Jacqueline, and thinking to do the right thing he spends his time trying to get a smile out of this poor, melancholy girl with listless eyes. Henri, isn't it about time you finished monkeying around with the kid? Jacqueline cries. She reminds him of his mother, always nagging.

• • •

IT'S ABOUT TIME FOR the child to start school. She's seven and she still hasn't learned her letters, she's never seen chalk on a blackboard, she's never been disciplined in a group, unless you count the cafeteria benches at Necker, where even the strongest children were still not well enough to be unruly. And right from the start, at roll call, she's in the wrong: Catherine Cremnitz, once, Catherine Cremnitz, twice. Calling Catherine Cremnitz, and either she's absent without an excuse, without properly informing the school, or she's being a smart aleck, hardly the kind of attitude that's going to help us get along here. The teacher gives up and continues roll call. Once everyone else has raised their hands, Catherine timidly raises hers: You haven't called me, Teacher, but I'm here ... She's sent to the principal's office for bad behavior, because she didn't recognize the name they're now insisting is her own. A troublemaker at school, a troublemaker at home: her mother, furious that the child has drawn attention to herself on the very first day, now has to explain to the principal that in fact she is divorced from the child's father. Once again the girl reminds her of her shame.

School is difficult for Catherine. She's far behind her classmates. Although she's seven, she traces her letters painfully, like a four-year-old. The teachers are disturbed by her delay: she's both distracted and a slow learner; she's always fidgeting, she keeps having to be sent to the corner or the principal's office, but punishments seem to have little effect on her, she crosses her arms and purses her lips. Her pride only makes her teachers crack down on her more vehemently, believing they must up the ante in order to beat some sense into this incorrigible dunce.

Catherine may not be much of a student, but she makes up for that with ballet. Her mother transfers her aborted dream of a career in dance to her lame daughter. Too bad one of the girl's legs is shorter than the other, but if she's scrawny, so much the better, dancers need to be slender, and in that regard Catherine's figure is ideal. And then she has courage and energy to spare, and she so wants to please her mother, she'd do anything to avoid disappointing her. At eight they start her on pointe work, on the tips of her skeleton legs, one leg three and a half centimeters shorter than the other, and by some miracle she compensates for that without tipping her pelvis; long-limbed, supple, graceful, she keeps her balance, in arabesque, in passé, she triumphs over the *pas de bourrée*, the *dégagés*, the *chassés*, the *glissades*, the *ballonnés*, she quickly moves on to tackle turns—the *piqués*, the *pirouettes en dehors*, *en dedans*, and, later on, the *fouettés*— she excels under the exacting eye of her mother, who never congratulates her, who always finds something to criticize, because that's how one improves. And Catherine improves, she's great at it, she's magnificent. Her body has only just recovered from illness, but her injuries calcify; soon it's difficult to distinguish between scar tissue and new calluses.

In dance class, Catherine finally makes a friend, Nini, her dear Nini. She, too, lives in Montreuil, but she doesn't go to the same school as Catherine. (At school, no one plays with Catherine; she sits alone at the back of the class, a pariah.) Catherine and Nini grow up together, and at puberty they are both flat as ironing boards, perfect profiles for ballerinas, in variations they alternate between boys' and girls' roles, they love dancing the *pas de deux*, they give each other real kisses on the lips during the *arabesques penchées*, in the bathroom they play doctor.

Now the boys whom Catherine had fought with during her entire school career suddenly begin to run after her. One who's a bit more of a wise guy than the others puts his hand on her ass when they're going up the high school stairs; she turns around, her arm spring-loaded like the flipper of a pinball machine, and gives him a slap in the face that sends him flying down the steps, his face bloodied in the fall. Uproar in the hallways. For the first time in her life, her mother takes her side. And with good reason! Such predators are a personal matter for her. No, her daughter won't let herself be pawed by some creep, it's outrageous that a fifteen-year-old girl is forced to come to blows to defend her honor!

Jacqueline begins giving dance lessons at a gym whose owner allows her to use the space during off-peak hours. She hopes to open a school one day; it's a start. Jacqueline and Henri are not spendthrifts, they're content with little, they're careful with money and have no desire to live beyond their means. Catherine wants everything that's off-limits to her, all that glitters, everything she doesn't have. She dreams of going on vacation somewhere other than the nondescript Italian beach where the young men call after her in a language she cannot understand. Every summer, the three of them—she, her mother, and Henri—leave for Rimini, taking the train to Turin, and then a bus. She'd love to go to Rome, can't they go to Rome? Just for the day? Well, how do you intend to get there? By swimming? Thanks to Henri's job, they get a good deal on accommodations in one of those new hotels facing the sea, a sea whose blue is obscured by rows of parasols, deck chairs, and beach towels. Catherine hates parasols just as she hates umbrellas, those hideous objects that confine their holders in little misanthropic bubbles. Catherine has some strange ideas. Catherine has always been different.

After Rimini, Jacqueline takes Catherine to a dance workshop in Royan (a coastal town southwest of Paris) directed by a former prima ballerina from the Paris Opera Ballet, which takes place during a month in the summer. These workshops are expensive, it's a privilege for her daughter to be able to attend, to train with such high-level professionals. There she learns not only ballet but also character dances, the fox-trot, the cha-cha, tap dancing, mime. Catherine is a born actress, and the professors soon take note of her talent, her discipline, spirit, perseverance. Unfortunately, the other students also notice that she is chaperoned by her mother, who won't let her out of her sight. On days off she's invited to the neighboring town, it's not far away, less than an hour by bus. The answer is no. Can she at least go for a walk downtown with her friends? Certainly not, does she think her mother is an imbecile? She's not going anywhere, and is that Catherine's way of thanking her mother, to make her feel that she's in the way, to use any excuse to drop her? Catherine doesn't protest, but seethes in secret. One evening she slips out with girls who have some boys coming to pick them up in a car late at night. They make a campfire on the beach and smoke cigarettes. The other girls allow the boys to feel them up, Catherine says no thank you, but she smokes a joint for the first time. When they return in the early morning hours, their giggling in the hallway wakes Catherine's mother. She has nothing to say to her daughter; she doesn't know what she's done to deserve such a child. Until their return to Montreuil, her mother refuses to speak to her, despite Catherine's tears and pleas, her desperate attempts to be forgiven. She didn't mean to cause her mother so much pain, she only wanted to have a little fun.

Her breasts develop all at once, she gets her period very late, at sixteen and a half, and as boys become interested in her, she starts becoming interested in her father, her real father, that is. She keeps pressing her mother to let her meet him; finally, her mother puts her in touch with a cousin of his with whom she's occasionally corresponded. It turns out that Catherine's father, Serge, has been living in Paris this whole time, or in the suburbs, not far away in any case. She meets him in a café, they have a beer together. He offers to take her on vacation to see his pal Jacky, who looks after horses for a traveling circus. If she wants to, she can go riding. She wants to. She doesn't need to be asked twice. Her mother is entirely against the idea, but Catherine goes anyway. She's seventeen and old enough to decide for herself. Her mother threatens to throw her out. She calls her all kinds of names, tells her she's a little slut, that she'd better not set foot in her house again. Catherine tells her that's fine with her. Slinging a bundle over her shoulder, she leaves that same night for Nini's.

The following week, she arrives at the bar where her father told her to meet him, but he isn't there. She waits. She orders coffee when the waitress comes back for the third time to ask if she's going to just sit there for free. She waits, staring off into space, she thinks he'll never come, she thinks he'll come, she counts on her lucky star, she tells herself there's no way she can be so unlucky. Finally she sees her father arrive with a lady in heels. She hesitates, unsure of what to call him in this context. She makes up her mind: Papa? He doesn't acknowledge her right away, the lady snickers. Is that your daughter, you bastard? That's a laugh! Catherine reminds him of their meeting, he explains that something came up, he won't be able to leave until the next day. She says she's run away from her mother's house and she has no place to stay. He says, okay, he'll take her in. She spends the night at his place, a one-bedroom on the third floor of a building blackened with grime, although the construction seems new. She sleeps on the couch. They make a lot of noise, he and the woman who'd mocked her. The following day around sundown they leave town, heading south, he says he likes to drive at night. His rig is a sort of camper; he explains that, for a long time, he lived in it. She's relieved to see that the woman isn't coming with them. They stop midway, at about three a.m., to get a bite to eat at a highway rest stop that he knows well because it's the only one in France that's open all night. He tells her he assumes she doesn't have a dime. She responds that she took all her savings with her. He has her pay for dinner. As they leave, he asks if she knows how to drive, he's beat. No, unfortunately not. No worries, he'll teach her. During their stay he has her practice on back roads, he shows her how, by turning the steering wheel just so, you avoid having to slow down on curves. She learns race-car driving, her foot pressed all the way down on the gas.

Once they've arrived, she gets on a horse for the first time and instantly falls in love with riding; with her dancer's posture, she's great at posting to the trot. Serge's friend Jacky is impressed. And Catherine's not afraid, not at all, right from the start, she goes over jumps. She shares a bed with her father, a fold-out bed in his camper. He goes to sleep after she does, he drinks a lot, he stays out late with Jacky and the circus troupe. There's a dance hall at the campgrounds near the big top. She meets a boy there who makes eyes at her, he's from Paris like her, he's a pretty boy, that's as far as her interest in him goes. One night her father slips under the sheets and gets close to her. He grips her, his whole body lassoed around her, she freezes. She feels something hard rubbing against her lower back, she isn't sure what it is but she suspects it's not an elbow. She's never seen a penis, let alone an erect one. Her father's hands press against her firm breasts and dig into her belly, his fingers, she thinks they're his fingers, she's not sure, pull down her underwear, he's hurting her but she keeps quiet. A moan. A warm liquid spreads over her ass. She stays silent. Motionless, she waits for dawn. She's going to go find the boy from the campgrounds and ask him to make love to her. If she's going to lose her virginity, she prefers that it be with someone other than her father. And it's done.

When the time comes to return to Montreuil, she says she doesn't want to go back. She faints. There's no reviving her. She has to be carried, unconscious, to the hospital. From the hospital in Antibes, Serge calls Jacqueline to ask her to come pick up her daughter. She arrives with Henri, who is in a panic. The doctors talk euphemistically about mental illness, they recommend at minimum a stay in a rest home. Her mother takes her to Épinay-sur-Seine, on the outskirts of Paris. Catherine spends a month there in a lithium haze. The day she gets out she learns that Granny is very ill. The little tree frog has neither the will nor the strength to be at her bedside. Soon after, Granny dies. Catherine doesn't go to her funeral. Her mother reviles her, how could she be so self-centered, how could she be so shameless and selfish. Catherine doesn't say goodbye to her grandmother because she has it in mind to follow her; she can't attend the funeral because she chooses that moment to disappear for good. She returns from her first suicide attempt a little dimmed, like a star shrouded by clouds, faded but not entirely lost. Her time has not yet come. The fight must go on. There follows a longer stay in another rest home. She shuffles through life without desire. At seventeen, she feels damaged. Without offering a clear diagnosis, the doctors speak of mood disorders, psychosis, the necessity of long-term psychiatric care. They talk a lot, but they do little besides inject her full of drugs. She emerges from her treatments dazed, her will broken.

• • •

CATHERINE DROPS OUT OF HIGH school. Still against all expectations, she becomes certified as a ballet teacher, passing the competitive exam by adapting the variations to her good leg. Her mother doesn't tell her how proud she is, but her eyes are shining. During the long weeks of preparation, Catherine manages to pull herself back from the brink of despair by punishing her body with relentless practice, until her muscles shake with exhaustion. She follows the courses at the conservatory that one of the professors from Royan has invited her to take. She doesn't spare herself because of her infirmity, she does everything like the others, she wears herself out with pain, and one evening when she's returning to Montreuil by subway, exhausted, her feet bloody, she overhears two boys whispering as they pass on the platform: that's a beautiful girl, too bad she limps. From that day forward she wears only high heels, to better hide her handicap. Too bad if they hurt. You have to suffer to be beautiful, dancers know that better than anyone, and as for physical torture, she's been used to that since she was a toddler. She'd gone back to living with Jacqueline and Henri. Catherine helps her mother with the dance classes. Jacqueline is lacking in fundamental skills and competencies, so Catherine backs her up and lends her legitimacy. That summer, Nini is awarded her high school diploma with distinction, and to celebrate the two of them borrow an old Renault 4L and set off on an adventure to visit some of Nini's cousins. They haven't got a dime, they smoke P4s—the cigarettes of the poor, Parisienne cigarettes sold in packets of four, so vile that they make them cough even more than the Renault's exhaust—and for their meals they buy jam and baguettes and picnic in the villages where they stop overnight.

Right after she arrives, Catherine meets a young man a few years older than she is, who comes from Marseille even though he doesn't have a southern accent. You might mistake him for a movie star, James Dean or one of those boys with angelic faces on the posters young girls pin to their bedroom walls. He has a job and a car and pays Catherine the sort of attention that renders his affection unmistakable. Catherine falls madly in love, and so does he. He's too shy to do more than kiss her on the neck. They're nineteen and twenty-four years old respectively, and they hold hands. He promises to come see her in Paris, to write to her every day. When she returns home, she waits desperately for the mail to arrive. He writes her wild love letters in which he compares the color of her eyes to dunes in the desert; he can see in them the rest of his days flowing by, like sand in an hourglass. She sleeps with the letters pressed to her chest, she rereads them one after the other, in chronological order, she reads them to herself slowly, her finger following each line. Her mother intercepts one and exposes her secret: she fears the worst for her daughter. What is this about, what now? Who is this guy? And I was just beginning to believe in you! What have I done to deserve this? Catherine tells herself that the boy who really loves her will love her as she is, dishonored, fallen. Yes, he'll love her for who she is, he'll love her madly. Catherine writes to him—Nini helps correct her spelling—to say that she can't wait any longer, that she wants to return to him. Nini asks if she's really sure, they'll be so far away from each other if Catherine goes to live in Marseille. Catherine tells her that she'll come to see her. The boy responds with a formal marriage proposal. He knows about the attempted suicide, Catherine told him. He also knows that his future wife is no longer a virgin, he knows and accepts her just the way she is. In June 1967, they marry. Catherine is twenty years old.

The boy's name is Paul. She takes his last name, whatever it is; she changes names easily; she's already done it three times before. She creates a new identity for herself, in Marseille, she becomes someone else, she's no longer what's-her-face, or a Cremnitz; she's very happy about that. She's very happy to belong to a man, a man who wanted to give her a name. From then on, no one in her life will ever call her anything but Catherine. Never Cate, and certainly not Cathy. Her only stable, fixed identity will be her first name—what women keep for themselves when they set up house. Catherine and Paul are magnificent newlyweds, their photo shoot in the Bois de Vincennes looks like something out of a magazine. They take their vows standing before the altar in the church at Montreuil, and then in the town hall of Marseille's 6th arrondissement—just behind the basilica of Notre-Dame-de-la-Garde, which watches over them—and she hears herself being asked, *Catheurineuh, Jacqueulineuh, Piérrêteuh,* do you take this man . . . ? Yes, she does. She'd packed her bags as quickly as possible, so happy at last to leave behind the gray skies of Paris, the pavement, the pale, ugly faces of commuters. In Marseille, the bartenders' faces are leathered like the copper counters of cafés. The sun is so blinding that you develop small lines around your eyes from squinting; even the notion of old age, of wrinkles, entices Catherine here. The city is always aglow, bathed in light—light that throws a bougainvillea or a hedge of oleander into high relief, that shimmers in a rearview mirror or picks out something sparkling in a shop window. Everything seems so beautiful to her that she could cry, and at first she often does cry. Paul asks her if she's sad, he's concerned and caring, but she promises that she's not sad, she's just terribly moved by it all. She cries the first time they make love—he insisted on waiting until they were married, which she finds almost unbearably romantic. She gasps with pleasure; she's not sure it's an orgasm, but a weight is dissolving, a weight below her chest, between her thighs, along her legs. Her whole body is dissolved, dissolved so she may be restored. She eats. She discovers that she likes to eat, the Mediterranean cuisine is delicious, Catherine adores the *rascasse*, the red fish that her father-in-law catches on Sunday mornings for their weekly *bourride*, and aioli, and bouillabaisse, of course, and *panisses* (flatbreads made of chickpea flour) and tapenades and *navettes* (shortbreads flavored with orange-flower water) and pastis, the anise-flavored liqueur they open on holidays or for special occasions. Her mother-in-law's accent would warm her heart, if her heart weren't already fit to burst; the daughter-in-law is welcomed with a spontaneous affection that reminds Catherine of Granny, her granny whom she misses so. Yes, she adores her new life. She is happy.

Without a penny to their name, but emboldened by their love, the young couple doesn't worry about the future. They live with Paul's parents, who are overjoyed to shelter them for as long as they wish. *Catheurineuh* is marvelously helpful at home, she assists her mother-in-law with shopping, cooking, washing the dishes, doing the laundry, ironing, sewing—behind the dancer lies a homemaker. And then she finds a job as an instructor in a neighborhood dance school. The students idolize her, and noting her clipped Parisian accent, the mothers admire the chic girl who studied dance in the capital. Pretty soon, she begins speaking to Paul about opening her own place, a studio for children and ladies, housewives to whom she'd offer exercise classes when their young children are at school. He encourages her, he admires her ambition, even if he doesn't have the faintest idea of how to go about raising the necessary funds; he doesn't have the means, nor do his parents, and her own parents wouldn't risk lending her the money for a security deposit, but she doesn't lose hope. Paul works in a real estate agency, he has an entry-level job, secretarial work, mostly. He didn't continue his studies after high school, he'd been good at writing and a sensitive reader, he was highly literary, but no one around him had any idea how to put such skills to use, although he had used them to write beautiful letters to win over the love of his life—that was at least something. One day as she's wandering along the Corniche—she is still unfamiliar with the city and frequently gets lost—she notices an abandoned retail space on the ground floor of a dilapidated building, and she says to herself, that's it, she's found her dance school. Paul helps her locate the owners, who agree to rent it for next to nothing, they don't understand what the young woman wants to do with this filthy basement, but whatever, it's hers.

To say that it needs a lot of work would be an understatement. She gets a loan from the director of the savings bank on the place Estrangin-Pastré, on the strength of her ambition, her talent, and most of all her beauty: during the interview she's wearing a new dress, nipped in at the waist and in a shiny silver gray, which she'd stolen from a downtown boutique. She'd gotten into the habit of stealing from stores to be able to give gifts to her mother and to Nini. In the beginning, she'd tell the recipients of these gifts that she'd stolen them, she'd brazenly confess her larceny, which she considered a feat. The fact that she'd committed a crime hadn't occurred to her, she'd simply taken what other people had the means to pay for and she didn't. That reality seemed to her as arbitrary as the prices of things, as the changeover from the old to the new francs, as the growth of the gross national product during the decades following the Second World War. But her mother had given her such a hard time about it that now she swiped things in secret. Those were prosperous times, between 1967 and 1973, it was easy to get a bank loan, and even easier if you were a lovely young woman in a pretty dress. Neither she nor Paul knew how they would pay back the sizable loan, but that scarcely bothered Catherine, she was sure she'd succeed.

Her school opens in September, at the same time, coincidentally, as that of her mother, who a few years earlier had bought a space in lower Montreuil, a co-op with an apartment above the dance studio, but the construction work had been delayed so often that she'd lost all hope that it would ever be completed; right when Catherine leaves for Marseille, however, it all starts moving again, as if by magic, as if Catherine just had to clear out for things to get going. The ever-changing social landscape of Montreuil had altered dramatically in the time it took to construct Jacqueline's Beauté-Santé dance studio. She had to lower her prices in order to attract a wider range of clientele beyond ballet aficionados, who in that neighborhood proved to be few in number. The public-assisted housing and high-rise apartment blocks that began to appear after the war had by now spread out across the neighborhood. Croix-de-Chavaux, the big housing project right across from Beauté-Santé, gets under way at the end of the 1960s. It introduces a level of racial diversity for which no one in this working-class suburb is prepared. Jacqueline hadn't expected her clientele to be so varied, but when you have a business to run, you don't turn up your nose.

Catherine and Paul move from Malmousque, where he'd grown up, in a home that had been in his family for generations, to be nearer to the Corniche and thus closer to the school. At the beginning she keeps her job as an instructor at the neighborhood school so as not to lose the income, but the enrollments at her new studio pile up and the demand grows so quickly that she soon devotes herself full-time to her studio, teaching from morning until late in the evening, including on weekends; she works relentlessly, she wants to get on in life. She'd so love for her mother to admire her achievement. She tells her about her successes when she goes to visit her in Montreuil. Jacqueline got a poodle to defend herself against potential burglars now that she's a homeowner. She doesn't congratulate her daughter, but she models her own school on Catherine's. Catherine explains her school's structure and schedule in detail, and Jacqueline imitates it. By the time September rolls around again, Catherine feels that she's created a new family for herself with her little ballerinas, most of whom are as talentless as they are earnest, but it doesn't matter, it's the journey that counts, not the destination, and her teaching, a mix of patience and discipline, of firmness and encouragement, enchants the mothers of her charges; they are astounded by their children's progress and enthusiasm for *Madameuh Catheurineuh*'s dance class.

Shortly after opening her school, Catherine becomes pregnant. Legally, she's an adult, twenty-one years old, just a few months older than her mother was when she was conceived. It's impossible. It's unthinkable. She can't repeat the same story. She doesn't feel strong enough to shoulder the burden of being a mother. She finds some-one to perform an abortion through a friend who is in her last year of medical school and who knows quite a few nurses who carry out the practice in underground clinics for a tidy sum. The abortion goes as well as can be expected, that is, she gets out of there mostly unscathed, a knitting needle inserted into her uterus, a little blood at first, then a lot more later that night. Her stomach hurts but she'd expected worse, and the blood clots that she passes over the course of a few days don't worry her that much. The next month she doesn't get her period but she doesn't fret about that. The following month, she's more worried about her bloated stomach than she is about any absence of blood. She finally decides to go see a doctor under pressure from Paul. He would have loved to have kept this child, but he's understanding, patient, they'll have a child later on, when she feels ready. Of course he came along to hold her hand in the underground clinic. The doctor's verdict is final: she's pregnant. Four and a half, perhaps five months pregnant. It's impossible, Doctor. She tells him about the abortion. He reminds her that abortion is a crime. He gives her a lecture and explains the risks she is running. She's risking a lot, there's a very strong chance that she could find herself with a child who is deformed, retarded. She is both enraged and terrified, but she doesn't lose her cool. Thank you, Doctor, she says, and leaves. For the next three days she searches for a way to get rid of this fetus, which has grown monstrous in her mind. No one agrees to help her, it would be unconscionable, it would be criminal at this stage. She contacts her father, whom she continues to see when she's in Paris or when he is traveling in the South. He didn't come to her wedding because her mother had expressly forbidden it, but she sees him from time to time, he's her father and she loves him. He'll find a solution, she is sure of it. And she's right. He tells her that he'll take care of it, those midwives are fucking profiteers, that bitch didn't give a shit whether it worked or not. It's not rocket science, he'll take care of it.

On Saturday she and Paul take the train to Paris. They arrive near Pantin, at the foot of the same building where, a few years earlier, she had spent the night. Serge's current live-in companion is a nurse. Paul had only met Serge once, in a restaurant in Antibes, where he'd been surprised to see his wife pick up the check, though at the time he didn't say anything. Serge has turned his kitchen into an operating room. He's used to this. He and his girlfriend make a business out of it. He settles Catherine onto the table, with stools on either side of her in lieu of stirrups. Paul holds her hand again this time, but he can't bring himself to look. Serge inserts a speculum into his daughter's vagina, and places a catheter in her cervix, a catheter attached to a syringe filled with a dark liquid, a homemade potion that will take care of things. Catherine grits her teeth, but the sudden, shooting pain is overwhelming, she screams and a defensive reflex makes her clench her thighs as well as her jaws. Serge pushes them apart while scolding her, yelling at her to keep calm. In any case, it's already over. No sense being such a drama queen about it. He pulls the catheter out with a yank, and a veritable geyser of blood erupts, leaving no doubt as to the remedy's efficacy. Within a few seconds the kitchen floor is gleaming where the thick bright blood has pooled. Catherine falls unconscious. Her face turns ashen as her body empties itself. Everything goes haywire, Paul wails, he swears, begs God. He gets hold of himself and yells at Serge to call an ambulance, now! Right now! She's going to die! For fuck's sake, what the hell's going on, Serge keeps repeating. He helps Paul wrap his daughter in a wool blanket to absorb the bleeding, which they cannot stop, then he lets Paul carry her downstairs alone, because he doesn't want the paramedics rummaging around his place. Paul feels Catherine vanishing in his arms. No, no, not that, I'm begging you, Catherine, my love, he sobs and pleads. He reminds her of their promises to each other, of all the things they're going to do together, that she's the love of his life, that he adores her. Her hair is plastered with sweat, she's at once burning and cold, he swears to her that he won't let her die, he'll save her. The ambulance takes Catherine to the emergency room, where a curettage and intravenous antibiotics manage, just barely, to save her. They show her the fetus to teach her a lesson. What she's done is monstrous. Groggy, she tilts her head up to look and puts it back down. She saw. Monstrous is the word.

She heals relatively quickly and the case is closed. She insists that Paul tell no one, not even her mother, especially not her mother. The doctor who looks after her tells her that he'd had to give her a partial hysterectomy, that she can no longer have children. She believes him. She's not sad, surely it's better not to transmit these genes to anyone, not to keep this story going any longer. She tells herself that perhaps one day she'll adopt a little orphan from somewhere, yes, it's better that way. She doesn't get her period anymore, which she assumes is normal, given what she was told. She forgets ever having had it, except when she changes the sheets and notices the old bloodstains that even after dozens of washings never entirely disappear. She and Paul get a dog, a miniature poodle like Jacqueline's, which Catherine names Vauban, after the boulevard where they were married. Vauban like the marshal under Louis XIV, known for his fortresses: Vauban the fortifier. The dog, Vauban, becomes the mascot of Marseille-Danse, he sits, gives his paw, and performs many tricks, he's a good dog, clean, very well behaved, he's perfect, his owners adore him and so do the pupils. Preparations are under way for the end of the year performance. Catherine produces seventeen dances for different groups of students, from the little four-year-olds to the elderly ladies who come to fitness classes, whom she has do *ports de bras* to the sound track of *Danses de travers* by Eric Satie. The show is such a triumph that she resolves to do it again, and next time in a much bigger theater! Two years later, Catherine rents the Théâtre du Gymnase, with a lighting and sound engineer, a stage manager, and a box office. She encourages Jacqueline to rent a big theater, too, but her mother is more restrained, she makes do with a gymnasium. There are two months between the two shows, which allows Catherine to be involved in both performances. She is credited as a dancer in her mother's program, under her mother's maiden name. The name of Cremnitz has entirely disappeared. Jacqueline alone is credited as artistic director. Catherine tells herself that if her mother has appropriated her work, that means she must have admired it. And then, compared to her own show, this one is so lousy, she's better off not being credited.

As his wife's star is rising, Paul stagnates professionally, but he doesn't begrudge her her success; on the contrary, he's very happy about it. The show at the Théâtre du Gymnase is the subject of an article in *Le Provençal* newspaper, in which Catherine is described as a born show woman. Paul helped with publicity for the show, thanks to the school at which Catherine had registered him the previous September, a school for press attachés in Paris. She had assured him that everyone graduates from the school with connections and the guarantee of a prestigious, lucrative job. The money Catherine earns makes it possible to pay for the courses, which he follows at an adjusted schedule so that he can continue working part-time in Marseille.

Catherine would have liked to live without counting pennies, not that she was incapable of making a budget and sticking to it, more or less, but she would prefer not to have to do so; she would prefer to concentrate on her choreography, perhaps even start a dance company. She would like Paul to have a career, for him to be able to support her financially rather than the other way around, she would like to be able to look at him with the admiration with which she sometimes feels him looking at her. She's been married for seven years, she's become a woman, she's become more confident and has developed her skills, she's learned to explore her strengths, her areas of expertise, what she is good at and where her gifts might fail her, all without fear of abandonment. When she asks Paul if he'll love her for the rest of his life, or asks him to swear that they'll be together forever, it isn't so much to hear him promise something of which she is at this point largely certain, but rather to convince herself that this is what *she* really wants, and that he won't let her go, he won't let her give in to her desire for flight or folly. She becomes less self-conscious, she takes pride in how men stare at her. Whether out of modesty or respect, Paul would never look at her like that, with such naked lust. Catherine doesn't know what she's looking for exactly, but she's looking for something. He is the only one she's ever made love with—the first time didn't count—and she wonders what it would be like with someone else. She possesses neither the frivolity nor the poise of an adulteress, she has no desire to sleep with just anyone, merely for the thrill of it. She loves her husband, and she convinces herself that she'll stay with him, that their love will continue to grow, God willing.

Paul and Catherine go up to Paris together for his graduation from the publicity school. The ceremony takes place at a theater in the 8th arrondissement, near the Champs-Élysées. Catherine gets dressed up and she buys her husband a new suit for the occasion—or rather, she steals it, but never mind. The theater is full, it seems to them that everybody who is anybody in Paris is there; Paul hasn't made a lot of friends, they don't know anyone. They make their way through the lobby and Catherine, intimidated at first, collects herself, holds her chin up. Her astonishing beauty makes the crowd draw back. It's impossible not to notice them, or at least her, she's stunning. One of the school's department heads, to whom their backs are turned, nabs Paul to shake his hand, congratulating him. The school's president—whom Paul vaguely remembers running into at some point—is determined to congratulate him as well. The president? Yes, he's here, of course. Mr. President, what an honor, thank you. But not at all, sir, the president responds, it's to you that my thanks are due, your presence here and that of your wife honors us. I bow before you, madam. Please allow me, he says, as he kisses her hand. She pulls it back, troubled. Please join me this evening after the ceremony, I'm organizing a cocktail buffet in a private room at Fouquet's, nothing formal, just a little supper among friends, come, be a good sport, join us! Dazed and a little intoxicated by this sudden, unexpected attention, they nod their heads a bit stupidly, Yes, yes, we'll come, thank you very much, that's very kind of you.

Catherine feels herself being observed throughout the ceremony, like a young woman from the provinces who makes her entrance into society and discovers that Parisians go to the theater not so much to see what's being performed onstage as to perform and be seen themselves. The department head who presented the diplomas walks them to Fouquet's, strolling down the Champs-Élysées with the other invitees, a lively cohort among whom Catherine feels so out of place, she could cry. They've scarcely arrived at Fouquet's when Catherine pretends to feel suddenly unwell. Paul believes her. They offer awkward apologies, thank you again, and please thank Mr. President for us. Once back in Marseille, Catherine has little time to recover from the impression that the president's kiss on her hand has made. Two days after her return, forty-seven red roses are delivered to her at the dance school, accompanied by a note: *The roses of tenderness have come to trouble my waking hours. I am waiting for you. Antoine.* She spends the night studying the ceiling of her bedroom, as if trying to divine the future overhead. He left her his phone number. And if she called him—no, she should know better than to call him. So what, then? Don't call. Ignore him. Forget him. Pretend it never happened. Impossible. She gazes at the inscrutable ceiling above her, as shadows or ghosts dance heedlessly across it. And if her life up to this moment were nothing but a blank page? The next day she comes up with an excuse to return to Paris, alone.

ANTOINE INVITES HER TO LUNCH at Maxim's. Catherine has heard of the place, but she can't imagine that there are real people who lunch there, who look each other up and down and secretly compare the length of their respective biographies in *Who's Who*, people who acknowledge each other in public with knowing nods. That day it is with a certain flattering complicity that men greet Antoine and the woman whom they presume to be his latest conquest. Antoine pulls out all the stops, his hand over his heart, citations from poets she's never heard of, the Dom Pérignon, the Chassagne-Montrachet, the Romanée-Conti—she tells him she likes burgundy, not knowing how to respond when he asks her what kind of wine she would prefer, after the glass of champagne—Rome, Venice. You've never been to Italy? Yes, to Rimini, she responds, reluctantly. Ah, I don't know it, but it must be magnificent! Celestial beauty, I beg you, don't turn Rome into my object of resentment! (Corneille, *Horace*.) I beg you on both knees: Come with me. I'm due there next month to participate in a conference. I hate traveling alone, I'm afraid of flying, and the truth is that I hate traveling. If you won't come I'll just have to cancel the whole thing, I won't go. What do you say? Yes, I know, you're married. Listen, let's take this opportunity, we have only one life to live! Just three days in Rome and Venice. What's the harm? No one will find out. If, at the end of the trip, you can't stand me, I swear that I will leave you alone. May I take a day to think about it, monsieur? Monsieur! Come now, you're making me feel like an old dodderer! Call me Antoine. Of course, think about it and write to me with your response. Catherine goes to Nini's house to think things over. Nini is also married, and has a little boy who is five years old, the age of the child Catherine didn't keep. The child I will never have, she tells herself. Nini thinks the whole business smells fishy, in fact it stinks to high heaven. Does Catherine realize that she's going to have to put out as soon as she arrives in Rome? Yes, she realizes this. It makes her laugh, she may be an idiot, but she's not that stupid. Nini thinks she risks throwing it all away for a guy who apparently has nothing to lose himself, who seems like a predator. Plus he's married? Separated, Catherine responds optimistically. So he says! I'm telling you, it's a dirty trick, watch out.

When she gets back to Marseille-Danse she finds seventy-three red roses waiting for her, seventy-two roses for the hours they'll spend together should she accept his invitation, and one more for good luck. She thinks about the lunch at Maxim's, about the maître d's attentive service, about the taste of champagne, about the sound of his voice pronouncing sentences that she never imagined hearing other than in films or onstage, she sees again the dark green Jaguar he suggested she get into—his chauffeur would take her wherever she wanted—she keeps remembering the sensation of his fingers caressing her wrist, she feels she's being followed everywhere she goes, she thinks she sees him appearing twenty times a day, every dark-haired man in a suit must be him coming to get her in person. She pretends to hesitate but she knows she's going to go. How can she resist the prospect of taking a plane for the first time, the idea of rediscovering the odor of his vetiver, traces of which linger where he touched her, there where he took her arm as they left the restaurant, setting down the ephemeral imprint of his perfume? She's spellbound. She's not in love, it's something else: she's been swept off her feet. Yet her chest is so heavy she feels she can no longer breathe. Three weeks and twelve letters later, she meets him in the Horizons restaurant at Orly Sud, en route to Venice.

She arrives early, a weight in the pit of her stomach. She goes through all the stages of waiting: sadness, anger, renunciation, hope. She couldn't care less about the sumptuousness of the place, this airport whose metallic architecture was, for its time, remarkably innovative, nothing seems remarkable to her. At that precise moment all she does is wait. Antoine arrives at last with his chauffeur pushing a cart on which a mountain of monogrammed Louis Vuitton luggage is precariously balanced. He gesticulates, his hair unkempt, sweaty, insulting poor Sancho (who keeps repeating in a Portuguese accent that it isn't his fault), and he explains to Catherine, in a tone that could make her believe that she too was guilty of some unpardonable crime, that some asshole ran into them on the highway, that they had to file a claim, and of course it had to happen just that day, it's unbelievable that they gave an asshole like that his driver's license, a guy who takes forever to fill out his goddamn form, your typical French hick with his redneck Citroën! No time for lunch now, we have to rush. Catherine is astonished by the number of bags but she follows along as he leads her frenetically to check-in, gesticulating the whole time.

In the plane, he takes out a bottle of Schoum—a neon green potion—and takes a big gulp, swallowing some pills along with it from a first-aid kit that he'd dumped at his feet. The full contents of his bag, scattered across the floor, form heaps of strange and disparate objects: an old Bible, an address book bound in crocodile, a thick leather wallet, a hairbrush, menthol-scented Kleenex, four packets of sugar-free gum, several sets of keys. Are you ill? she asks timidly. No, it's preventative! She bursts out laughing. Do you find me funny? He's quite serious, his brow is furrowed, he seems distressed. I don't know, I find you incredible! After all, you're really something. Ah yes. He smiles. I must explain, travel makes me terribly anxious, I'm naturally very anxious and I find trips deeply disturbing, it's the memory of the exodus, the war, you know, when at eleven you had to depart, leaving everything behind, it marks you for life, and you never get rid of that fear. It's the distinction, in Freud, between neurotic anxiety and realistic anxiety, you see, phobic anxiety is infantile anxiety that stands in for a frustrated libido, so it transfers itself onto a situation, it displaces itself. It's a problem of displacement, and later on, when realistic anxiety is added onto it, well, you're screwed. It's all screwed up, and it's been that way for quite a while, screwed, in a word, really screwed. I'm happy that you've come. Thank you for coming with me. I'm going through a hard time with this separation, it's very complicated, it's all very confused, you're going to help me think it through, I have to find some solutions, the situation is no longer tenable. Catherine doesn't understand what he's talking about, she's distracted, making a mental calculation: if he was eleven years old during the Second World War—she suspects it could only have been that war, as for the exodus, she's not too sure, but let's say around 1941—and if she, having been born in '47, is twenty-seven years old, that means that he must be—no, she's going about it the wrong way, it's too complicated. If he was eleven years old in '41, 41 minus 11 makes 30, that's easy, so in 1974 he would be forty-four years old. Yes, that seems plausible to her, forty-four years old; that means that he would be, give or take a few years, the same age as her mother. Yes, that makes sense. She'll notice a bit later, glancing at his passport as they pass through customs, that he was born in 1929, so she wasn't that far off the mark. On the plane he holds her hand like a madman, and then he falls asleep during takeoff. Her stomach sinks as they take off, a feeling she adores, that she knows from roller coasters, she's in a trancelike state. He snores for the whole flight, competing with the engines. She doesn't dare touch the tray they bring her, she's not sure it's hers, she's afraid of betraying her ignorance, and she doesn't dare wake him, either. He finally wakes with a start when the wheels hit the landing strip, and expresses his regret at having missed the meal.

At the Hotel Danieli, Catherine is astonished by the gilding on the staircases, the rugs, the tapestries and drapes, the ceiling heights, the views, the headboard of the bed, the immaculate sheets, the marble bathroom, the bathrobes, the mirrors, the fact that you can pick up the phone and order just about anything, and they bring it to you. *Pronto! No, non parlo italiano, francese,* yes, French, very good, well we would like, as soon as possible, two bowls of minestrone, your famous tagliatelle with white truffles, and some fish, whatever you have, and steak, filet mignon, yes, perfect, and some *zabaione,* and a bottle of champagne and a French wine, you must have a Bordeaux, a Grande Bordeaux, the best you have (within limits), we understand each other, I trust the sommelier, yes, *grazie mille!* There's at least one thing done. Good. Catherine is speechless. You're hungry, I hope? She doesn't know, she doesn't know anything anymore. I suppose that's what it means to be blown away, she tells herself, but she would be quite incapable of putting words to so much enchantment. She watches him hang up the phone and then pick it up again, covering the receiver to explain to her that he has to call his mother. She nods her head, pretending to understand, but it all seems insane. He speaks very loudly; she smokes a cigarette at the window. She hears him say that he can't speak, that she's there, yes, her name is Catherine, no, Maman, I'll explain, but I'm telling you she's right here, right next to me! She'd like to disappear. He doesn't look at her, his body hunched over the receiver, he talks for a long time, such a long time that Catherine eventually asks herself what the hell she is doing there. She hears names that she doesn't recognize, she understands that he has a lot of worries, but she doesn't know what kind, exactly, it seems he has all kinds of problems, money problems, work problems, problems of the heart, health problems, psychological problems, clearly, a seemingly infinite number of problems. A discreet knock on the door of the room relieves her of this torpor. He finally turns toward her, apparently he hasn't forgotten her. He signals to her, with exaggerated hand movements, that she should open the door. When the waiter has laid out, on a sparkling tablecloth spread with a magician's dexterity, a constellation of silver cloches, and she is prepared to close the door behind him, Antoine suddenly interrupts his conversation: Wait! He shouts to Catherine to find him his bag, which she hurries to do without knowing where it is, she searches, she turns around, but where is it? There, silly! There? No, over there! She sees him take a bundle of lire out of his wallet, selecting a bill from it in a denomination that seems to her improbably large. He gives it to the waiter, tells his mother that lunch is served and that he'll call her back. Click. He's very hungry! Come on, let's have lunch! She doesn't ask any questions, she does as she's told. One mustn't eat to live, but quite the contrary, live to eat! (Molière, *L'Avare*.) Isn't that right? He must be right, she doesn't contradict him. He tells her about Montesquieu— who died in his mistress's arms while composing an essay on taste— he talks to her about aesthetics, about books he has written, his career, about his brother the art historian, who committed suicide. Atrocious, a terrible story, with the gas pipe down his throat, and his daughter found his body—atrocious! She's too disconcerted to eat, hesitating about which fork to use as each dish is uncovered. She's taken aback by his story, his digressions, by the strange way he chews, and she's also surprised that he doesn't kiss her, that he's not in a hurry to make love to her. And she's genuinely alarmed by the way he eats. He sends food all over the place, speaks with his mouth full. He keeps filling and refilling her glass with wine, he keeps serving and re-serving her meat, pasta, fish, in complete disorder, insists that she eat dessert. Then suddenly he needs a coffee, he has calls to make. Would he prefer that she go out? Yes, that's a good idea. Go visit the Piazza San Marco, it's just downstairs, and get a gondola to take you to the Bridge of Sighs. He offers her some bills. She tries to refuse, but he insists. Don't be a fool! You can't do anything in life without money.

She's too disoriented to be offended at having been called a fool or sent out by herself alone in a strange city. She asks the way to Saint Mark's Square, which she doesn't dare pronounce in Italian, she's too unsure of the accent, but the way is pretty clear, she finds it. She wants to marvel at it, but she finds the esplanade crushing, she feels dwarfed by the columns, the immense arcades on the tops of which she glimpses figures staring back at her from on high, she feels oppressed by the swarms of pigeons whom she fears at every instant may attack her, hundreds of pigeons. She turns back to the Grand Canal, where she gets into a gondola. A circular movement of her hand is enough to indicate that she would like to take a tour, that and the bills she proffers. She tries to admire the palaces but all she can see are couples embracing in the boats that cross her path. What does he want from her? What is she doing in this postcard city? Why her? She feels out of her depth. The waves make her seasick. She wants to return to dry land. *Scusi, ma non capisco, signora, mi dispiace*. All she retains of the splendor and poetry of the canals of Venice are the smell of sewers and the sensation of being swallowed up in a maze of dead ends. She finally returns to the hotel, her complexion livid. She goes to vomit in the bathroom of the restaurant. She splashes her face with water above a gilded basin in the form of a shell. Looking in the mirror she tells herself: Catherine, watch out, this whole story smells fishy. She goes up to the room, determined to demand an explanation.

Antoine is seated at a table, writing. She sticks her head in at the door. He glares at her. What's wrong? Is he angry? My God, never in my life have I seen such a beautiful woman! He rushes over to greet her as if they hadn't seen each other for months. He kisses her hands, bows down at her feet, he kisses her ankles, her calves, her knees. Stop, stop, come on now, get up! She can't help but smile. He nestles his head between her hips, and caresses her thighs with his cheeks. Slowly, languorously, she runs her fingers through his thicket of dark hair. He lifts her dress, she lets him. He bites her gently and she cries out a bit more loudly than she would have preferred. She gets him to straighten up by picking him up under the arms, she has him stand but he almost stumbles. She laughs. She leads him toward the bed with a drunk's wobbly steps, their balance precarious. They make love quickly and badly. She's neither happy nor disappointed. Her heart beats fast. He plays with her breasts, distractedly. When his fingers slide between her thighs, she stops them. Don't you want to come again? His question stuns her. I don't know. She discovers with him that one can talk about sex that way, that it's a question that can be asked. The advantage that you women have over us, is that your orgasm is without limits. You can come an infinite number of times. She's never heard such a thing.

The next day, their Italian romance is abruptly truncated. While they're preparing to leave for Rome, for the famous conference where Antoine is to be an honored guest, everything collapses, there's a sudden reversal of the situation: against all odds, his ex-wife, well, his wife, actually, has decided to join him. Catherine must understand, he still loves his wife, they have a little girl, a three-year-old, and over-night his wife had dumped both of them for the man of the couple with whom they'd been sleeping. And he'd found himself with the other guy's wife, Claude, and their little girl now divides her time between her mother and Claude, it's very complicated, it's very bad for the girl, who is very disturbed by this situation. He'd like most of all for his wife to return to live with them, and now it seems she may be willing to do so, she's agreed to meet him in Rome. You must understand, it's for the sake of the child. Catherine, in a state of shock, says that she never asked to go to Rome or Venice, she hadn't asked for anything. He has the concierge of the hotel change her flight, he hands her her plane ticket. She departs for Paris in a few hours. With-out further ado, she packs up her things in her old suitcase, taking care to leave behind the overnight bag he gave her as a gift, as well as the souvenir Murano glass paperweight. Okay, *ciao*. And above all, he shouldn't try to see her again. *Basta così*. She slams the door of the room violently, to the sound of his pleas: but for goodness' sake, she has time, her plane isn't leaving for several hours! She bawls during the entire trip back, from the steps of the Danieli to the tarmac at Orly. She arrives in Marseille a wreck.

Months pass during which Antoine sends apologies, love letters, and mind-bogglingly gigantic bouquets. He begs her, he threatens her, he adores her, he implores her. She's afraid. She feels lost, she is attracted and repelled. He promises her that the situation with his wife has been settled once and for all, he swears on all that is sacred, on the heads of his six children—four from his first marriage, then a love child, and finally the little girl from his second marriage—that Catherine is the only one in his heart, that he can't live without her, she must give him one last chance. Paul remains innocent, ignorant. He senses that his wife is distant, agitated, irritable, he blames it all on her work, which is so demanding, she has so much to do, she is so brilliant, it's necessary for her to be free to express her creativity, between her courses and the administration of the school, she never has enough time to produce her ballets. Seven months after her return from Italy, she agrees to see Antoine in Paris. He suggests they meet at the Crillon, since with the child it's still complicated at home. She arrives late on purpose but he's even later. She becomes indignant, angry tears start in her eyes. Just as she approaches the revolving door to leave, he appears.

Catherine doesn't know what she's gotten herself into, or how she's going to get herself out of it, but she knows the situation is dangerous. She saw that in Antoine's eyes the first time he kissed her hand, in the reflection of his pupil she saw her own image multiplied ad infinitum, she saw her future possible selves. Never mind the dance school, too bad about Vauban, never mind the love and stability that Paul and his parents have given her, too bad about the Mediterranean sun, it's too bad, she's going back to Paris and not to her shitty suburb this time, not to the Marais, she's going to move into a 2,700-square-foot apartment on the third floor of a grand Haussmannian building, number 18, avenue de Friedland, above a statue of Balzac, which she will only notice months later, when she takes her new dog out for a walk. With Antoine life will be carefree, she can be careless, because they can afford to make a mess of things, a maid is paid to clean up after them, and whatever breaks can be replaced. Catherine packs her bags one morning after Paul has left for work—she takes almost nothing, Antoine has already begun to buy her a new wardrobe in Paris. She leaves a note on the nightstand.

What can a letter written on a notepad possibly say? Thank you? Forgive me? I love you? I loved you? I'm in love with someone else? Don't try to win me back? All good things must come to an end? Paul finds out that she's already given the school away to a friend. He calls Jacqueline, who pretends not to know anything. He calls Nini, he even calls Serge. Serge! Serge doesn't know anything, but he reminds Paul about the cash he's owed for the goddamn ambulance, not to mention the problems he's had with neighbors because of the bloodstains in the hall. Paul, desperate, calls Nini back and begs her to tell Catherine that he must see her. His wife agrees to meet him in a café near the place de la République: the Barometer.

HER FEET NO LONGER TOUCH the ground. Antoine tells her a hundred times a day that she's the most beautiful woman in the world, that he loves her more than anything, he only calls her Catherine in public or when speaking of her in the third person: he calls her my beloved whom I adore, my darling sweetheart, my exquisite angel, my treasure. Paul had never told her he loved her unless she asked him to do so. Paul was circumspect; Antoine is extravagant. When she gets out of the bath, it's compared to the birth of Venus, she becomes Aphrodite rising from the sea, a blond nymph, Galatea. What is she doing with this atrocious Polyphemus, this monster standing next to her? To make up for his grotesque appearance—he's always sarcastic about his looks, a self-mockery which she constantly tries to counter, she thinks he's magnificent, magnificent in every way—he showers her with gifts, spoils her outrageously, believing that in this way he can buy the feelings that she already has for him. He takes her shopping in the Jaguar, avenue Montaigne, place Vendôme, boulevard Saint-Germain, he buys her Van Cleef jewels, outfits signed Yves Saint Laurent, a mink coat at Rebecca, evening pumps at Lanvin, Emmanuelle Khanh sunglasses, an Hermès handbag, Montblanc pens. He encourages her to redecorate their apartment, where he used to live with his ex-wife, from whom he is now really separated, not officially divorced, but yes, separated. He gives her carte blanche and an unlimited budget. He gives her bundles of bills and promises more if those run out. She enjoys hunting for antiques in the flea market, she buys Persian rugs and a big marble table for when they have guests in the dining room. They go out a lot. He's very much in demand and there's always something, high-society cocktail parties, dinner parties, opening nights at the theater, lectures and courses to give. She enjoys dressing up like a great lady, she has a rare skill for putting herself together; she's been onstage, and can do her own hair in extravagant styles, crowns of braids, imperial chignons, curls, and ringlets. With the grace of a dancer, it isn't hard for her to make a good impression. That is, until she opens her mouth. She guesses, without even hearing them, the comments of the society ladies, old bags as ugly as sin, or so Antoine assures her when she comes to him crying at the latest humiliation, complaining that she just doesn't belong, doesn't know anyone, doesn't know the codes or understand the references, hasn't read the right books. He corrects her mistakes in French, the syntactical errors that betray her lowly background. And then, perhaps she could read a little? Educate herself? She's dying to do so. She studies the shelves of his personal library with the scrupulous attention of a jealous wife going through her husband's pockets. She applies herself as she never did in school, she attends his lectures at the Sorbonne, she asks him a thousand questions, she's not ashamed to admit to him that never before in her life had she heard the name of Immanuel Kant. He explains transcendental idealism to her, he tells her the story of Descartes and the ball of wax, he teaches her the meaning of ontology, he talks to her about metaphysics, about empiricism, about skepticism. And finally he introduces her to his mother, whom he encourages her to call Grand-mama, this woman to whom he'd spoken on the phone for hours from Venice, a bitter memory Catherine carried into her first encounter with this pedantic matriarch who sought immediately to flatten her.

As if guided by a pendulum's swing, Catherine's life oscillates between fortune and misfortune, a black-and-white universe, no room for nuance or complexity. So Antoine's family welcomes her with as much coldness and disdain as Paul's family had pampered and cherished her. The children from his first marriage, the eldest of whom is scarcely seven years younger than she is, consider her a slut, a gold digger. It had been hard enough for them to accept their father's second wife, let alone to see a new one barge in, even younger and more beautiful than the last. That's leaving aside Grand-mama, who swears that her son must have fallen on his head, a dancer from Marseille! Does he have any idea what a fool he's making of himself? This young woman can't put two words together without making a grammatical error or spewing nonsense. I mean, come on now, it's time her son came to his senses, the whole thing is completely absurd. It's heretical! Grand-mama makes no attempt to keep such insulting talk from Catherine's ears, on the contrary. The more Antoine tries to silence his mother, the more she raises her voice. She couldn't care less for the feelings of that hussy! Antoine refuses to follow her advice, yet he still listens to her patiently. Catherine is alarmed to realize that they must revisit this scene every blessed day, for at least an hour, and patiently receive her vitriol.

With Paul, Catherine had led a well-ordered life. Their sex life had unfolded without surprises, without frills or embarrassing demands, without words. Catherine could write epic novels with what Antoine says to her in bed. Pornographic, sure, but also poetic, in the way of Sade or Bataille. Antoine starts off buying lingerie for her, a woman who didn't even own a bra! She has to conquer her initial fear but she enjoys performing and she goes along with his games. He does it in stages: after lace comes leather, followed by blindfolds, whips, ropes for bondage. She accepts everything, no questions asked, obedient, by turns submissive or dominating, ready for anything. She sees herself surrender in ways that a few months earlier would have seemed, at minimum, improbable. She discovers the pleasures of the flesh, listening to him quote Rabelais; like good Rabelaisians, they eat and fuck in equal measure.

Antoine is a regular at 2plus2, one of the top libertine clubs in Paris, where his tips and his loyal patronage secure his excellent reputation. Catherine arrives there without any thought of what to expect, with a virgin's naïveté. Antoine encourages her to have a few drinks in order to relax, and after four or five cocktails, each of which she downs in one gulp, she begins to feel at ease, that is, drunk and uninhibited. She gets up to dance, and it would be difficult not to notice her supple, svelte body, her rhythmic, swaying walk, the movement of her slender arms. She grabs the room's attention—swingers suddenly transformed into spectators—a beam of light settles on her shoulders, gleaming in her strapless dress. Antoine tells her to choose a girl to her liking, and the one who approaches her at that moment has very big green eyes, or gray-green eyes, with the strobe lights it's difficult to tell. Her long, curly hair is red—unless that's merely the effect of the color filters above the dance floor. The girl kisses Catherine on the lips, their teeth clicking together briefly, the girl's hands sliding down her back, beneath the fabric, under her skirt. Catherine hikes up her own dress to free her leg and slides her knee between the girl's thighs. The girl lifts Catherine's breasts out of her bustier, one at a time, licks them. A crowd gathers around them. Catherine feels hands touching her from behind, she doesn't know whose, she's closed her eyes, she's lifted up by the waist, her heart is beating alarmingly fast, she doesn't feel the orgasm coming, it takes her by surprise, she's overcome, she doesn't understand how, or who did it, or where it originated, she'd like to leave, she'd like it to stop and also go on, but differently, elsewhere, not like this, not here. Suddenly she smells Antoine's cologne next to her, him, phew, it's him. She pulls his shirt, his collar, she cries out to him in a deep sigh that resembles a moan that she wants to leave, please, get me away from here, let's go. Antoine agrees without trying too hard to change her mind. They talk about it later that night. They must agree upon signals to communicate with each other in such situations. They're going to have to establish some ground rules.

AT THE BAROMETER, Paul proposes that he and Catherine share custody of Vauban, he could bring the dog to Paris and she could return him to Marseille, let's say every other week or month if she prefers. But what she prefers is to make a clean break of it. And then she's already had enough of shared custody with regard to Antoine's youngest, the little girl who now lives with them every other week, that is, when her mother agrees to take her back, which isn't always the case. Antoine insists that Claude continue living with them for a little while, in their guest room, just temporarily, until the little girl gets used to things. He promises Catherine that there was never really anything between them, he'd never been in love with her, it just happened, she was there, and he needed a woman to help him with daily life and the child, et cetera. Antoine had never lived alone. He had married at nineteen—him too!—and had had four children immediately afterward. His first wife was scarcely a year older than he was, neither of them were legally adults, and they had started a family while still being kids themselves. They'd been unfaithful to each other from the start, which is to say that neither of them knew anything about sex, so they had to learn somehow, and since they didn't have anything to teach each other, they had to go looking elsewhere. Thus the extramarital relationship from which another child was born. And then afterward the children grew up, and Antoine fell madly in love with one of his students. He divorced, he remarried, and voilà, now she knows everything. Everything, in a manner of speaking, it wasn't a story that could be told in three sentences or in a single conversation, and his narrative technique consisted mainly of digressions, but now she had the main points, that was pretty much the gist. During this time, Antoine founded a school for press attachés, after having studied philosophy more or less as a dilettante, so that he failed the *agrégation*, the high-level competitive examination for teachers—to the great dismay of Grand-mama, who was outraged that her son was taking the plunge into business, which was traditionally Jewish work, well, for Jews from the garment district, not secular Jews like themselves, intellectuals, ambassadors of French culture. It was a good thing his father wasn't around to witness Antoine's descent into vulgarity—his father, a high-ranking civil servant, a famous historian, a recipient of the Legion of Honor, secretary general to the president of the Republic under Paul Doumer, managing director of fine arts before the war, a member of the Senate after the war, a great man to whom poor Antoine would never measure up, Grand-mama is certain of that, he's a crackpot by comparison. Well, what can you do. At least he has enough money to pay for his women. And women he has, everywhere, including at work, including his subordinates, women who are under his authority at the school, which is very convenient for him. Catherine isn't jealous as long as he doesn't make it obvious, she's not obsessive about his infidelities, she's not a prude who insists on monogamy, although she'd like them to agree on a few details, such as what he does with his dick when they share their bed with another woman. She finds that at the very least she should be acknowledged as his official, primary lover, even if she's not his one and only; if he has a fling here and there, so much the better for him, but at home, she'd like to be able to feel that she's mistress of her own bed, and to watch him sticking it to another woman right under her eyes, that's a bit much. He more or less puts up with this rule, that is, until the first night Claude spends outside of the guest room. After having made Catherine come two or three times, Claude lowers herself down on Antoine's cock, until Antoine and Claude receive two hard face slaps each. Don't you two ever pull a stunt like that again, get it? They learned their lesson.

Despite this incident, Claude and Catherine become close, they get to know one another, and learn to appreciate each other, bonding in part over the little girl. Claude doesn't want children, she's never wanted them—she finds it demeaning for women to submit to being wives and mothers, she prefers to be a friend, a lover, to be herself above all. She has no desire to take care of this kid, and if she's agreed to stay on for a while, it's initially out of compassion for Antoine, whom she sees is in despair over his wife's departure, and later on it's because of Catherine, whose company she begins to desire more and more. With regard to the child, Catherine says she can easily give her love, it flows effortlessly from her, and since she can't have a child of her own, she might as well lavish affection on this girl. She has some experience with children this age thanks to her dance school, where she had to do quite a bit of babysitting in addition to teaching them the *pas chassés*. And the truth is that she adores children. She loves their gaiety, still unsullied by the wear and tear of reality, their eccentric spontaneity, their fantastical games— the zanier, the more preposterous, the more incredible, the better. Catherine loves making up stories, playing the clown, miming a tightrope walker, a puppet, an acrobat, her games also make Antoine laugh a lot, Antoine whose youth hadn't left much room for tomfoolery, for reasons quite different from Catherine's, but which nevertheless haunt him just as much. Antoine's family isn't welcoming, so she assembles an alternative network of supporters. Claude reminds Catherine of her dear Nini. Perhaps if Nini hadn't been quite so sensible or if Nini had loved women and Catherine had been able to admit her attraction to them, they would have been lovers. But she had needed a man in order to declare her passion for her own sex, she had needed a mediator, through whom she could convince herself that she wasn't a lesbian. No, really, she loves women only through the intermediary of a man, for his pleasure, to seduce him. Antoine allows her to discover a propensity for something that alters her identity. She loves women—that is to say, the partners they dig up at 2plus2 or at Castel—but she really loves Claude. Claude's not just one of those girls with whom they spend the night, Claude lives there part of the time, is at home; Claude has fits of jealousy, Claude listens to Catherine's stories about her childhood, her past, Claude helps her to learn calmly what Antoine tries to teach her with his jumbled anecdotes and obscure references and associative leaps; Claude becomes not only her lover, but her best friend, her confidante, her devotee, her tutor.

It's for the best that you lost your virginity to a nobody. It's always awful the first time. Claude says that with her, Catherine will never experience pain. She doesn't ask Catherine to choose, not right away, she's patient, she waits for the right moment. She recognizes that Catherine has artistic aspirations, she encourages her ambition, her ardor, her creativity. She makes her promise never to listen to advice from anyone, not even from Claude herself. Live your life as you wish, be confident in yourself. Claude encourages her to read, women especially, but also great Jewish writers, sensing in Catherine's disordered stories how important her father's religion is to her, for during that time her only link to her father is through his Jewishness. Catherine never talks about what happened between them. Not to anyone. Never. Claude acts out scenes from plays with her, she recites poems to her, she reads her passages from Nathalie Sarraute; she explains the philosophy of Hannah Arendt, of Simone Weil. She gives her a very prettily bound edition of Stefan Zweig's *Twenty-four Hours in the Life of a Woman*, which she found among the green book stalls on the quays. Through this gift, she subtly encourages Catherine not to settle for or with Antoine. On the title page, as a dedication, she writes: *To my dear Catherine. Beware of moderation, as others must beware of excess. For you, prudence and convention are the most dangerous enemies of success and happiness.* Claude is not going to accept the fact that the woman she loves is in love with someone else, but she is patient, she takes things one day at a time, attempting to forge an unbreakable bond between them. She tries her best to conquer Catherine, absolutely, desperately. She promises that she will never impose upon Catherine the yoke of male domination, that between them there will be no constraints. The voraciousness with which their bodies possess each other confounds Catherine and comforts Claude. How can Catherine reject the one person who finally takes her seriously, the only one who is interested in her intelligence, who acknowledges her talents? Have no fear, love me, Claude whispers to her, pulling her close by the belt of her jeans. Love me, my sweet, love me, she repeats, her fingernails grazing her sides, opening with one hand the fly of Catherine's old Levi's. She pulls her jeans down suddenly, decisively. The skin between Catherine's thighs swells and opens like a wound, moist, sensitive to the touch. Her wetness, its taste, sticks to Claude's tongue, to her hair, their mouths wide, hungry for more kisses, stray strands of hair caught in their lips. Catherine twists and trembles, until daylight dissolves under her eyelids. Claude trusts their physical bond, the sensual pleasure she gives Catherine is unmistakable, she believes she'll convince her, in time. No, yes, perhaps, later on, we'll see, no, yes, I don't know, yes, of course I love you. Claude grants her every delay. She lets her get away with anything. She adores her. She has no choice but to wait.

Antoine and Catherine live only part-time in Paris; they're often traveling or on vacation or spending the weekend in the country. Every time they go away, as Catherine packs their bags, she recalls the scene of their encounter at Orly—it's unbelievable how many bags and suitcases they drag along, full of clothes they'll never wear, books they'll never read, provisions in case they find themselves starving, old magazines. He constantly berates her for not packing quickly or well enough, for not knowing how to close a suitcase properly, for having forgotten something, for being inefficient. Catherine's not the type to allow herself to be trampled underfoot for very long, and if he wants to play that game, if he continues to run her down, he'll have to manage his luggage on his own, and anyway, she bursts out, beginning to scatter the clothes she'd spent hours folding, dumping out every last item, you can go ahead and pack your own fucking bags! On that note, they head off to spend the weekend at Grand-mama's country house, that is to say, the house of his dear departed father, the former mayor of the village, a legendary personality, the house where the grandchildren and their companions and longtime friends gather around a table that Catherine lays out thoughtfully, eager to win the family over. Catherine loves playing mistress of the house, though no one grants her the title, she ends up cooking the meals and setting the table and clearing it and no one complains, but nobody thanks her either; they ignore her. Catherine tells herself that she'll wear them down in the long run. But will she?

During the summer, the same scene, more or less, is played out on the coast of Brittany, where Antoine has spent all his summers since his early childhood, a vacation spot frequented by eminent company—by scientific researchers, including several Nobel Prize winners, by painters, novelists, musicians, and philosophers. When Antoine and Catherine are not in the country or on the coast, they fly to prized destinations where he's been invited to participate in symposia or give lectures or set up businesses. In London, they stay at the Park Lane, in Athens at the Hotel Grande Bretagne, in New York at the Pierre, in Seville at the Alfonso XIII, in Frankfurt at Hessischer Hof, in Bologna at the Baglioni, in Cannes at the Majestic, in Saint-Paul-de-Vence at Le Mas d'Artigny . . . The hotels all end up looking the same, running together, the two of them only leave their rooms to go shopping or to go where Antoine is expected. Tourism bores him, and though he encourages Catherine to go to museums, it's always begrudgingly, she senses very clearly that he prefers she wait for him, that she be at his disposal, so she smokes cigarettes at the window while he talks on the phone. They collect bathrobes, ashtrays, paper with the hotel's letterhead, and other baubles that Antoine can't resist swiping on the fly. Catherine looks at him, flabbergasted, the first time she discovers this tic of his, which reminds her so much of herself that she can hardly believe it: Are we allowed to take all that? Well, I suppose we can grant ourselves certain rights. So too, Catherine notices the surprising habit Antoine has of pilfering empty prescription pads during routine doctor's visits or emergency house calls by SOS Médecins, because he often worries that he's about to have a heart attack, that his headache may be symptomatic of an aneurysm. His hypochondria is commensurate with his fits of rage. So the fact that Catherine also has a screw loose doesn't necessarily displease him: they're perfect for each other, as long as their follies remain harmless, as long as no tragedy intervenes. But the tragedies come in waves.

MANY YEARS EARLIER, there had been the suicide of his older brother at thirty, the facts either unknown or largely hidden from the family. Suicide using both gas and barbiturates, the two of them, to be certain of achieving his aim. Then Antoine's eldest son suffered a terrible car accident, he was hit by a semi on the highway, his car was totaled and he was crushed. Catherine is responsible for being there when the ambulance arrives, she's the only one to see him in the condition in which he'd been found, that is, damaged beyond recognition. He survives for a few days in a coma; it's not clear if he can hear his parents telling him that they love him, pleading with him to keep fighting. He is twenty-five years old. He dies without having regained consciousness. Catherine doesn't know how to console the father for this inconceivable loss; she forgives his excesses all the more, as she imagines Antoine in mourning for a long time, she imagines that the death of his son continues to haunt him. A few months later, the daughter of his brother who committed suicide throws herself from the Eiffel Tower. This time it's Antoine who has to identify the body at the morgue. Grand-mama hadn't wanted her granddaughter to be confined to a mental institution, for her it was unthinkable to put the girl in the loony bin.

Catherine can't help but remember her own suicide attempts, her stays at clinics, the lithium, the barbaric treatments she had been subjected to as a child, as a young girl, and as a young woman. She mixes up her different hospital stays, she confuses her memories of early childhood with those from the sanitarium. The nightmare she hasn't had for years suddenly comes back to her, without warning: Men in white coats tie her to a metal workbench, perhaps an operating table; they tie her down with straps, they hurt her, she can't see their faces, she doesn't know who they are, they're not doctors anyway, they're impostors, torturers. Panicked, she realizes that she can't move, she's paralyzed, the doctors or the men in white have disappeared, but suddenly all around her appear torsos with severed limbs, severed heads, all these fragmented bodies encircling her like a bloody carousel, laying siege to her in a horrible *danse macabre*. She begins to get an idea of what's in store for her, she hears clanking noises, sawing noises, she screams, she tries to struggle but she is paralyzed. Then Catherine wakes up one morning and she really is paralyzed. It's nerves.

Antoine asks Jacqueline—Catherine had finally introduced him to her mother, whom Antoine hadn't quite dared to flirt with—if it had ever happened that her daughter had found herself in such a state. Yes, no, a little, not really, paralysis, no, she never pulled that one on us. She tells him about Catherine's first suicide attempt, when she was about seven, well, that's how the doctors talked about it later on, it wasn't so clear at the time, she was always looking for trouble, she was a problem child, always problems. Seven years old! Antoine responds, horrified. He'd always thought his older brother was very precocious, having first tried to kill himself at thirteen. Seven! How is it possible? Catherine had told him in rather general terms about her childhood. He'd listened solemnly, but he'd never really grasped the weight of it.

She spends three weeks in a clinic, undergoing a sleeping cure, taking antianxiety medication, antidepressants, and sleeping pills. Claude spends entire afternoons at her bedside, holding her hand. Nini also comes sometimes. They'd reconnected when Catherine had come back to Paris, but Nini's existence is far from luxurious, she leads a very simple life, with a teacher's salary, her husband a construction worker; she doesn't always understand or agree with Catherine's choices, she doesn't recognize her old friend in her new guise as a member of the *grande bourgeoisie*, but she loves her as she is, she doesn't overthink things, she'd told her from the start what she thought of the whole thing. Then one day, as if by miracle, Catherine recovers. She has only a very vague memory of the weeks that have just elapsed. She goes back to live at the avenue de Friedland apartment, where her wild life of luxury and lust resumes its course.

Antoine begins to pay closer attention to Catherine's eccentricities. It's true that he swipes odds and ends from hotels, and sometimes
from restaurants, and then there are the doctors' prescription pads, but
those are all things to which he feels he is more or less entitled, he's not
really stealing. One day on a little tour of the Côte d'Azur, when they
stop to do some shopping at Saint-Laurent, Catherine leaves the store
smirking. What's with you? Antoine asks her a few streets further on,
when they've gotten into their rented convertible. Look! Catherine
cries, lifting up the dress he'd just bought her: one, two, three, four!
Four dresses that she'd layered on in the dressing room. Are you completely out of your mind? You must be stark raving mad! I could have
bought them for you! How humiliating, now we can never go back to
that store, how embarrassing, don't you understand? Catherine doesn't
think there's any harm in it, he fails to see the relationship between
what she's just done and his own milder kleptomania, and anyway, it's
funny! Just think of the look on the saleswoman's face, funny, isn't it?
Antoine doesn't find it funny in the least. When his reputation is at risk
he loses his sense of humor. But he is nothing if not full of contradictions, having chosen a woman of the people to aid him in his quest for
high office, glory, and the admiration of his peers.

Catherine isn't going to help him find his place among the ranks of
ministers, professors, or stuffy academicians, whose society and support
he strives for, in order to perhaps one day get himself elected to one of the
elite clubs whose membership he covets. He dreams of the red rosette on
a gold ribbon that his father sported in his buttonhole, his father, a veteran
of the First World War, recipient of the Croix de Guerre, bestowed with
the honor and dignity of *Grand Officier de la Légion d'honneur*, obviously,
the ne plus ultra, the pinnacle, beside which all the rest of it is merely shit.
Antoine had written books, among them textbooks which had sold by

the hundreds of thousands—a fact which counts against his reputation, commercial success being something French intellectuals frown upon— and he'd had a proper education, he was, after all, his father's son, he could have become a high-level public servant, but he chose the world of business, he chose money, he didn't pass the *agrégation*, he didn't go to one of the elite *grandes écoles*. And on top of everything else, Antoine always had a taste for girls from the lower classes, from the gutter, Grandmama complained, indignantly. To her credit, Catherine has the kind of beauty that transcends riches, or education, or even refinement, the kind of blinding beauty that confers its own status, that causes you to set aside her upbringing and improprieties. Almost. But Catherine goes too far at times. During one of those important dinners where Antoine makes her promise to behave, and not drink too much—she quickly develops a liking for champagne and fine wines—she responds to an asshole who makes a point of telling her that, when you're lucky enough not to look Jewish, you're better off not bragging about it, you don't say it out loud, and she answers him: Oh really, you don't say it *out loud*? Well, look, is this loud enough for you, she yells, throwing her glass of red wine across the table at him, a gesture greeted with horrified gasps by the assembled guests; Antoine is petrified, he doesn't know what to do with himself, he hopes maybe people have forgotten that they came in together, but she stares straight at him and declares that she won't stay a moment longer, that if he can live with himself, a self-hating Jew with his eyes set on society's little prizes, well, so much the better for him, but she's leaving.

BY THE TIME CATHERINE AND Antoine have been together for two years, their fights are out of control. Claude and Antoine have become rivals, and while he doesn't exactly throw her out,

Claude understands that she is no longer welcome. Claude tries to convince Catherine to come live with her. Catherine could resume her teaching—when she first moved to Paris, she had taken a job at the conservatory of Sèvres, but it annoyed Antoine that her schedule made her less available to him, so after a few months, she had given it up—and she could finally put a dance company together, take up choreography again. Claude is a journalist and while her work isn't terribly lucrative, she makes a living, they'll live comfortably. Catherine doesn't identify as a lesbian, but is it necessary to give loving a woman a name? She feels reassured with Claude, similar to the way she'd felt with Paul. Catherine finds herself once again caught between two loves, two lovers: loved, she feels light shining on her; loving, she projects her own light onto the other. She hesitates, vacillates.

Christmas arrives, their second Christmas together, and Catherine, who adores presents—who will never forget the painful memory of her mother taking her window-shopping during the holidays, outside in the cold, among crowds pushing and shoving, crowds whose bags were filled with toys and the latest fashions, while Catherine had to content herself with looking at the displays in the frosty windows of Printemps or Galeries Lafayette, having taken the subway there from Montreuil—Catherine now goes Christmas shopping for the little girl, she takes the Jaguar and raids the boutiques, filling the trunk and backseat with packages. She spends a whole week decorating the tree in the living room of the avenue de Friedland apartment and putting up garlands in the child's room; Catherine is preparing the most beautiful Christmas of all time. The little girl is five years old, and she's over the moon with excitement, telling anyone who will listen about the amazing holiday Catherine is preparing, Catherine this and Catherine that. And the mother, Antoine's ex-wife, is sick of hearing about Catherine, we'll see who's preparing the most beautiful Christmas! That's her daughter, she'll have her know! And though she'd left the girl with the father (and Claude and Catherine) for months at a time, now she has settled down with her new boyfriend, and they are taking her back, full-time, and no, the girl won't see her father for Christmas, she's taking her skiing or to her grandmother's house, in any case, Catherine and Antoine will have to make do without her for the holidays. Catherine is sick at heart over this. Antoine tries to calm her down, he tells her that they'll go on a trip instead, but Catherine couldn't care less about traveling, she wanted to have a family Christmas, all together, and she mopes under the covers for days, she doesn't get out of bed, she's despondent. Antoine begins to worry that she's going to pull the paralysis trick on him again, but no, it's different this time, she says she's at the end of her rope, and she cries and cries, she can't stop crying. Antoine can't stand seeing her like this, he starts crying, too, he doesn't know how to distract her, he won't go into the office if she prefers, but then he'll spend days on the phone, and that's even worse! Catherine usually has such a good appetite, but now she doesn't want to eat anything, not even the *choucroute* that he has delivered from Brasserie Lipp, not even the shrimp salad from Lenôtre that she loves, not even the lemon macarons from Dalloyau that she could never resist. No, it isn't at all normal to feel so out of sorts. She's constantly nauseous, and Antoine tells her she has to take a pregnancy test. She assures him that she can't possibly be pregnant, but he convinces her to do it, it doesn't cost anything, he'll bring her a packet of Predictor tests, which for a little while now have been sold over the counter in pharmacies. And bingo! She's pregnant. No! But yes indeed. No, it's impossible, these tests aren't reliable. She makes Antoine take a test himself, to show him how unreliable they are. No, Antoine isn't pregnant. But she is. Shit. One doesn't bring a child into the world under these conditions, Nini, the voice of wisdom, tells her. Of course she's right, they're already having enough trouble with their current arrangement, a little brat's not going to make things right between them. Antoine had given her a dog after she'd moved in with him, another poodle to replace Vauban, whom she said she missed; the dog disappeared after a few months, she'd forgotten him, tied up in front of a store, and only remembered him hours later; someone must have taken him, how crazy to steal a dog! What would happen to a baby amid the tumult of this life? Catherine imagines Antoine's child growing inside her, she sees herself becoming a mother, this time she allows herself to imagine it, she conceives of it. As if the little girl's absence had allowed her to sense the presence of this new life inside her, she feels for the first time that maternity is a possibility for her. And she believes it's fate, yes, a higher force was at work, deciding things for her. She'll keep the child. The baby is expected in the summer of 1977. She'll be thirty years old. She's ready.

Catherine shares the news with Paul, who has been hoping all this time that his wife will eventually return to him. Now he asks for a divorce; she says: So be it. Claude takes the news as badly as Paul did, if not worse. Have your kid without me! It's the worst mistake of your life, my poor darling. You're going to end up like all those kept women who only live vicariously, putting their lives on hold. You can say goodbye to your dreams of being an artist. You're signing your own death sentence. Mark my words—from the moment your kid is born, you'll be nothing. Jealousy has turned her sweet, gentle Claude cruel. Never mind, she's made her choice.

Antoine's older children are scandalized, there's a general out-cry; their father is going to be forty-eight, they're old enough to give him grandchildren, he should be preparing to become a grand-father, he's too old to become a father all over again. They convene a family meeting, with their mother, who is of course on their side, and Grand-mama, who presides over the table and declares em-phatically: Catherine must get an abortion. Terminating a pregnancy is finally legal, the *Loi Veil* is there for a reason, isn't it? Antoine is crushed, his family is accusing him of disgracing them, of being ir-responsible. He doesn't protest, keeps his mouth shut. Okay, okay, he tells his family, but he tells Catherine: Don't worry about them, they'll get over it soon. The ex-wives are now lined up against Cath-erine, the most recent ex-wife in particular, she can't stand having been replaced. You'd think Catherine had committed a crime, given the atmosphere around her, the ex-wives and their children together plotting their revenge. The ambience in the countryside is tense, to say the least.

It slowly dawns on the adult children that their father must think they're morons: Catherine is still pregnant, she's growing rounder. If that's how it's going to be, then Antoine and Catherine should stay in Paris, stop visiting the family. Her obstetrician assures her that she has no reason to believe she can't bring a pregnancy to term. Moreover, it's surprising that without using contraception she hadn't become pregnant earlier! It's not so surprising, given their sexual practices, but she's careful not to discuss her private life with her doctor. She asks if she really has to stop smoking. She's so addicted to her red Roth-mans, the very idea of stopping smoking makes her panic, she thinks maybe she'll need some kind of treatment in order to stop, antianxiety medication, tranquilizers. She explains a bit about her past. But you don't need to stop, madam! the kind, obliging doctor reassures her. Just limit yourself to five cigarettes per day, and the baby will be none the worse for it. It's just that the babies of mothers who smoke tend to be smaller; assuming you have a vaginal birth, that might be a blessing! And alcohol? Same, don't overdo it, but one or two glasses of wine a day never killed anyone. And meds? Do as you normally would, relax and enjoy yourself above all, the most important thing for the baby is the mother's well-being. You must take advantage of your pregnancy. Pregnancy doesn't last a lifetime, enjoy it! Catherine, whose life as a small child had been entirely entrusted to medical professionals, listens to her doctor. Or she almost listens. Antoine still wants to go out a lot, and she drinks less, but she still drinks a good deal. One pack of cigarettes a day instead of two. But she does enjoy herself. While her mother had watched with horror the transformations in her own body, Catherine admires hers with sensual pleasure, she's proud of the changes in her body, they astound and delight her. She's never been so fat. At six months, she catches sight of her backside in the mirror one morning as she's leaving the bathroom, and thinking to please Antoine, who sometimes complained, mostly to tease her, about her small butt (he who dreamed of Mediterranean hips), she plants herself in front of him and asks if these hips are to his liking. And they are—he adores her pregnant body, her rounded silhouette. It's scandalous to love a pregnant woman's body so much, but she is scandalously beautiful, he can't stop himself from biting her, from devouring her. I'm sure you're lying! You don't love me that much, and God knows you've seen plenty of pregnant women. Not like that. Not like you. Liar! He who lies like Homer . . . / is no liar. You're such an asshole! Not me, that's La Fontaine! She laughs. They laugh. They're in love and the child compounds their love. Everyone swears they're insane.

During the sonogram, the obstetrician informs them that it's a boy. Antoine doesn't care so much, a boy is just fine, but Catherine is thrilled, deeply relieved that she's not having a girl, not like her mother, yes, she's better off having a boy. For the first time, although this is his seventh child, Antoine attends childbirth classes, he helps Catherine practice Lamaze techniques, he breathes with her, he holds her hand. She'll give birth at the Belvédère clinic, the chicest clinic in all of Paris, actually just outside of Paris, in Boulogne-Billancourt. The baby is due at the end of June. They'll spend the first part of the summer at the family's country house and then in Brittany. The family has been forced to accept the situation. Antoine photographs Catherine from every angle, naked, dressed, standing, in profile, sitting, lying down. He buys almost as many packets of Polaroid film as cartons of cigarettes at the Drugstore on the Champs-Élysées where he goes to stock up on Sunday evenings. One of his eyes is always plastered to his SX-70, like a pirate with an eye patch. These photo shoots didn't start with the pregnancy, they'd been part of their games from the beginning: stripteases, pornography. From behind the lens of his camera, he can objectify her further, turn her into an idol, an object of worship, to be symbolically possessed. Under Antoine's exalted gaze, Catherine becomes a metaphor: she is lust made flesh. And isn't her pregnancy proof of his virility?

Nine months pregnant, Catherine isn't one to complain. She still shows up in nightclubs and devotes herself to helping her darling, the poor genius who can't do anything on his own, not even pull on his own socks. She brushes his hair, she helps him to shave, she squats, her enormous belly sagging between her bent legs, to grant his desires, whether lecherous or practical, no matter; she is happy, or rather, she is proud to be his lover. He worries that she's not eating enough, and though she shows him the circumference of her thighs to convince him that she's not about to waste away, he asks her in the middle of the night if she isn't a little bit hungry, if she wants something in particular. Doesn't she have any special desires, the cravings of a pregnant woman that he could hasten to fulfill? If he insists, okay, maybe, why not a *choucroute*? Yes! A *choucroute*! It's four o'clock in the morning, but who cares! Catherine doesn't fear labor or the child's arrival, she feels fabulous, she's not apprehensive at all. Physical pain has never frightened her, on the contrary, it reassures her. Pain has something of a nostalgic quality for her. Grace and suffering are inextricably linked in her mind, that sensation of bruised flesh seems to her inseparable from the feeling of being fully alive. Her body no longer belongs to her, it belongs to him and to their child. She surrenders to his desires unconditionally. She's no longer afraid of anything, she can do anything for him, for them, she feels invincible.

She finally gives birth twelve days late. She doesn't want a cesarean, no, she can't imagine having a doctor cut her open to steal her child from her, she won't let them. She insists on waiting, until one day the doctor tells her they can't wait any longer, and then, as if by miracle, her water breaks. She spends thirty-six hours writhing in pain, her contractions and contortions so terrifying that Antoine sobs. He's never been present at a birth. He doesn't want to leave his Catherine, he can't stand the idea of not being near her, so he's constantly spritzing her at inopportune moments with his spray bottle of mineral water, to refresh her. Does that help? he asks her with tender concern. Incomprehensible groans are her only response, but she nods her head, so he keeps going. He has her drink big gulps of whiskey, he tries to massage her but he doesn't know how, he's so clumsy, until she finally begs him to stop, everything, the caresses, the spritzing, I beg you, don't touch me, she's in agony. The doctor says that's it, we're not waiting any longer, we'll have to do an emergency cesarean, but the baby's on its way, the baby is coming, she yells, the baby is coming. And her baby does come, cuts her open lengthwise, her baby is a girl whom they place on her breast, and if the surprise of not having given birth to a boy makes her hesitate for a fraction of a second, she is fully a mother the next instant, a mother absolutely, she gives in to the adoration of her child completely, her tears and her milk issuing out of her simultaneously as if they came from a single source. They look at each other, the parents, they look at each other and they are so proud, they've made a magnificent little girl. What will you call her? the nurses ask. Oh that! They have no idea. Catherine says the baby's eyes are so deep it's impossible to think of this life as new, Catherine believes she's known her forever. Elsa, Antoine says. The eyes of Elsa, as in the poem by Aragon. Yes, they'll call her Elsa.

Jacqueline meets her granddaughter, and Catherine is surprised to see her mother so moved before her daughter's creation. Catherine discovers an affectionate side to her mother which she hadn't suspected, and her pride alone prevents her from shedding tears over the tender scene. She promises Henri that he will be the child's only grandfather. In any case, she hasn't seen Serge since returning to Paris, as if Antoine had obliterated the presence of her father in her life. When she'd separated from Paul, her mother had said to her: Well, I'm glad we went to all the trouble of making such a beautiful wedding for you! But now the baby shuts her up. She's moved, simply moved by her grandchild. All the same, her mother says, Antoine would do well to marry her. All the same.

Antoine is still married: his ex-wife is very happy with her new partner, but is in no hurry to remarry, and maybe out of spite, to punish Catherine, she refuses to get a divorce. Recognizing a child out of wedlock as his own is no longer as scandalous as it was in the 1950s, when Antoine first tried his hand at it, but it's still tough. Catherine doesn't worry about a thing, she's busy with her breasts, which are overflowing, which leak into her blouse, occupied with the baby who sucks at them, with the rhythms of the child's eating and sleeping, with constantly caressing the blond peach fuzz on the skull of her little angel. At the family house in the country, Grand-mama receives them for the month of July with unconcealed loathing. Ah yes, the little girl is magnificent, she's so beautiful one wonders whose daughter she is, really. She looks a lot like Catherine, but not you, it's strange, isn't it, that she looks so little like her father? Grand-mama tries in every way to convince her son not to recognize the child, after all, where's the proof that the girl is really his?

Catherine doesn't listen to her, she barricades herself in her room with her baby, using the rain or excessive sun as alternating pretexts to remain indoors. When the baby naps, she reads books on child psychology: Françoise Dolto, obviously, and also Fitzhugh Dodson, the American psychologist whose worldwide bestseller *How to Parent* had come out a few years earlier. Catherine reads distractedly, in the midst of a paragraph she leans over the crib to admire her daughter, whose beauty surprises her a little more each time. She discovers that everything in a person's life is decided during the formative years, before the age of six. If that's true, Catherine thinks, then she herself was, is, a lost cause. She also tells herself that she's not going to repeat her mother's mistakes, that she's going to do everything differently, she's going to take the opposite tack from start to finish, and she's already telling herself that she's going to need to have a second child, because she knows what it means to be an only child and she doesn't want that for Elsa.

The summer is relatively uneventful. The atmosphere in the family is chaotic, to say the least, but Catherine doesn't let herself be maligned, she's busy with diapers and nursing, her focus is elsewhere, on Elsa, on Elsa's eyes. And then September comes and Antoine has planned a series of lectures in the United States, where Catherine must accompany him, it's out of the question for her to remain behind. Their daughter will be looked after by her grandparents, with a nanny to help them, because *they* happen to work, and Jacqueline—unlike her daughter—hasn't just handed her dance school over to a friend on a whim. Catherine weeps on the day of her departure, she's not going to see her daughter for three whole weeks, it's too horrible, and then she drops her off and the weeping stops. A huge weight is off her chest, she's once again alone, without a baby at her breast or in her belly, she's a human being in her own right. The weaning had been abrupt. She falls ill from it, with pains through her entire body and a high fever, she spends the first two days of the trip confined to bed in a hotel suite with a view of Central Park. Scarcely recovered, she goes out to dinner with Antoine and his friend from New York University who helped organize the tour and who was preparing to award him an honorary degree, which would in fact be a great honor for Antoine, who loves that sort of thing, certificates and encomia. At dinner, the friend's wife, a woman embittered by her husband's flagrant infidelities, extols the clear advantages women like her have, women who never had children. It's a question of independence! Once someone has children, they can never again be independent! And then, look at Catherine, she says, turning to her dinner companion on the left, look at Catherine, who was so beautiful, with her dancer's figure, look how much becoming a mother changes a woman! Catherine excuses herself from the table, she's not feeling well, hasn't fully recovered.

She doesn't make a scene, you see, I didn't make a scene, she says late at night when Antoine finally gets back to the hotel. That bitch, do you realize what she said to me! Catherine must be exaggerating, she must have misunderstood. No, I understood perfectly well. She wanted to humiliate me in front of everyone, because she's jealous, because she'll never know what it is to be a mother! Catherine had gained more than forty pounds during her pregnancy, mostly from late-night *choucroute*. It's his fault, he practically force-fed her, now she looks like a whale, and the proof is that she's the laughingstock of the whole world! But what are you talking about, you're magnificent, my darling, my adored one, they're all jealous, let her say what she likes! What she likes! Believe me, she's not going to like it when I have my say! She'll see, that one, how becoming a mother changes a woman.

Catherine spends the next three weeks running around American campuses to find rehearsal studios where she sets herself up with her own cassette player. It had been a year since she'd slipped on a leotard—before becoming pregnant, she'd continued dancing, and teaching a bit in a fancy school on the avenue George V run by a famous dancer (to whom her former teacher had introduced her)—but now she bought herself all the gear: a unitard, leg warmers, ballet slippers, a wrap sweater. She puts herself on a draconian diet, helped along by the amphetamines that a friend of Antoine's—they'd met up at a hip nightclub—had very kindly given her. They're frighteningly effective! Over the course of exactly nineteen days she sheds the extra weight. Antoine doesn't need to be asked twice to go to Saks Fifth Avenue, where Catherine locates a pair of supertight leather pants, which she wears with a see-through blouse to a dinner where they'll see all their friends, including the couple from New York University. Catherine receives compliments from the offending wife, who is dumbfounded by the transformation, while Antoine accepts his new title on a little platform with a long speech peppered with aphorisms and flashes of wit. They return to Paris, thrilled to see their daughter again, or almost thrilled.

While they were away, the baby was thriving, according to the updates Catherine had checked in regularly to receive. The baby is doing very well, she's put on weight, she's growing, she takes the bottle. But upon her return, Catherine finds everything changed. She doesn't recognize her daughter, she's different suddenly, and Catherine no longer knows what to do with her. She'd been in the habit of nursing the baby when she cried, and now she doesn't know how to appease her, the baby cries constantly, and only the nanny seems to be able to calm her. Her own body has changed, and then there's that new perfume, maybe she shouldn't have switched. Early on, Antoine had bought her Fidji by Guy Laroche, and she'd become attached to it, it had become her odor, a second skin. In the plane on the way to New York she had allowed him to give her a bottle of First by Van Cleef & Arpels. She'd been wearing it for three weeks, and perhaps her daughter didn't recognize her mother's scent anymore. She'd been gone for too long, she shouldn't have gone at all, they shouldn't have left her, she feels guilty and she worries that she'll never again know how to take care of her daughter, that she won't be able to manage it. She decides to switch back to her old perfume, but now it disgusts her. She's disgusted with everything about herself, about mothering, just looking at powdered milk makes her want to vomit. She's stopped taking the little pills that served as her meals, and now she's constantly worn-out, exhausted. She drags herself around all day, and everything exasperates her, she's on edge, she's useless and helpless. It's only in the evening that she manages to recover her spirits with the help of spirits. She has to meet Antoine at his cocktails, and dinners, and after parties. The nanny sleeps in a maid's room on the building's top floor. She's supposed to stay in the apartment with Elsa until the child's parents get home, but one night she's busy with something else, and the baby is screaming, screaming at the top of her lungs, so much so that the concierge finally takes notice and finds the child alone in the big apartment. Panicked, she frantically calls every number she's been given, finally reaching Jacqueline, who wakes Henri, and the two turn up at avenue de Friedland to retrieve the child who's been bawling herself hoarse for hours. Horrified, they take her home with them. It's not until the following morning that the nanny breezes in as if nothing happened and discovers that the baby is gone. Catherine, still drunk, tries with difficulty to understand the incoherent story told by the poor girl, crazy with worry, who swears that it's not her fault, who—seeing Antoine gesticulating and screaming more loudly than any child—swears even more, lies about leaving her watch, denies everything. Antoine recovers some presence of mind and calls the concierge as a last resort. She recounts the whole incident, the cries, the grandparents, et cetera. Catherine finds herself lowering her eyes before her mother's damning stare. The judgment cuts through Catherine with the cold finality of the guillotine. Catherine tells her: It was a momentary lapse, I know what I'm doing. Of course, that's obvious, Jacqueline responds. Her daughter tells her mother that she didn't ask for her help and certainly not for her condemnation. Oh, that's good to know! Does she want to talk about the three weeks she just spent changing her granddaughter's diapers? Was she not asking for anything then?

· · ·

CATHERINE IS UNWELL. She doesn't feel normal, not that she can say what normal is supposed to feel like. She tells herself she must find a way to reconcile her life as a liberated woman with the demands of motherhood, but she's losing her grip, she feels as if she's drowning. The tears return. She's trapped in a whirlpool of dark thoughts, she can't stand her daughter's crying, she could throw her out the window, she could throw herself out the window, she doesn't want Antoine to touch her anymore, she doesn't want to go out anymore, she doesn't want to do anything other than cry and sleep and if possible never wake up. Antoine has a doctor make an emergency house call one morning when he can't rouse her from her alcoholic stupor. She'd gone a bit overboard with the sleeping pills, the ones Antoine takes to help with his bouts of insomnia. A touch of the baby blues is the doctor's diagnosis—neither a psychiatrist nor even a psychologist, just a keen observer, just a man of the world. Try getting some fresh air, perhaps take a trip somewhere, someplace exotic? Antoine had also called Claude to the rescue, Claude, who hasn't seen Catherine since the news of her pregnancy. Of course Claude still loves her, she's there for her, she'll be there for her. Antoine suggests that he pay for them to take a vacation in a place of their choosing. They decide to leave for Dakar, for the Méridien on the Pointe des Almadies, just after the New Year, to be warmed by the sun in the middle of winter.

Claude cut her beautiful hair, which Catherine had so loved watching her brush through the half-open door of the bathroom, as she lay on the bed in Claude's Montparnasse studio. She now sports thick bangs falling from a side part over her forehead. It looks good on you, Catherine says timidly. It has been over a year since they've seen each other. I just couldn't deal anymore, Claude responds with an extravagant sigh, mimicking Catherine's own complaints about her hair, teasing her with affectionate glee. Before their trip, Catherine stops in at Alexandre, avenue Matignon—hairdresser to the stars. It's worlds away from the beauty salons of her past, with their helmet hair dryers, Formica countertops, and flecked tiling. Catherine has made an appointment with the sphinx of hairstyling, whose logo was designed by Jean Cocteau. She turns into a platinum blonde, with a pixie cut à la Jean Seberg. From that day forward her bourgeois chignon, held together with tortoiseshell combs, is gone. Her haircut is even shorter than Claude's, whether out of a spirit of competition or to prove her commitment. Regardless, from now on her hairstyle will become a political statement, a sign of her allegiance with women who defy the masculine fetish for long hair, that symbol of archaic, servile femininity.

At the end of the first week, they decide to stay another week, and then a third. Catherine refuses to go home. Antoine sends her letter after letter, telegram after telegram, he begs her to return, he and their little Elsa are waiting for her, they miss her terribly, we miss you, I beg you, come back soon! Claude swears never to leave her, they'll work something out, she's prepared to share her. They return. Things will be all right. She breathes forcefully, a deep breath, in through the nose, out through the mouth, she reminds herself every ten seconds that she must breathe, she smokes even more than usual as an exercise in inhaling and exhaling deliberately. Catherine sees a psychiatrist and agrees to undergo a mild treatment with mood stabilizers. The doctor tells her to watch her alcohol intake, the mix is contraindicated. Yes, yes. She gets better. Life gets less unbearable. Yet being a mother continues to be difficult. Caught up in memories of her own childhood, she's obsessed with not repeating the past, but her determination to avoid acting like her own mother doesn't mean she knows what to do. And then she feels harassed by constant demands for attention from both the child and her father, contradictory demands. She feels this dichotomy in her flesh, she's afraid she'll lose it all, she's afraid she'll lose it again, she's always afraid of getting it all wrong, of fucking things up for good. The image of her daughter screaming, abandoned, comes back to haunt her: that child was her, it was she who had been abandoned, not her daughter. No, she's here, she's always been present, she's a loving mother, she's always there for her daughter, it's her own mother who had given her up. She buries the memory of her own failure by transferring it to her past, fabricating memories. The guilt associated with what actually happened is too much to bear. She finds it impossible to face her libertine lifestyle, the debauched parties she and Antoine continue to attend. She refuses to examine her own conduct, or she can't. All she sees is her devotion to her lover's desires and her irrepressible love for her child, the impossible tightrope act by which she tries to bridge the two.

Catherine begins to want some commitment from Antoine. If they're not going to get married, perhaps he could buy her an apartment? Antoine had always been against owning real estate, he'd seen his mother spend her life tangled up in roofing and plumbing problems, in the country, in her apartment in Paris, in her house in Brittany, and he'd always told himself that she really would have been better off renting, as he did. They'll get married, Catherine shouldn't worry about that, it's just a question of time. She's thinking about having another child. She doesn't talk to him about it, she knows he'll say that he's too old, and doesn't she think things are complicated enough? They celebrate Elsa's first birthday during the summer of 1978. They spend it in Brittany at the house of Grand-mama, who bullies Catherine to her heart's content, criticizing her for her laxity, her methods of child-rearing inspired by the worst pseudo-psychological manuals. Catherine is thrilled by her daughter's every milestone. Elsa walks! Elsa babbles! Elsa points with her finger! If only they could live this way all year long, Antoine is there, by her side, he's at ease, he laughs and sings, he's not getting worked up about office problems, his insane schedule, his endless projects and indomitable desires. At least here there are no skirts to chase and the marathon race for social recognition pauses for the summer vacation. The house is so dilapidated and the staircases so hazardous that Antoine relieves himself in a chamber pot so as not to have to go downstairs in the middle of the night. He dumps it out the window in the mornings, and when Catherine warns him that one fine day somebody's going to get soaked in his piss, she can't have imagined that someone would be her! You don't think that, with your daughter's diapers, I'm dealing with enough *pipi-caca* as it is? He finds this hilarious, he almost falls out the window from laughing, and to her own amazement, Catherine, sopping wet and stinking, guffaws too. How on earth did she find herself mixed up with such a crazy guy? Their eccentricities unite them, they share the solidarity of the mad, their raucous laughter aligns them against the world and its norms.

In August, Catherine decides to take advantage of the respite country life offers them to tell him she's pregnant, which isn't yet true but she wants it to be, so it's her way of preparing the ground. She needs him to be in a receptive mood, and that time is now. And anyway it's bound to happen and when it does there will still be time to stretch the truth. It happens in September, there's only one month's gap, but she has to play her cards close to her chest. She counts on the baby's late arrival, which happened with the first one, and in any case Antoine doesn't have much of a sense of time. They finally marry, after Christmas. This pregnancy is perhaps even more marvelous than the previous one, she develops a passion for fruit jellies, and candied chestnuts, and salads with lots of vinegar, and gargantuan platters of cheese. The only thing giving her trouble is her bad leg, which is acting up, her back hurts a lot too, but she's not one to complain. Using the pads Antoine swipes from the doctor's office, she prescribes herself anti-inflammatories, opioids, and steroids, until the cocktail works and she feels no pain whatsoever. For her wedding, Catherine chooses an Yves Saint Laurent pantsuit in black velvet, which she wears with a deep purple ruffled blouse and a hat accompanied by a little tulle veil with black polka dots. She can't close the pants, but the suit jacket is wide and a bit flared, like a peacoat. She looks stunning, with her face rounded and rosy from the pregnancy, a surprisingly jovial bride wearing black. Antoine's children join the party, plenty of sarcasm in the eldests' toasts, which everyone laughs at, the newlyweds included. Catherine has won, they'll have to accept both her and her children now. Claude doesn't come to the party, though she was invited. Let's not push things, she gets it, she's just Catherine's lover.

Driven everywhere by his chauffeur or by Catherine, upon whom he can always count when he's really running late—when she's driving, he clutches the phone box on the dashboard during the hairpin turns, hits his head on the Jaguar's ceiling when she climbs onto the sidewalk, screams: No, Catherine! No, no, no, dammit, don't go the wrong way down a one-way street! You're going to kill someone! but she always gets him where he needs to go without killing anyone and almost on time—Antoine, out of practice as a driver for a long time, takes the wheel one day when Catherine, eight months pregnant and exhausted, asks him to drive them to the country, and

he runs smack into a tree on the highway, with Elsa in the backseat yelling: Papa boom! Papa no boom! Shortly afterward, Catherine
goes into labor, and their second child is born almost the same day as
Antoine's second brother dies as the result of a similar car accident,
although this one might have been deliberate, a suicide. Antoine has
now lost both his brothers, his niece, a son, and—almost—a daughter, who remains paralyzed following a motorcycle crash. Catherine
considers all this carnage and is horrified. Who's next? Could it be a
curse? They call their second child—another girl!—Violaine, because
at the time Antoine happened to meet a very pretty woman who bore
that name. Finally they can agree on something, Violaine is classy, it's
poetic, and it sounds good in French. Catherine's every suggestion
had been turned down. If it's a girl—she declined any attempt to
know the child's sex in advance, thanks but no thanks—she would
have liked to give her a Jewish name, perhaps Rebecca. Why not
Rachel while you're at it? Rachel, when from the Lord! What's that
got to do with anything? Proust, my dear darling, it has to do with
Proust. Ah! The day of her birth, May 8, the anniversary of the Liberation, Antoine suggests calling her Victoire. Catherine, who didn't
get a graduate degree in history—as opposed to her late father-in-
law—asks what right France had to claim victory, after Pétain, Vichy,
the collaborators, and all the rest of them. Violaine will do. Yes, it's a
pretty name.

Married, with two kids, everything will fall into place now,
Catherine tells herself, confidently. We have a family, we are a family, Antoine will calm down. She'll achieve some sort of stability.
But if getting ready for trips was a trial when it was just the two
of them, with four, Catherine finds out, it's an apocalypse. Antoine
turns their home into a war zone, he fancies himself a general bark-

ing contradictory orders as he stalks through an apartment ransacked and pillaged by enemy forces, mother and children against father. It isn't so much the little baby's fault but Elsa keeps making a mess of things. Catherine tries to close the suitcases, while Antoine continually reopens and rummages through them, convinced that his wife and daughters are mixing his things up on purpose, important correspondence, documents of inestimable value, they don't realize how serious this is, if those papers were to get lost, go now, leave me alone, get out of here, I need to put some things in order, I can't cope anymore! Antoine often works late, he spends whole nights either writing or organizing the shelves of his library. His family is absolutely forbidden to touch anything. Catherine never displaces even a pen, but he accumulates so much paperwork—bills, correspondence, newspapers, brochures, magazines, publishing contracts, expense reports, everything from butcher wrapping paper to documents worthy of the national archives—that piles tip over, and in his agitation, in his attempt to set things right, he makes even more of a mess, until everything is in chaos. Fine, we'll wait for you in the car, pack your own fucking bags, we don't have to listen to your indignant squawking.

Did they really need another dog? Catherine asks herself in these moments of exasperation. She was the one who chose the enormous pet this time, perhaps she thought his size would mean stability, longevity, a jet-black sheepdog who licks Elsa's feet and watches over the baby wedged into her Moses basket in the back of the car. Catherine's priority, when her second daughter was born, was making sure that Elsa didn't feel jealous of the new arrival, fostering a bond between the two sisters without rivalry. Elsa calls her little sister the baby, and Catherine lets her touch the baby as much as she likes, with her hands covered in dirt, purée, germs, it doesn't matter, she encourages her, she coaxes her: Yes, my love, the baby is your baby, too, my sweetheart, she's the baby of all three of us, you, Maman, and Papa. Elsa is twenty-two months old, and she keeps kissing her little sister, she's so proud of her, the baby, her baby. Catherine feels her heart split in two. Her darling big girl, the flesh of her flesh, can no longer be her only reason for living. She had told herself, in moments of overwhelming distress and sadness, that if anything happened to Elsa, it would be so easy for her to end her own life. But now if she lost one girl she would have to survive for the sake of the other. The idea obsesses her. She thinks that her own survival now depends on that of her two daughters. It's as if she had to give up the greatest love of her life, because she had to make room for another love, she tells Antoine one evening in tears, crumpled against his chest, and it's so beautiful to imagine loving so much twice, but it's also hard, it's so hard. For the baby's first bath, she asks her big girl to help her, they'll do everything together, yes, my love, it's your baby. Elsa almost drowns her little sister, and Grand-mama, who prowls through the hallways of the country house where they've moved for the summer, is glad for the opportunity to scold her daughter-in-law: Catherine! You privilege psychology at the expense of prophylaxis! Big words don't frighten her anymore, and anyway she knows the meaning of these ones well. Grand-mama, with all due respect, please fuck off, she responds without skipping a beat. Their relationship has not improved with time.

A procession of nannies followed the one who'd let baby Elsa wake up her grandparents on the other side of town in the middle of the night, an incident best forgotten, never to be mentioned again. Catherine has tried them all: the English nannies and their infuriating strictness, the young au pair girls whom her husband would happily bed, the kind but wimpy, the impertinent, the impatient, the ones who are too old, the ones who don't speak French, the ones who can't work nights. It seems impossible to find a suitable match. And in fact, it is impossible. Nobody's perfect, my sweet beloved, says Antoine, except for you, of course. And the perfect is the enemy of the good! Catherine assures him that her most recent hire was far from good, she was a walking disaster, and she starts another round of ads and interviews, which leave her drained and discouraged. The truth is that Catherine isn't at all sure she wants to have someone else looking after her daughters, and when she compares herself to any random nanny, they inevitably fall short. How can you replace a mother? She lets her aging housekeeper, a wonderful stand-in for a grandmother, look after the girls for a couple of hours each day. At night she gets babysitters to come after she's put the girls to bed herself. The trade-off is that she gives up going to cocktail parties, and she often arrives late to dinner parties, which gets on Antoine's nerves. She doesn't want to travel as much now that Elsa speaks, now that Elsa realizes that Maman is going away, Catherine can't stand hearing the girl beg her to stay, it breaks her heart, it makes her feel so guilty. And then she loves bedtime. She loves telling the girl stories that she invents night after night, installments that follow each other with the logic of dreams, adventures for which Elsa provides details or plot twists. Catherine nurses the baby for longer this time, and the baby refuses to take the bottle, so she continues to give her the breast, relieved to have found a reason to maintain this bond, which anchors her in maternity, in an identity. Elsa asks right away for the baby to share her room. She wants to be able to see the baby in order to fall asleep. She wants to see the baby when she wakes up. She wants to see the baby always beside her. The baby is also her baby, she takes her role very seriously, she watches over her, she doesn't take her eyes off her.

What does daily life consist of? Work, routine, constraint. For most people, that is. In her domestic setup, Catherine has no firm obligations, no structure. She gives herself tasks to accomplish, she takes care of her husband, whose name she has even adopted, yet another name. She takes care of her children, and she manages the staff, who take care of everything else. She prepares meals for the girls, and she'd like to cook dinner for herself and her husband once in a while, but Antoine hates dining in, and even more than that, he hates the idea of a meal prepared in advance, with a fixed menu. One evening when she convinces him to eat at home—Just this once! One time won't hurt!—she prepares a pot roast, because she knows it's one of his favorites, and cooks various first courses and side dishes to make him feel that he has a choice, to offer him the possibility of picking at different dishes as he likes to do in restaurants, where he always orders enough for twelve, only to be able to taste everything, so that afterward he won't regret not having ordered something else, but that evening he sits down to the meal begrudgingly, under orders from his wife. Scarcely seated, he leaps up as if his chair had caught fire and begins opening all the cupboards and emptying them of cans, and frantically, using a rusty can opener and risking tetanus as in his impatience he manages to cut his palm, he dumps the contents of old jars of cassoulet and other delicacies relegated to the back of the pantry onto the table at random, and with his demonstration completed, he declares: There, I like to have a choice! Catherine, hurt, angry, fights back tears. Her pride gets the better of her. Fuck it! She dumps her pot roast into the toilet, and she flushes it before he has the time to catch up with her and tell her that she's mad, stark raving mad, that he would have eaten her pot roast, why, you're totally insane! What a waste! Yes, it's such a waste. You ruined everything. The madwoman is going to bed.

WITH THE EXCEPTION OF VACATIONS and weekends in the country, Antoine doesn't see the children much. He's an important man with an important job, a man of his times, unapologetic, who wouldn't dream of sharing domestic tasks, a man who admires his daughters when he has the leisure time to do so. He is a loving father in his own way, however, he finds it terribly moving to see his wife nursing his child, and Catherine's second daughter resembles him, she's the spitting image of her father, so no one in the family dares open their mouth, no one dares go there anymore, and in any case it's too late: they're married. She's pulled it off, they got what they wanted. But what was that, exactly, does anybody know? An open marriage, a family, a certain conventional respectability they then threaten with their antics, a permanent high-wire act, a crazy wager from beginning to end. The babysitters who sometimes sleep in the guest room next to the children's room are awakened by the sound of raucous sex—all manner of partners cycle through Antoine and Catherine's bed—issuing from the master bedroom. They quit, one after the other. Elsa, on some weekday morning, discovers a woman passed out on the toilet. She asks her mother who is the lady sleeping on the potty, with no clothes on? Claude, circumspect, refuses to participate in the chaos, to take part in the spectacle Antoine and Catherine make of their debauchery.

If she must do without family dinners, stability, routine, if they won't walk the straight and narrow path, as Antoine would say, Catherine returns to the prospect of owning something together, an apartment, a house, she'd like some kind of security, and if it can only be financial, or in the form of real estate, well, that would at least be something, an anchor. But Antoine continues to tell her that investing in brick and mortar is for the petit bourgeois, that they themselves have the means to live even beyond their means, that they lack nothing, that she has everything she could possibly want, what is she complaining about? She'd just like to have a safe place, to know that her daughters are covered, not in cashmere buntings and outfits from Baby Dior, but with a roof over their heads that actually belongs to them. It's such a drag, her obsession with owning a house. She goes to see a real estate agent behind his back, she visits dozens of apartments, persuaded that she'll end up convincing him when she's found the right one. But Antoine isn't buying it, literally or figuratively. Catherine, naïvely, doesn't think about being strategic with her demands. He said no, and he doesn't mean to be cruel, but a thousand times no, and nagging won't get her anywhere, and anyway, he has no savings, not enough to buy a house or an apartment, just enough to pay their day-to-day expenses, and the very thought of scrimping and saving nauseates him even more than the idea of dining in. He might as well wear a beret and buy his baguette while returning home in the evening, after having clocked out of his job as a civil servant, like a good little Frenchman who puts pennies aside every month in order to buy himself a little apartment in the suburbs, is that it? Might as well drop dead right away. Catherine also doesn't want to live the way, say, her mother does, obviously she rejects the model of Jacqueline and Henri in Montreuil, with their jealously protected nest egg that they go on growing incrementally thanks to whatever conservative investments the nice banker at their local branch suggests; nevertheless, she'd like for each of her daughters to have a bankbook for a savings account in which their parents could deposit a little bit every year, so that the girls will each have something when they reach adulthood. Do you mean saving? Yes, exactly, saving. To live cautiously, parsimoniously, within boundaries, with constraints, to think of the future, to foresee and forestall, all these distressingly mediocre concepts are anathema to Antoine. No, not at all his cup of tea. He sees his life unfurling on the big screen, not on some redneck's little TV set, otherwise why not start chugging beer out of a can while we're at it? There can be no half measures, no compromises: he wants to live big, which also means burning through cash to brighten up the gloom of everyday life, to make it glow. And can he make it glow! Sometimes the fire is blinding.

One winter Catherine joins Claude on a visit to her parents in Corrèze. She falls in love with the region's rural landscape, the undulating fields, the unadorned villages, as simple and solid as the massive stones out of which its buildings are constructed. The land itself makes her feel robust, she feels she could stand on her own two feet in such a place, experience, for once, a sense of groundedness. She and Claude start looking at For Sale signs, just in case, you never know. On an exploratory drive, they stop in front of an abandoned train station to have a drink in a bar that has strangely remained open there, an incongruous relic of bygone days. The waitress sets down their half-pints of beer and asks what they're doing in the region—one can see you're not from around here, oh, of course, Parisians, that much was obvious from the start. She says that on top of the hill, all the way up, in the village, there's a house for sale that belongs to her old aunt, who hasn't lived there for ages, so it's fallen to ruin, it's been so many years since anyone lived there, a tear-down really, a lot of work, so much work, no one around here has the money to do it. Catherine likes the sound of it. They go up the tiny, winding road, at the base of which a rusty sign points to Puypertus. Her chest begins to tighten, her heart speeds up, she feels that she's been here before, or has always wanted to be here, that she's home. She asks Claude to pinch her, she must be hallucinating, it's not possible, she sees rising before her in this shambles the house of her dreams, Claude hugs her, she doesn't try to question her, simply shares her joy, kisses her hands and her lips, folds her in her arms. Catherine negotiates with the barmaid's old aunt, or rather she doesn't negotiate, she agrees to pay the price she is asked. It's a deal! I'm ready to sign.

She returns to Paris and announces this extraordinary news to Antoine, who at first assumes she's kidding. She's completely off her rocker, he'll never set foot in Puypertus, a godforsaken hole, in the middle of nowhere, and she bought it to do what, exactly? She bought it to please him, to make a home for their daughters, a family home for them all, to have a place of her own. It's a drop in the bucket, it costs practically nothing, and what the fuck do you care, with the money you throw around on all sorts of stupid things? I give a fuck because it's my money and I do what I want with it, and I'm not buying a house in *Corrèze*! And all the work, the renovation, the plumbing, and the hassles you have no idea about, you don't have a clue about what you're getting us into, you're perfectly clueless! And do you realize how far it is? How will we ever get there! Catherine pleads, scolds, curses, sobs, cries. She says there is a train—a beautiful old-fashioned train, the Corail, with a full-service café car—she says they'll be so happy there, he doesn't realize it yet, he just has to see it, she says. He says he's made up his mind. I said no, for fuck's sake! So she steals money from his safe in secret, over the course of several months, and when she's finally put the sum together, she leaves from the Gare d'Austerlitz on the Corail to Brive-la-Gaillarde. She tells Antoine that Claude bought the house for her, just to make him jealous. Claude doesn't contradict her. Finally he agrees grudgingly to pay for work on the house, but all the same he's never going to set foot there, let that be clear, never.

And then, and then. What happens next has already been told. In broad strokes, a few details saved from oblivion.

CATHERINE STAYS WITH ANTOINE for a few more years, during which time their girls grow up, she opens a dance school in Boulogne, the sheepdog is killed by neighbors in the country, Grandmama continues to be a surly mother-in-law, they get another dog, who disappears one fine day, they replace him with a cat who jumps out the window and doesn't land on its feet, they get yet another dog, they continue to make the rounds of the Paris clubs, Catherine continues loving Claude in her spare time, and then Antoine becomes infatuated with a very young woman, a cocaine addict, sublimely beautiful, in front of whom Catherine finds herself at a cocktail party, both of them wearing the same Saint Laurent dress, which Antoine had bought in duplicate. Of course, he's had flings, of course he's fooled around left and right with young women, high-class call girls, out-of-towners, so be it. He inadvertently tries to pick up his own wife in a boutique one day. Her back is turned toward him and he doesn't recognize her from behind. Of course he's been unfaithful, but she's his wife, for fuck's sake! All she's demanded over the years is a minimum degree of respect, a minimum, just enough so that he doesn't openly fuck with her, so that he doesn't humiliate her in public! Apparently that's too much to ask. The girls are four and six by now. Antoine spends most of his nights at his whore's place. He doesn't even come home anymore, he's too afraid of facing Catherine's rage, she's gone out of her mind, she's lost all sense of proportion. A sane man might have thought twice about buying a revolver, keeping it loaded and within reach at all times, as a way of protecting himself from a crazy woman in an apartment where two young children were also living. But he thinks that, just in case, it might come in handy, when she's really acting out, maybe he could use it to scare her. It dawns on him that it was perhaps a bad idea only when he sees Elsa pointing the weapon at her little sister, her finger on the trigger. Catherine, meanwhile, allows herself to be picked up by the first asshole who comes along. He happens to be the father of two of her daughters' classmates at school. He's divorced and he promises her the moon and the stars, and he agrees to have dinner at home, and to create a big new family with her.

Catherine has enrolled her daughters in a bilingual American school, because she wants them to have access to everything that she herself was deprived of, including a progressive education, at once rigorous and child-centered, with teachers who listen, who encourage their students rather than crush them. And then she wants above all for her daughters to speak English, she makes it her personal mission, because her mother had forbidden her to learn the language. That is, her mother had prevented her from going on a language study trip to London with an English teacher with whom she was madly in love. She was fifteen years old, her mother was resolutely against it, and knowing how tricky her daughter could be when she got an idea into her head, she had insisted on meeting with the teacher. Their meeting had so humiliated the lovelorn adolescent that she never returned to class after that. All Catherine had retained from this incident was an irrevocable ban. Her mother had prevented her from learning English, out of bitterness, meanness, stupidity, or malice. Since for her it is imperative that her daughters' upbringing not resemble her own, their learning English becomes for her a top priority. Nevertheless, Catherine's mother is a perfect grandmother, who takes wonderful care of her granddaughters, looks after them on a regular basis. When dropping off her children in Montreuil, in the apartment above Beauté-Santé, Catherine watches the girls running to embrace their darling grandma. Hello, Maman, says Catherine, her air-kiss barely brushing her mother's cheek, with a pettiness that's unlike her. Well, I'm off. Elsa, Violaine, be good girls with Grandma and Grandpa. Don't drive them up the wall, okay? And getting into her car, parked out front, her brand-new Opel— Yes, I've changed cars again, she tells her mother, who is astonished that she's bought a car, a new one, yes, the Jaguar is impractical in Paris—she rolls down her window to wave to her girls, who blow kisses to her from behind the macramé curtain. Catherine recalls the odor of hair spray when she hugged her own grandmother, and her grandmother's trembling fingers, which she warmed by rubbing them together under the lining of her felt coat. Catherine lets out a loud sigh, exasperated with herself—what sentimentality, what pathetic nostalgia!—she exhales the smoke from her cigarette and dries her tears. She's proud to have managed to conserve that relationship between her daughters and their grandmother, between her daughters and her ingrate of a mother, who is perpetually full of reproach.

Catherine has become a member of the *haute bourgeoisie*, her mother watches her strutting around in her furs and her Van Cleef jewels and wonders who she thinks she's fooling. She knows very well where her daughter comes from. Jacqueline doesn't refuse her daughter's gifts—Catherine gives her many very beautiful gifts—but she finds it unreasonable and absurd to spend so much cash on such idiotic things, that aren't at all useful, that won't put a roof over her granddaughters' heads. Catherine would tend to agree with this, but how can she admit that her mother is right? It is far better when it is useless! Antoine says, quoting Cyrano. In front of her mother, Catherine takes Antoine's side. She takes the side of love, she starts from the premise that the important thing is to love, to love unconditionally, and when her mother reproaches her for not being strict enough with her daughters, for not teaching them good manners, for letting them continue to bottle-feed until well past the appropriate age, for not punishing them enough, and for raising them without an ounce of common sense, Catherine tells her that she loves her daughters, and that's the most important thing, and if only her mother had realized that a bit earlier in life, the centrality of love, perhaps things would have gone a bit better between them. Oh, and by the way, I don't need lessons from you. Catherine's confidence has grown along with her standing in society, and becoming a mother herself has given her the nerve to tell her mother to fuck off when she sees fit. Her money gives her authority. It's so much easier to get people to fall in line when you've got cash to throw at them, Catherine would frequently say later on in life. People always line up behind the big bucks. Her husband has at least taught her that.

Antoine still loves her, and she still loves him, that's what drives her insane. His ungainly body, his skinny calves, his paunchy belly, his scrawny shoulders covered with long, curling hairs, his crooked feet with ingrown toenails, his clumsy hands, his dazzling mind, his fabulous erudition, his love notes, his flowers, his stupid fuck-

VIOLAINE HUISMAN

ing flowers—everything that he represents, his body, his mind, his whole being is so much a part of her, it lives inside her. The years have not extinguished her passion, on the contrary, his constant indiscretions seem to have fed it, fueled it all the more. She becomes indignant at his setbacks, she takes pride in his successes, she is his wife for better or for worse, she is his lawfully wedded wife, after all, and it doesn't seem too much to ask to impose a minimum of rules and basic decency around their life together. Why can't they try to live like normal people, for fuck's sake, why can't they try just once, to live the way normal people do? Normalcy—a vast subject of inquiry! Antoine responds. As a couple, they're not in the least bit normal: they're a pair of weirdos, iconoclasts, they can't do anything the way everyone else does it. Even shitting doesn't happen normally at their house: they have to talk about it for hours, every day there's something going on with it. They shit too much or not enough. No, there is nothing normal about this family, but there is love. They love their daughters madly, they kiss their adorable little feet, they tickle them, they tickle them everywhere, even on their privates, their little apricots, so pretty, on which they deposit kisses as if that's the most natural thing in the world. They go into raptures over their beauty, and roar with laughter at their funny faces, their antics, they hug them and spoil them and tell them just how much they love them, more than anything in the world.

Claude thinks that perhaps her time will come, that she has a fighting chance. She waits because she loves Catherine. She doesn't have much of a choice. Catherine starts a new dance school, where she hopes to regain the self-confidence that she had in Marseille, she tries one last time to get Antoine to buy an apartment, right next to the school. She believes it will happen, without reason, simply by force of will. And when he doesn't, when Catherine has to face the fact that he's a bastard, and decides at last to leave him, where will she go? Claude holds out her arms to her. Claude says to move in with her, not to be so timid, not to care about what people will think. You, Catherine, is it possible that you're afraid of being seen as a lesbian? You? No, it's not just what people will think of her, it's not that she's afraid or ashamed, it's that she needs a man, any man, to put her in her place, to give her her rightful place. She tells herself that maybe yes, maybe she'll leave and move in with Claude, she tells herself maybe but she knows very well that at one time or another she'll stumble upon some guy who'll come and pluck her like a flower. Still, Claude waits for her.

The guy in question is a *pied-noir*, which perhaps reminds Catherine of the stories her stepfather, Henri, often told about his military service in Algeria. He has two children and his ex-wife is English, hence the bilingual school. Catherine allows herself to be seduced, they begin an affair, which she doesn't have any trouble hiding from Antoine, though it's less easily hidden from Claude. She leaves on a trip with him under a false pretext that Antoine probably doesn't buy but doesn't bother to expose, he's been having a rough time with his whore recently. Elsa and Violaine spend more and more weekends and vacations with Grandma and Grandpa. They are always happy to have them and this pattern allows Jacqueline, when she sees Catherine, to argue that she's the one raising these children. The professional rivalry between mother and daughter that had been put on hold during the early years of Catherine's marriage comes roaring back as soon as Catherine's school takes off. The registrations pile up, and she runs the school more or less effectively, even though she's perpetually high on prescription drugs, mixing antianxiety and pain medication, downers to go to sleep, uppers to wake up. And then she drinks, at times troubling quantities of alcohol, often alone, at home, to calm her nerves. It's complicated with the girls, she has no patience, and she's very aware of how much they notice her absences. They see everything, and their gaze makes her feel unbearably guilty; she'd rather blind them than catch them looking at her like that. Maman! Maman! Maaaaaaaam! The girls call her, over and over, they cut her off when she's speaking, they interrupt her when she's on the phone, she can't even piss in peace, they're constantly in need of something. Maman? Maman, where are you? Elsa and Violaine sing in a chorus of voices echoing across the apartment's long hallways. I'm here, for fuck's sake! I'm here, she screams at the top of her lungs like the Queen of the Night: I'm. Right. Here. Is it possible to take a piss in this place? I can't take it anymore! I'm just not going to make it if you keep harassing me like this. I'll never make it, do you hear me? The girls fall silent, petrified. They begin to cry. We're sorry, Maman, we're so sorry, sweet, sweet Maman! She's mad at herself for having screamed, it's not their fault, it's not your fault, my darlings, I'm the one who must ask you to forgive me, forgive me, please, I love you more than anything, you're my adored darlings, but Maman is tired, she's just so tired. The guy keeps pressing her to move in with him, he's ready to take her in, with her daughters of course, yes, they'll have a big family, lots of children, so much the better. Claude's patience is at an end, there are jealous outbursts now, she sees clearly that Catherine doesn't give a damn about her, does she intend to keep making a fool of her until the very last moment? It's been ten years, ten years of her living with Antoine while fooling around with Claude, a decade isn't nothing. But what Catherine would like is for Antoine to pull himself together, for them to find a way to live harmoniously, as a couple, for them to manage to balance their desires. As an ultimatum, she writes him a twenty-page letter, a letter riddled with spelling errors and poetic inventions, curses and swearwords. He doesn't respond. Has he even read it? She's not sure that he's read it. She could die from the pain, but for the sake of her daughters she must move forward, something's got to give.

Antoine tries to keep her from going, all the while continuing to lie to her. He promises to break things off with his floozy, but he does nothing of the sort, he wants to have it both ways. You're going to fuck it all up, she taunts him, and for what? Do you really think your high-class hooker isn't going to get tired of you? I give you two months, my poor darling, in two months you're going to come crying on my shoulder, with your tail between your legs, and it will be too late! She speaks to him this way on days when she feels strong, days when she manages to forget how much she loves him and can concentrate on the disgust he inspires in her. On those days she hates him, she'd like to hurt him so bad that he'd never recover, to watch him suffer a slow, painful death. But there's no justice in this world: it's Claude who falls ill, stricken with a terrible disease. Breast cancer, Stage IV: tumor, ganglia, metastases. She'll go fast, in excruciating pain. Catherine responds with horror and then with inconceivable coldness. She abandons the invalid, her lover, because, as far as Catherine is concerned, she has to move forward. She goes to see Claude in the hospital two or three times but as soon as the end draws near, she stops. Claude will die alone, just as Catherine was absent from the bedside of Granny, her granny whom she adored. She abandons her lover to her fate. How unlucky, really, poor Claude. Catherine leaves Antoine in the month of June 1984. The girls will spend the summer at their grandparents' place, while she fixes up the guy's apartment, at 59, rue de Varenne. The four children will share a bedroom, in which

Catherine has room dividers installed, so that they'll each have some privacy, while all being together. She informs the girls, solemnly, at the end of the school year. Faced with their tears, she too bursts into sobs, she puts her arms around them, my loves, my darlings, of course Maman still loves Papa, of course he'll always be your papa, of course he'll always love you. I swear to you that if I could have done things differently I would have, it's not what I would have wanted either. My loves, my darlings, don't cry like that, I'm begging you. Catherine promises her daughters that they'll see their papa every evening, and that they'll spend their vacations all together.

And in fact, the parents do go on vacation with their daughters, to a big bungalow with a private pool in a five-star hotel. They do love each other after all, the first night is fine, they sleep in separate rooms, but from the second night onward, things take a sharp turn for the worse. She grabs her children and flees to her mother, who is only too happy to rub her nose in it, to put her down and to mock her. Yes, all right, all right—wiping her tears— could you dial it down a bit? The girls aren't doing so bad, the girls will be fine! Yes, everything will be fine, a separation isn't the end of the world, lots of parents divorce these days, there are definitely worse things than that in life, the girls will get over it. And they'll see their father every day, he promised, he'll stop by every evening, he's used to making his nightly rounds and visiting his old mother. When September comes, they move into the new apartment, and Antoine does stop by every evening just before bedtime, to see his daughters and his wife from whom he is not yet legally separated, and the girls hope that it means all this is temporary, that Papa will come back for good one day, that order will be restored, or at least the old disorder to which they've become accustomed. Catherine manages to get custody of her new lover's children, thanks to the best lawyer in Paris, a friend of Antoine's with whom he suspects her of having an affair, or at least a fling, but really, that's the pot calling the kettle black!

The guy is of no interest at all, he's so boring it's hard even to describe him. He's got a perfectly boorish face, a macho square jaw, a flat nose, a crew cut, vicious little eyes, pinched lips, a double chin, sagging jowls, in short, a nasty face, nobody can figure out what Catherine sees in him, but Catherine decides, as if at random, that he's the one. Catherine is an exemplary mother, she drives all the children to school and back in the Volvo station wagon that they bought together, she plays taxi driver in order to ferry the whole little band to their extracurricular activities, and after dinner she welcomes her ex into their home so that he can kiss his daughters good night. Their relationship is complicated, they're not so sure they've made the right decision, especially her, he knows that she wanted them to stay together, and of course she was right, the floozy took off shortly after Catherine's departure. And of course he found another one, because he can't remain alone for a second, and because he has, one must admit, plenty of women to choose from, nevertheless, she's the one he loves, he begs her to come back. It's too late. The children are settled, their classes have already begun, she's registered them all for tennis and dance lessons, and at least here they have family dinners, and then there is Corrèze, where the house is finally habitable. No, it's too late. After a year the guy begins pestering her to get a divorce. After two years she divorces. Three years later, she remarries.

•   •   •

CATHERINE CELEBRATES HER fortieth birthday. Surrounded by her new family, she blows out the candles on a giant cake in the shape of a fish, what a joke, to be born on April first, things got off to a funny start! The children grow and she organizes birthday parties, extraordinary surprise parties with costumes, magicians, clowns, and tons of guests. The four children divide their vacations between Papa and their respective mothers, ski vacations and Corrèze, the house in Corrèze that Catherine has turned into her family home, yes, she's succeeded in doing that, and she is so proud of it. The major construction on the second wing started just after the wedding, and it was all hands on deck, between preparing for the wedding and digging the pool and building the tennis court and managing the children and running the dance school. The guy blends in with her new life, but he might as well be transparent, invisible, she's not sure that she knows him, she's not sure that they have much in common, but is that really necessary? She trusts him to be a good father, to bring their boat safely into harbor. But which harbor? And what boat? She lets herself be carried along by the current and her little boat resembles the one that travels along the Enchanted River, the first ride you come upon in the Jardin d'Acclimatation, the amusement park in the Bois de Boulogne. Everybody on board, hooray, perfect! Had she really allowed herself to be taken for a ride? Yes, but she'd gotten into the boat herself, of her own free will. After all, it's Catherine who asks this guy, soon to be her husband, to leave their home when her ex comes by, so that her ex can see his daughters without his rival being in the way. The guy didn't have to be asked twice. He has dinner and then promptly returns to his nearby office, and sometimes as a result, he gets caught up in the piles of work, and in fact yes, he comes home a bit late, the children are already asleep and his wife is too. She doesn't question the business trips he goes on, men take business trips, men like him, who wear pin-striped suits and leather loafers and carry monogrammed briefcases. She's completely shocked when she discovers that he's been fucking his secretary for months already, and that it isn't his first infidelity. She's stunned because it isn't at all like the portrait of the man that she'd painted for herself, the picture of the life that she thought she'd hung above her mantelpiece. But it's not just the picture that's been damaged, it's the wall, the entire structure that has crumbled. She didn't leave the man she loved, loved body and soul, to find herself fucked over by this asshole.

Catherine goes into a rage. Medea is not insane. She's been ridi-culed, humiliated, betrayed. She is a queen, yet she's been dragged through the mud. Medea is not insane, no. She avenges herself by destroying that which is most dear to her. Her life alone can't measure up to the enormity of the betrayal. Her own life is not enough, it's bigger than she is, she has to take on all of humanity, humanity in all its rottenness, and in particular the vileness of men. Because men are vile, abject, pigs who only think with their dicks, filthy swine, all of them, and she knows something about that, she's the daughter of one of those bastards. Medea is not insane; she's that marvel who warns of the will of the gods. And the gods—not always, but nevertheless, once in a while—the gods show up to put their foot down, to say, frankly, that's a bit much, we won't have it, it's all wrong. Really. All wrong. Catherine could kill them all if only she had taken Antoine's revolver with her in her suitcases, but lacking a weapon, she begins by setting fire to the dance school, so as not to have to admit to her mother that she needs to hand it over, at least temporarily, because the administrative tasks, the management of the personnel, the look-ing after the children, the stretching classes for elderly ladies, she can't deal with any of that right now, she's going to have to take a break to settle scores with those scumbags who turned her body, her life into a garbage dump. For fuck's sake. They haven't yet felt the full force of Catherine's anger. She is not just furious, she's become a fury.

As for the secretary, who was heavily pregnant, she could have skinned her alive; she could have ripped the little runt from the woman's womb with her bare hands, tearing it out with her fingernails and drowning the bastard in its mother's blood. She could have done so, but she won't go that far. She limits herself to dissecting the little dog—she's lost count of how many pets her family has been through—in place of a voodoo doll. When Catherine discovers the dirty little secret, the secretary is seven months pregnant. She's engaged to be married, but she'd been fucking her boss for quite some time, so who knows who the father is? What kind of a whore doesn't know whose child she's carrying? It's so sordid, so disgusting, too pathetic. Catherine had had her tubes tied. When she left the father of her children, she was sure of one thing: she'd never have children with anyone other than him. What an outrage, to imagine her husband impregnating a whore! To have children from different men had always seemed to her the height of vulgarity, totally déclassé. She's shocked, she's revolted, and she would like her vengeance to fall upon them, the whole lot of them, with the overwhelming force of the divine. Animated by a higher power, she feels capable of crushing her oppressors with her fist. And she takes her revenge in the worst manner possible, that is, she takes revenge upon herself, she manages to set herself on fire without ever realizing that she's the one being sacrificed. She begins by burning down the dance school, and then she murders the little dog, and then she destroys her husband's career by informing his managers of his secret little deals, embezzlements, and misappropriations that have been going on for a while. He finds himself slapped with a lawsuit and their marriage falls apart, to the sounds of shattered glass and cries of shame and horror. The children are terrorized, hidden away in their room, from which they no longer dare to emerge, not even to go to the bathroom at night, so the youngest, age nine, starts to wet the bed again. And then Catherine herself flees. Too overwhelmed to find a new place, she follows the advice of Antoine, who tells her to move back into the apartment on the avenue de Friedland, which he's been using as his office.

Antoine has remarried. At the same time as Catherine, he too remarried. He's no longer available, or at least not to return to live with her, to piece together the fragments of their family. Catherine goes back to their apartment, with the navy blue carpet she'd had installed there, the sofas she'd chosen for them, the rugs she'd found rummaging in antiques shops, the marble table in the dining room, their bed, the curtains. She'd like to hang herself with these curtains, impale herself on the rod: to end it all. Yes, it must end. Claude's death comes back to her, Claude's ghost returns to haunt her on the rare nights when she can sleep. Despite the sleeping pills and the whiskey, she wakes with a start, in a cold sweat, her hair sticking straight up on her skull, someone's pulling her hair from behind, she feels that someone's pulling her hair out. The men in white from her old nightmare return, the torsos, the chain saw, the clanking noises. No, no, not me, not that! It's not her fault that Claude died, it's not her fault that men screwed her over, it's not her fault. Paul chooses that moment to write to her, after fifteen years of silence. Not knowing where to find Catherine, he sends the letter to Jacqueline. He leaves a work number in Rouen. Catherine calls him. Paul. Finally a man will come save her. Paul is coming back to save her. Thank you, God. Thank you, Paul.

Catherine tells Paul to meet her at the Barometer, like the last time. The weather matches her mood. She arrives soaked, still beautiful, a little thin, a little pale, her features drawn, she's no longer a young girl but she's magnificent. Paul has also remarried, he has two boys, each of them a year younger than her girls. But yes, he still loves her, he'd never stopped loving her. She finds Paul's arms again, his calm, his attentiveness. He spends the night with her in a hotel, a shabby little hotel the likes of which she hadn't seen in fifteen years, and she cries when he makes love to her, she cries the way she cried the first night. Dry your tears, my Catherine, I love you. Everything will be all right, don't worry, you've always been so strong. Paul tells her that his wife would like to meet her, that's why he'd been in touch with her, his wife has heard so much about her, adorable Catherine, marvelous Catherine, it took his mother ten years to stop calling his new wife Catherine . . . It's because your wife wanted to meet me that you wrote to me, she asks in a hollow voice, haggard, her eyes fixed on the ceiling, like that other night, when she debated whether to see Antoine again. Her wide-open eyes are staring at a crack that she thinks she can see opening, discharging a swarm of strange creatures, insects, nameless things, now she feels them entering her body. Please make them go away, she screams, the things, things, go away, please, make them. She can't breathe, how will she make it, she's not at all strong anymore, she doesn't know how she's going to get up, she can't bear it anymore, how will she ever get up from so much pain. She's in such pain. It's too much pain! She rolls out of bed, collapses in a corner of the room, hiding from something only she can see. For fuck's sake. Can't you tell? I'm dying! I'm fucking dying! Now the noises are no longer words. She's left the world of men, entered a realm beyond reason.

Catherine thinks about Serge, her bastard of a father, and she retraces her fight, her battle as a child, her struggle to survive, the head physician at Necker, and then the abusive grandfather, who beat Granny and whipped her black and blue, and Henri, who had no balls, who never defended her, who'd never take her side even when he knew that her mother was wrong, and Paul, who wasn't up to it, Paul, who didn't keep his promise, Paul, who let her go even though he'd sworn he'd keep her forever, and Antoine, that scumbag, Antoine who'd destroyed her in the end, and the last one, Ducon, Mr. Asshole, Ducon, fuck me! For the third time, she'd taken her husband's name. Who goes around calling themselves *Ducon*? Seriously, Catherine, you were a bit slow, not the sharpest knife in the drawer, to marry a man named Asshole! Duh. What a dumb bitch. Were you at the back of the line when God gave out brains, my poor Catherine? Who gets it wrong so many times? Who, except for you? How did you manage that, you poor dear? And how are you going to get out of all this shit now?

BACK IN THE APARTMENT on avenue de Friedland, she no longer sees clearly, no longer stands up straight, she is overwhelmed by memories in this haunted house. She brings back her piano from the rue de Varenne, the black lacquer Yamaha that she'd bought with Antoine so that the girls could learn to play, the only thing, apart from clothes and jewelry, that she'd taken with her. She plays the *Moonlight* Sonata, the first movement, the piece she'd learned by heart for the recital that her mother was so insistent upon—her daughter's knowing how to play an instrument was firm proof of their upward social mobility—and Catherine had played her sonata brilliantly, the public had applauded, the whole audience had given her a standing ovation, and she still remembered it, fingers on the keyboard, playing her sonata ceaselessly, relentlessly. She never learned to read music, but she knows the first movement by heart, and with a cigarette between her lips, ashes falling between the keys, she plays it over and over again, blowing away the gray dust. She stops only to light one cigarette from another, then replays her desperate sonata, her sonata from beyond darkness, her moonless sonata, her own funeral march. She forgets to go pick up the girls at school, she forgets everything, she's forgotten everything, she no longer knows where she comes from, who she is. What's her name, anyway? She's changed her name six times in forty-two years, it's too much, she can't remember, she no longer knows exactly who is who. Ah yes, that's it, Cremnitz. Her name is Cremnitz. Her father died in the camps. Yes, she's Jewish, that's it, her father died in Auschwitz, in the death camps, those convoys that left from the Gare d'Austerlitz, everything's coming back to her now, the Gare d'Austerlitz, that's where she said goodbye to her father, where she saw him for the last time, the convoys were leaving from the Gare d'Austerlitz, yes, she remembers that train station now, the death camps, yes, death in the gas chamber, it's all coming back to her now. Night and day she plays her sonata, her fingers play it on their own, her long, thin fingers stretched over the keyboard, blinded by the footlights, soon the applause will come, she will take her bow, her hands split far apart on the last chord, sigh, she sighs, the very last chord.

Antoine still comes to see them every evening, her and the girls. He shakes her until her teeth rattle, he yells at her: Catherine, for God's sake! Catherine, get hold of yourself! Catherine, what the hell are you doing? Think of the girls, dammit! Catherine gazes at him blankly, dazed by lack of sleep, by alcohol and drugs. She stares past him with her glassy eyes, without seeing, she frowns, her cigarette smoke traces a question mark in the air. Ah, the girls . . . Yes, the girls! Ah, right, the girls . . . Antoine threatens her, Antoine tells her he's going to have her committed if she continues with this bullshit, she needs to check herself into a hospital, she's not acting normal. Ah, normalcy . . . she says. A vast subject of inquiry. Eye roll. Catherine, for God's sake! There's no more Catherine for God's sake, there's no Catherine at all anymore, Catherine has given up, it's all over for her. Catherine is shot. She's about to get it over with, for herself and for her daughters, she'll do it for the three of them. Careful, she mustn't mess up her chance. She doesn't want to frighten them, no, above all, don't frighten them. Gas won't work, the apartment is too big, the kitchen too far from the bedrooms. She has to think about the best way to get it over with, for the three of them. Together for all eternity.

After Catherine totaled the Opel on the avenue George V, Antoine sends his chauffeur to pick up his daughters at school and drop them off at their classmates' house, so that they won't worry, and to distract them. Catherine senses the tide turning and flees to Nini's house. Nini has followed her childhood friend's misfortunes, the collapse of her world, and though powerless to help, she wishes she could. Catherine begs to borrow her car, and she says yes, how could she refuse? Catherine knows that Antoine is on her heels, she knows he wants to have her locked up. But she's not going to put up with this, she won't go to prison, she's not guilty, they're the ones who should be convicted, those bastards, those murderers. Antoine asks Ducon to intervene, but Ducon has very little to say for himself, he doesn't want to have anything to do with her, she's a nutjob, hysterical, she'd almost bumped him off, he never wants to see her again. Antoine asks Jacqueline to do something, shit, it's *her* daughter! Jacqueline says that she knows what her daughter is like and she doesn't want to get involved, her daughter is subject to violent, uncontrollable outbursts. He's the only one left who can do something. Antoine musters up the courage and asks his chauffeur to drive him to Puypertus, where Ducon is convinced she's hiding out. He has an ambulance come from the hospital at Tulle, where there is a psychiatric wing. An antiquated hospital, but a great hospital, founded under Louis XIV, a historic hospital. They put a straitjacket on Catherine, the way they put handcuffs on criminals. Catherine is hospitalized at Tulle in the fall of 1989. From Tulle, she's transferred to Sainte-Anne, the paragon of psychiatric asylums in France, the place where the first antipsychotic medication was discovered, a Mecca for the teaching of psychiatry, with an emergency room open 24/7, for all the crazies of Paris.

Catherine thinks about digging a grave in the air, there's room for everyone, in this park for lunatics. She is done with pain, she thinks, she is done with the cursed pain of living. Finally, to be done with it, in this hospital that stinks of piss and bleach, like the one she grew up in, the rancid smell of bedpans that has followed her everywhere. She's had enough, yes, enough of this bullshit. She refuses to see her daughters. She refuses to have them see her like this, in this place. Perhaps she remembers her mother's absence from Necker. The hospital is a place for orphans. Catherine tells herself that she's not going to remain under the earth for all eternity. Better fire than worms. She prefers to turn herself into dust, dust in the black milk of morning.

• • •

THUS A NEW DECADE—the 1990s—begins under the sign of absence, abandon, the little cut metal kittens that the patients at Sainte-Anne make in their handicrafts workshop. In the fog of antipsychotics, the seasons blur together. Catherine celebrates her forty-third birthday with a cake in the shape of a fish, which Nini brings her to make her laugh. But she no longer knows how to laugh. And then Mother's Day arrives. At school, her daughters write poems for her. (In the hospital, patients less crazy than Catherine are also encouraged to write poems.) She doesn't dare open the envelope that was just handed to her. The messenger is the mother of one of the girls' classmates. Would you like me to read them to you? Yes, I'd like that, Catherine responds. The mother begins with Elsa's poem. If Maman were a flower, she'd be a white rose, for her purity. If Maman were an animal, she'd be a she-wolf, for the way she protects her young. Catherine is crying from the first line. She cries in silence. *Elle pleure toutes les larmes de son corps:* she cries all the tears in her body, a beautiful cliché. The reader puts her arms around her. She hugs her tight. Catherine asks her to read Violaine's poem. Please, I'm ready to hear it.

> *Maman, maman,*
> *You who love me so,*
> *Why without telling me would you go?*
> *Because now I am hurt,*
> *Hurt that I cannot hold you against my heart.*

She sobs audibly now. Thank you, I get it. I'm going to get through this. I'm going to get through this. I'm going to go home to my girls.

In *Saxifrage*, after the reproductions of Elsa's and Violaine's poems, Catherine writes, again and again, *I have to get through this*, makes stanzas out of the refrain, a kind of mantra. And then, on its own page, floating in white space: *You cannot throw your hands up in defeat when your children hold theirs out to you, hoping to be rescued.*

Catherine did get through this. She held on. She came home to her girls. She held on for almost twenty years.

PART III

MY SISTER TOLD ME ON THE phone from Paris that Maman had died. I was in New York when she said the words: It's over. She's gone. I was waiting for her call. Unable to sit still, I had walked from my Brooklyn apartment on Pacific Street toward the East River. When my cell phone rang, I was on the walkway, between the two bridges that link Brooklyn to Manhattan, facing the gap where the Twin Towers had been. After that call, every time I'd look out the windows of the elevated train, I'd locate the pain of that moment in space, as if it formed part of the shore. For a split second, I could feel the train derailing, I could feel myself plunging into the river, as if plunging into the Acheron. A few months after her death, in a taxi approaching Brooklyn from the Manhattan side, I saw again the section of the shore I'd been staring at as I received the news from Paris; the site had become a sort of memorial. From the taxi I noticed a highway sign indicating the name of the street just off the beltway: Catherine Lane. My city had dedicated a plaque to her, commemorating the instant when she slipped from the world.

I remembered the Twin Towers well, I'd worked next door to them for several years, at a small publishing house where, after the attacks, you had to make your way through the dust and ashes that hung in the air and show ID in order to cross the police checkpoints. I arrived in New York in 1998. I was nineteen then. I'd lasted in Paris exactly one year after finishing high school. I might not have finished school had Maman not been there to wake me, make me shower, drive me to the exams, and tell me that she'd be waiting outside, that she'd drag me back into the examination room by the scruff of my neck if I attempted to duck out. In retrospect I can't remember why I was rebelling, but I can recognize how silly and annoying my rebellions were. A graduate of the Lycée Henri IV—where my philosophy professor had suggested that I represent our school for the national exam in philosophy, an immense privilege, which left me perplexed, wondering if he'd taken a good look at me, me with my neon sarong wrapped around my waist, chain-smoking skinny Vogue cigarettes during recess, the alarming circles under my eyes deepened with kohl, my hair pulled back into a disheveled chignon barely held together by a Bic pen, and to whom I replied No, no thank you— I decided that, unlike my peers, I wouldn't be pursuing any more elite schooling. I hesitated even to enroll in college, but I went because in my country college was free and I had nothing better to do. My last year of living with Maman had been made all the more difficult by the absence of my sister, who had already left; she was studying international law in a prestigious program in London. Maman clearly sensed that my days with her were numbered. We'd spoken about it. She knew that at the end of the school year, after having passed the final exams and obtained my driver's license, I would leave home, it was my turn to go. Maman had managed to survive thanks to us, she'd say, thanks to her girls, she had kept on living in order to fulfill her role as a mother. Her sole reason to live was to remain our mother. What would become of her without us?

My sister and I arrived together in New York, that summer of 1998. My sister was interning at a law firm; I ended up where my father's connections could get me. We settled into a cute one-bedroom, which we rented with Papa's money, in the East Village, a neighbor-hood that at the time was still both run-down and hip, above a café called the Pick Me Up, where we did in fact manage to get ourselves picked up. I fell in love with an older boy, whom Papa approved of because he was erudite, and whom Maman liked because he was offbeat, and I announced to Maman during her visit that I intended to stay in New York. With a solemn tone that indicated the supreme effort she was making, Maman told me that not only did she under-stand my decision, but it seemed to her obviously the right thing to do, that I had to start my own life, that the pain and trauma she had imposed on me were too heavy to bear, that I had to leave and build my life somewhere else, not on the wreckage of her suffering, not on the minefields of our past, but on new ground, in a different city. Maman gave me that much: unconditional love and confidence in my ability to set out on my own. She said: Go, my darling, you're so right to go. And then, it's a good thing there's this boy around, it'll give your father peace of mind. It's a good thing. Don't hesitate to embellish your life here to impress him, assuage his fears, but don't worry, he'll be fine, and I'll have your back no matter what. She ex-plained to my father that it was important for me to leave Paris, to remain in New York, and Papa, never having been one to put his foot down, never having made much use of his paternal authority—for that he would have needed to be more of a presence as a father—let me go with money in my bank account and the assurance of more if I wanted it, money was not a problem, I wouldn't find myself want-ing for money. I broke up with the boyfriend I'd left in Paris, who had been patiently awaiting my return from New York—perhaps I had to devastate him in the way I feared I was devastating my mother; I had to make him do the penance I was avoiding, a displacement of the pain of separation.

I'd been living in New York for eleven years when my sister called me on that summer morning. Pina Bausch had died a few weeks earlier and the next day Merce Cunningham would die, two of the greatest choreographers of the past century, two monumental artists whom my mother and I admired, her death transpiring quietly between theirs. The date of her death is written in red marker on a mirror in Louis Malle's film *The Fire Within*, while Erik Satie's *Gnossiennes* plays in the background. I'd spoken with Maman the night before, meaning the same day for her, given the time difference. She'd seemed sad, but no more than that. She told me that she'd been to dinner at some friend's house. She'd paused for a second during our conversation, and I'd asked if she was okay. It's nothing, she'd answered. It's nothing, my darling. I love you, that's all. Maman had already made her decision when she bought her plane ticket to return to Paris from Dakar, where she'd been living for the past seven years. She'd wanted to die in Paris, perhaps to make things easier for us, or perhaps it was easier for her to die at home, in her homeland.

MAMAN HAD WAITED until nighttime. My sister was returning from Los Angeles, where she'd been sent for work, for the biggest case of her emerging career as a lawyer. Maman had waited until my sister was in the air to disappear, perhaps so they would cross paths in the sky. My sister always needed to speak with our mother before taking off, it was one of her superstitions, she never boarded a plane before speaking with Maman. But this time Maman didn't pick up, her landline kept ringing, and her cell phone went directly to voicemail. Perhaps she stayed over at her friends' house, I had told my sister to reassure her, even though I was just as worried as she was. My sister was certain that her mother would not have gone to sleep without speaking to her, knowing full well that her daughter needed to hear her voice before getting on that plane. Maman didn't have the strength to speak with you, I tried to explain later, when my sister asked again and again why Maman had called me and not her. I reminded her that she was the one who had always fought to keep Maman alive, that she would have heard in Maman's voice that something was off, she would have detected the false note, would have forced Maman to talk to her. What is it, Maman? What's wrong? Talk to me! She would have forced her to fight, as she'd always done, and Maman didn't want that, she had made up her mind, she didn't want to fight anymore.

Maman committed suicide in her Parisian apartment, behind the Musée d'Orsay, the apartment Papa rented for her, where she lived when she wasn't in Dakar, the apartment she'd moved into after we left home. My sister found her body—she had the keys to the apartment—immediately upon landing. I was the first person she called, no, first she called the police, then she called me. She told me: It's over. She's gone. I think I didn't believe her. I said: No! Try again. Call the fire department! Remember, the firemen always revived her. Remember, you have to keep trying! She told me she was sorry, so sorry, she began to sob, and she asked me to come as quickly as possible. Later I was upset with myself for having asked her to make sure nobody touched Maman's body. In shock, I said to her: Please, I beg you, I want to see her just as she is, I want to see her however she is. I'm begging you, don't let them touch her. There was a long silence on the line, the kind of silence that comes before a baby's wail, and then she uttered a piercing cry. I don't think that will be possible. *Chouchou*, please, please don't be angry, I don't think that will be possible. I scolded myself afterward for having tortured her with that demand.We each wanted so much to meet each other's demands, just as we'd always wanted to respond to our mother's demands, no matter how impossible.

One cannot be expected to do the impossible. And yet we had been raised without limits, we had been compelled to redefine the realm of the possible, overcoming all barriers and harboring within ourselves the fantastical power of keeping Maman alive. For so many years we felt we had worked that daily miracle but now we had failed. We had lost her and in losing her we'd lost the very meaning of our lives, the impossible project around which our lives had been structured. No matter how many therapists and solicitous professionals told us that we weren't responsible for her death, that we mustn't feel guilty, that we hadn't killed our mother, my sister and I knew what we knew: it had been our duty to keep her alive.

My sister didn't tell me right away that Maman had killed herself. She told me several hours after I arrived in Paris, on the terrace of a café on the place des Vosges, which we had turned into the headquarters of our mourning. My two closest friends had shown up as reinforcements, their hands tightly gripping mine. My sister said Maman had left a letter. The apparent cause of death was a drug overdose, it could have been an accident. But it wasn't an accident. She had left a letter in Paris, in which she made reference to another letter she had addressed to her lover in their home in Dakar. It was tucked away on a bookshelf, next to copies of *Saxifrage*, *Belle du Seigneur* by Albert Cohen (the book on her bedside table during my entire teenage years), *Tropisms* by Nathalie Sarraute, the child-rearing manual *How to Parent*, and a few other volumes which held some symbolic meaning

THE BOOK OF MOTHER

for her, her version of family portraits. Maman had written to us that she'd put that letter in a book by Stefan Zweig, her favorite author. You can't miss it, her note to us said, its binding is bright red: *Burning Secret*.

The book was hard to miss. A crimson gash in a row of flesh-colored spines. Bright red, the color midwives warn new mothers to look out for in their lochia. The copy I have beside me now is not the one that held the note—I realize that in looking at the publication date in the back of the book—but it is identical. My sister must have saved my mother's copy in one of the innumerable boxes that she refuses to throw away, piled one on top of the other in storage units which she rents exclusively for that purpose. The letter, she keeps in a safe. I had told myself that if I ever wrote the story of Maman's life, I would have to read Zweig. I had purposely avoided him, as if reading him would have been tantamount to involving myself in one of her affairs. *Burning Secret*: Really, Maman, it's a bit much, don't you think? Still, I had to examine this last piece of evidence. I preferred to think that she had addressed her final letter to Zweig, an Austrian Jew, who had killed himself as she had, and at the same age. I preferred to think that her ultimate letter was addressed to another writer rather than to her lover. For how could one of her boyfriends be equal to the burden, or the honor, of receiving her final words? Neither her last lover, nor any other man, could be worthy. And while I was aware of how immature that sentiment was, of how much it betrayed the persistence of my girlish idealization, while I was capable of painting a more nuanced, grown-up portrait of Maman—I could see clearly her failings and her strengths—nevertheless, for me, Maman still occupied a sphere above everyone else; she lived and died on a different plane.

In *Burning Secret*, a preteen boy recovering from a long illness is sent out of the city to convalesce, accompanied by his mother. There, in an old-fashioned pension, a man begins to court her. She's nothing special, according to the story, but the man finds her attractive enough, or he's bored enough, so that she represents a welcome distraction. I can't say what secret I'd imagined this book held, but the secret I discovered in it came as a shock. The child comes to realize that grown-ups are hiding things from him. As he begins to decipher the intrigue unfolding between his mother and the man, he starts to see his mother as a woman for the first time: Maman is a human being after all. Maman has desires that can be distinct from or even in tension with his own.

A mother and a whore. Neither, or both. Ever since she gave birth, Maman had felt stretched between those two impossible poles. Every woman must navigate the injustices and indignities of her gender. Except Maman couldn't manage it, no matter how hard she tried, no matter how she worked her ass off, as she would have put it. In *Saxifrage*, she writes: My ass, my ass, it's not for sale anymore! And I have finally acquired the right to tell you: *Merde*. Indeed, she had every right to tell the men who'd abused her, objectified her, humiliated her, to go fuck themselves. But even as she did so, she couldn't stop performing for men, responding to the relentlessness of their gaze, taking pride in it, how they stared at her ass, her beautiful ass. Until the very end, she was performing, even in this last letter to her lover, which she'd slipped into a book about a mother becoming a whore, a fool, and betraying her child. A mother and a whore, inextricable and reversible terms. Mothers have everything to lose and Maman had lost everything, little by little, starting with herself.

Once a man has found himself, there is nothing in this world that
he can lose. And once he has understood the humanity in himself,
he will understand all human beings.

I wasn't sure I grasped the meaning of this quote from Zweig, which Maman had used as an epigraph for her autobiographical prose poem. I thought she wanted these sentences to make the case for the moral value of what she had written: that all her introspection was in the service of understanding others—or something like that. Strangely, I never thought of looking for the meaning of these words in context, in Zweig's work itself. When I finally read *Burning Secret*, I was stunned to come upon them at the conclusion of another story in the collection, *Fantastic Night*: for me they only really existed in the pages of *Saxifrage*. The sentences float alone on the page at the end of the story, like ghosts, surrounded by white space. Here their meaning seems entirely different. Zweig is making a case for excess, risk, the imperious force of feelings kindled by extremes of sensual pleasure. The story offers his defense of a violent, passionate existence. A person is only truly alive if he or she experiences life as a mystery, rejecting all norms, all conventions. Well, of course. Maman wanted to live that way, or not at all. She preferred drowning to a still, smooth sea. If she'd asked me to suggest an author she might admire, might identify with, I would have chosen Virginia Woolf over Zweig. But she didn't ask for my opinion on this matter, and when I gave her advice of any sort, she'd scream: You live your own life, I'll live mine.

Our roles had been reversed for so long—my sister and I being the comparatively responsible ones—that without realizing it we ended up reproaching Maman for the same ingratitude that she had blamed us for. Each of her birthdays, every Mother's Day, offered her the chance to throw our gifts back into our faces, to complain about our inadequate attention. You didn't exactly break your back planning my birthday, did you? My sister and I would call each other after getting an earful from our mother in Dakar. Did she mention the scarf? Yes, she thinks you chose it: How did your sister manage to pick out such a piece of shit scarf? She didn't say that! I swear, she did. She's impossible. I made a point of saying that there are people out there who simply ignore their mothers' birthdays. I'll let you guess her response. Um, People are morons? Or, There's no shortage of assholes out there? We both knew her lines by heart. More than once, as I tried to halt her ruminations about this or that disastrous aspect of her life, she'd cry out to me, indignant: But, Maman! No, wrong. I was not her mother. That slip of the tongue gave even her pause. Forgive me, my darling, Oh my.

We had to go to the police station, the police to whom my sister had been required to make a statement on the spot, at the scene of the crime. She told me later that she'd hesitated to show them Maman's letter, because she realized that it would be confiscated as evidence. Later she was thankful she'd had the presence of mind not to hide it, though she'd wanted to give it to me to read directly from her own hands, without the cops' fingers staining it. She'd done the right thing, she would have faced serious legal problems otherwise. Killing oneself is considered a criminal act, witnesses must keep their distance, lest they be suspected of murder. Maman would have been depressed to discover all the petty ordeals we had to face. Her apartment had been sealed, the contents of her handbag inventoried. The police inspector made some insulting remarks concerning the number of medications Maman carted around with her. My sister and I had to take turns holding each other back so as not to curse whoever dared to speak against her. Our pain made us imperious, fearless, savage. Maman's body was taken from the apartment to the morgue—my sister had asked if it could wait for my arrival, and had been told no, absolutely not—where an autopsy confirmed the cause of death.

MAMAN HAD BEEN LIVING IN Dakar, she'd made a new life for herself, a life punctuated by stays in Paris to see my sister, to see me when I arranged to have my visits coincide with hers, and to stock up on medicine. Maman ached all over. She'd had two hip-replacement operations, first the left then the right. The last one had been followed by an infection, which had almost killed her. My sister and I had taken turns at her bedside, keeping constant watch over her. In intensive care, visiting hours were so restrictive that we'd hide in a closet during the nurses' rounds to avoid being kicked out. It was an opportunity to prove our devotion to her, as we had as children: there could be no wavering. The doctors said they were impressed by her progress. The nurses were impressed with our commitment. We would have stayed there all night had we been given permission. But we didn't actually ask for permission. One night, she called us, distraught, she was having some kind of panic attack, so we snuck back into the hospital when the guard wasn't looking. We had to give Maman one last kiss. Kneeling on either side of her recumbent body, amid the tangle of IV drips, we brushed her cheeks with our lips, we calmed her. A nurse caught us, and asked if we were half-mad. How did you get in here? Are you out of your minds? Get out immediately! Maman was so proud. My sister snuck back in one last time as I kept watch in the hallway. She promised her that we would be back first thing in the morning. I could hear her whisper, See you tomorrow, Maman. See you tomorrow morning, Maman. Maman! I love you, Maman. I love you madly for my whole life and for all eternity. Maman was a wreck. Her childhood illnesses, her ruthless ballet training, her wild life, drugs, alcohol, cigarettes had ravaged her body. Her face bore the traces of her past and the plastic surgery she'd undergone in order to erase it only made the traumas more apparent.

Maman was destroyed. At sixty, she looked like an old woman: limping, bloated, her silken hair thinning, her hands covered with swollen veins like worms, her skin ashen despite the tan that the African sun lent to her complexion. In Dakar, she could still be beautiful, she was a *toubab*, a beautiful blond *toubab* whose eccentricities might be mistaken for a white woman's foibles, her madness dismissed as cultural difference, her craziness easily forgiven since she always paid in cash. Her alimony—which Papa would pay forever—allowed her to live, if not a luxurious lifestyle, at least a respectable one—she was no pariah, loser, failure, nutjob; in Dakar, she was simply *toubab*. Yes, *toubab* was all right. Her lover was my age, six and a half feet tall. She'd met him while traveling with friends, who had convinced her to open an arts center with them, one of those ideas that was impossible to get out of her head. She was always becoming infatuated with new friends who were plainly opportunists, with whom she'd undertake the most improbable projects: a ranch-cabaret in the Atlas Mountains of Morocco; a chain of French salad bars throughout the United States; a Tunisian pottery business; a home for Romanian immigrants, which could double as an artists' retreat, and maybe also as an orphanage. During her last year in Dakar, she had decided to start an interior decoration business, by commissioning local artisans with whom she designed furniture in Kotibe and Dibetou woods, the African equivalents of mahogany and walnut, only much cheaper, she would make a fortune. She became indignant at the lack of enthusiasm my sister and

I showed for each new project. After a certain point, she became indig-nant a lot. With hindsight, we could trace the darkening of her already tumultuous moods back to a specific moment: it started with the death of Grandma.

Maman had always said that she couldn't wait for that bitch to croak, but when the day finally came she was quiet. She arrived in Montreuil directly from Dakar, wearing dark sunglasses, a cigarette between her lips. The glasses and the cigarette never left her on this trip. Maman had wanted to see her mother in the funeral parlor be-fore the coffin was closed. She had wanted to speak to her alone. She placed a letter beside the body; I didn't ask her about its contents, but she told me anyway. She said she'd written to her mother that she forgave her, that she wanted her to go in peace. Grandma had asked to be cremated. We fulfilled her wishes at the crematorium of Montfermeil, an awful place; Maman's face reflected, eloquently, her repulsion. On the way to the so-called Garden of Remembrance, where her ashes would be scattered, where, the undertaker explained, we'd have the chance to reflect on our grandmother's life, Maman decided to call her father. My sister and I knew she was still in touch with him. She told us then that he too was in bad shape, on the brink of death. She asked us if we wanted to speak with him. Our only response was to look at her in horror. And then, after the cremation, she turned to us and said: You little bitches, don't you even think of dumping me in Montfermeil! Fuck, I've never seen such a sordid place! She wanted her ashes to be scattered at sea, from the Pointe des Almadies in Dakar. Right, sure, we said sarcastically, assuming she was joking. Yes, in a pirogue with djembe players, and everyone wear-ing boubous. She was serious. Make it a party! We were to turn her absence into a celebration of her presence, not something dumb and depressing, a party, a happy occasion. A big party with everyone you love, she said. Invite all your friends, everyone. Have a huge party and remember me.

I was responsible for calling Maman's lover with the news of her suicide, and for telling him about the letter, where it could be found. I was chosen by default, because I was the only one who had met him, the only one to have gone to see firsthand Maman's life in Dakar. First he screamed, then he broke into tears. He asked me if he could see her one last time. He could only see her here, in France, in Paris. We had to find a way to get him here, we had to get a visa for him in time, while Maman still had a body. We had to do the impossible, but my sister and I were capable of that; nothing was impossible where Maman was concerned, except for saving her. In less than a week we had mobilized the Ministry of Foreign Affairs and the French consulate in Dakar. In less than a week he was in the air.

The summer after Grandma's death, with the money she'd left behind, we bought a little apartment in a handsome Haussmannian building, a Parisian pied-à-terre for Maman and me. It faced the Seine, in front of the Pavillon de l'Arsenal, with a view of the bridge, and on the opposite bank, the train station, Gare d'Austerlitz, and the Jardin des Plantes. When I stood there beside my mother and took in the panorama of my childhood city, my memories followed the shapes of buildings, connecting the different moments of my youth. My past was imprinted on the streets. And just as New York forms part of the collective imagination through film, so that many of its streets are familiar to those who have never visited the city, so Paris is layered over with correspondences from its literary history, a synesthetic maze of scenes and rhymes. And thus, all the rainy mornings of my adolescence, the sky weighed like a lid thanks to Baudelaire's alexandrine; Papa's favorite restaurant shared an address with one of Balzac's famous heroes; I measured my steps against Villon's verses, although at least once I twisted my ankle on the cobblestones. After the year 2000, the Eiffel Tower was illuminated at dusk. Watching the Left Bank sparkle, I thought of all the artists and thinkers who made Saint-Germain famous. But this literary history coexisted with or was supplanted by personal associations: our little dog leaping from the car window in order to pee on the lawn of the Invalides, a reception I had to attend as a child in one of the ministerial buildings behind the place du Palais-Bourbon, where my tights were itchy, my hair was pulled back too tight, I was hot, Maman kept scolding me—specific, individual memories, beneath the threshold of official history. As I looked on at the Gare d'Austerlitz, I thought of Maman boarding the Corail train, carrying bundles of bills hidden in her pants, which led me to recall a book of Sebald's which I'd read one winter in a café on the Lower East Side. Then my reverie broke against a nondescript brick building, right in front of our apartment. I asked Maman if she knew what it was. She came closer to the window, and blowing her cigarette smoke in my face, she said: No idea.

Papa would have known. Papa had often been forced to enter the building to identify members of his cursed tribe. That building was the morgue, the place where I saw Maman for the last time, the place where we had to say goodbye. I had wanted to see her as soon as I'd landed. To see her, at all costs to see her. But I had been forced to wait for the results of the autopsy, and only after six days was I allowed to see her body. I left my sister's house, where I was staying, not recognizing the address where I was going. When I found myself before the building I knew so well, I felt dizzy. It seemed unbelievable, implausible— like something out of a novel. I wasn't sure I could keep myself from collapsing when I faced Maman's body. The dead in this morgue are the victims of murders or accidents, mostly violent accidents, some are children who have burned to death or been riddled with bullets, whose wrecked bodies their parents must come in to identify. Later I would read a beautiful book, *The House of Death*, written by the director of this limbo. I don't know if the author was the woman who received me that day. I recall that she was elegant, not a hair out of place, that she wore makeup and a diamond ring. She looked into my eyes with compassion and with candor. She took my hand as she told me where we were going, she explained what I was about to see, how Maman would be presented to me, that we would see her from behind glass. I was crying now, and she pressed my hand with the gentleness of a loved one. I won't be able to touch her? We're going to go together, she said to me, then we'll look at her together from behind the glass, and maybe, maybe we can make an exception, maybe you can touch her, but you must help me, you must do as I say. I would have followed her into the depths of Hell, I would have followed her blindly, never breaking her rules. Her voice, her kindness, her calm and reverent manner, inspired in me absolute confidence. This woman was the guide who made it possible for me to kiss the forehead of my dead mother. She stayed by my side, she gave me permission and the courage to do it. She seems at peace, the woman said to me. It was true. It was also true that her features had begun to collapse, her lower eyelids had started to sink. She was covered with a sheet up to her neck. May I look at her feet? I asked, barely managed to speak. No, I couldn't look at her feet, they were too far along in necrosis. The woman explained the autopsy, she explained what the sheet hid, Maman's swollen body. I tried not to cry because I feared my tears might make the woman remove me from the room, but I could no longer hold them back. Maman's feet, their magnificent arches, her feet were dead too.

I hadn't gotten married, not even to obtain the papers that would have allowed me to live legally in the United States. I'd begun working at nineteen, continuing my college degree in literature by correspondence. I completed my master's; I went back to pass my exams at the end of the school year, I turned in my homework and my essays on time, I had been a pretty good student, all in all. Somehow I'd landed a job in a publishing house which arranged a work visa for me and offered me responsibilities that far outstretched my nonexistent experience and ostensible competencies. I would learn, my boss had insisted when I admitted my anxiety: *You'll learn.* And in fact I did learn, I acquired the knowledge and connections that I had lacked, and a green card, without Papa pulling any strings and without getting married, and I took a certain pride in that. I lived for six years with the man whom I'd met when I arrived, and then we separated, as might have been expected, perhaps rather later than might have been expected, and I fell in love, and I fell in love again.

My boyfriend at the time of Maman's death had found a nice apartment in Brooklyn for us; we'd moved a few months before I received my sister's call. He and I had known each other for a long time, we'd been involved on and off over the years. Is he *the one*, is it for keeps this time? Maman had asked me in one of our last conversations. What is it with this old-school question, darling Maman? Are you worried about your daughter getting hitched? Because it all worked out so well for you, did it, getting married? Hey, hey, that's enough! I never said I was a role model, she argued. And I was just asking, I'm not forcing you into anything. I told her that she was my mother, and that was a role model enough for me. The conversation ended there, we didn't get into a fight, we were just talking, we debated the value of marriage in our time, feminism, the perpetual disparities of gender. This dialogue was the sign that everything was all right, that all would be for the best: Maman was checking in on me, Maman remembered the circumstances of my life, Maman was even asking me about the future.

THE FUNERAL IN PARIS HAD to be planned. But one afternoon, sitting in the café we visited when we weren't at the ministry or the morgue or the funeral parlor, we looked at each other and, without pronouncing a single word, agreed: we would have to go to Dakar. We would leave right after the cremation at Père-Lachaise—we had promised, not Montfermeil; we would take our partners, our dearest friends, those who at all times, from childhood on, had always come to our rescue during the worst dramas of our life. And so eight of us would eventually leave for Dakar with Maman's ashes in our luggage. Come on, you can't be serious, our friends had said when we first informed them of our plans. Would we joke about such a thing? We had learned from Maman's lover that cremation was illegal in Senegal, and from the funeral parlor that it was illegal to scatter human ashes in the wild. We didn't go to the trouble of finding out whether it was legal to transport ashes abroad, in this case, to Senegal: we imagined the answer would have been no. We had a strategy for dealing with this, but first we had to take care of the funeral in Paris.

Our pain had abolished all sense of proportion, all restraint—we were shameless, feral. As long as we were still working on Maman's behalf, attempting to carry out her wishes in death, we were in some sense keeping her alive, and we would have been capable of coming to blows, we could have hit, scratched, or bitten any person who tried to stand in the way of our plans. The managers of Père-Lachaise wanted to put us in a lousy little room in the basement, but that wouldn't do, we made it clear that we couldn't care less about their logistical problems and reservations, and eventually we won the day, how could they defend themselves against our mixture of hysteria and obstinacy? We wanted the main chapel with a grand piano. Without waiting for confirmation that it would in fact be put at our disposal, we went in search of a pianist. We wanted him to be able to play the *Moonlight* Sonata and the *Farewell Waltz* by Chopin. One of the friends who never left our sides in those days—a kind of support group had formed, one we'd done nothing to organize—looked at us appalled. Okay, what's next? Then we'll all go hang ourselves? After a moment of silence, we burst out laughing. Between tears, rivers of tears, and drunkenness—rosé, torrents of champagne, because we'd started in on champagne: To Maman!—we'd laugh to feel human again. We'd laugh to return, wittingly or not, to the land of the living. Our friends kept us from complete despair. You're going through Hell, they seemed to say, but you're not going to stay there, we're going to get you out of there, we're here for you, hold on to us, hold on.

The day of the funeral, Papa had roses delivered; we'd asked for white roses. We turned the room into a stage—for her last act, her final performance, Maman in her coffin had to be sublime. We wanted the room to resemble a rose garden, we had put arches in place, and fake espaliers made of this and that, pyramids of white roses, only white roses, hundreds of white roses. We brought in a huge portrait of Maman that an artist friend of Papa had composed when they were still together, a charcoal-and-chalk drawing in black and white, which had hung over the piano when we were growing up. She loved that portrait, she recognized herself in it, but I found it too smooth, too literal, because it showed only her beauty. My sister and I were the only ones to speak. Papa, the great orator, wasn't around. Everyone in Paris was on vacation at the beginning of August, and that included Papa, whom an insignificant accident prevented from making the round trip from his house in Brittany. Only our friends had given up their plans to be there with us. As for Maman, she no longer had any friends. She'd worn them all out, no one could stand it any longer, not even Nini, her lifelong childhood friend, her closest and dearest. My sister and I had called her to tell her that Maman had died. She seemed mostly sorry for us. She wouldn't be coming to Père-Lachaise, she had to leave for a trip with her son and newborn granddaughter. We couldn't get over it. You're not coming to her funeral? We were incredulous, we were distraught. No. It was really too late, she'd put up with too much from her. She'd already mourned her, in advance of her death.

Our Senegalese stepfather still hadn't seen his wife's remains. They had married in the Senegalese tradition, to please his family, observant Muslims for whom their living in sin was inconceivable. Maman had changed her name a seventh time. For the occasion, she wore a moussor and a ring of gris-gris around her neck, her soon-to-be relations—grandmother, sisters, cousins, and neighbors—kept her company on the big day. The bride and groom sealed their union in front of a marabout; after a meal of *thieboudienne*, they were left alone to consummate it. They'd gotten married almost right after meeting in order to be able to live together, and, some months before her death, Maman had expressed a desire for us all to get together—my sister and I, our friends, her new family in Dakar, her lover who was our age—in order to make their union official to us, too. She'd abandoned the plan for reasons that were never made clear; I had the feeling that her marriage was already floundering. She was impossible, especially during periods of crisis; her pain, both physical and mental, could make her so difficult. She hurt everywhere, her belly, her lungs, her hips, her soul. She was in terrible pain, a pain which none of us, her caretakers, had ever fully understood.

Before they closed the coffin, before we got into the hearse to drive to Père-Lachaise, we went to see her for the last time, her new husband, my sister, and I. We went by Maman's apartment, her apartment which smelled of piss, her bed soaked with what had issued from her body when she'd died. The apartment would have to be cleaned, her effects sorted, but we had a few weeks to do that, please, not everything at once. We found unexpected letters there, letters that Papa had sent her after my sister's birth. They chronicled Maman's serious postpartum depression. And they mentioned Dakar. According to the telegrams, she had stayed at the Méridien, with a woman whom we had heard a lot about, but whom we had never really known. We found her Saint Laurent blouses, clothing which reminded us of the years of her marriage with Papa. There was one that was very loose fitting, a deep purple ruffled blouse, perhaps the one she'd worn on her wedding day, when she was pregnant with me. I decided to wear it to the funeral. I had prepared a speech. I had resolved not to cry.

For this last trip from the morgue to Père-Lachaise, we arrived with armfuls of white rose petals, with which we had planned to fill the coffin. My sister, who hadn't seen our mother since she'd discovered her body, found her very changed. We had picked out some clothing at her apartment, unassuming clothing. Her husband had written her a letter, which he insisted on showing us before placing it on the bosom of the deceased. He had signed it with a drop of his blood, and despite my own arms being full of flowers, I found the gesture a little extreme, a little childish. You self-righteous little shit, I heard Maman say to me. Self-righteous little shit! I was startled by my sister's grieving. She covered the collapsing face of our mother with tears and kisses. She began to scatter the petals all around her body, wildly, compulsively. We had asked that Maman's hands be uncovered and placed on her torso, but the undertaker had warned us that it was unlikely they would be in any state to be displayed. Her corpse was twelve days old, twelve days is a long time for a cadaver. My sister wanted to see, she tried to raise the sheet, she loosened the hem of Maman's blouse, pulling on it, the way a nursing child might undress her mother in public; beside her, I softly begged her to stop. She stopped cold when she saw what was under the clothes. Shock gave way to a strange, childlike expression of pouting, the same distraught face she made as a little girl when she tried to get over Maman's nonsense. The coffin was closed. And after the sonata and the waltz and our speeches in the chapel of Père-Lachaise, the wooden coffin was burned in a fire out of which emerged a marble urn filled with ashes.

MY SISTER AND I WERE the same age as Maman when she'd had us: thirty and thirty-two years old, respectively. She had brought us to that point, to the age when she herself had become a mother, she had succeeded in giving us that. Now we were side by side, the sole survivors; it fell to us to publicize the news of her death in the obituary column. Her mother was dead, and at last her father was, too. We were adults, we were grown women, but finding ourselves orphans made us feel like children again, children in need of protection. It was only at that moment that I began to take the full measure of the psychological catastrophe that the death of Maman's parents had been for her. The dam had burst. She gave herself permission to leave for good after them. The day of her cremation, my sister and I constantly clutched each other's hands, as if we were clutching a branch extending over an abyss. We searched for other supports among the company in that solemn room where we were honoring her corpse. I no longer had the strength of mind to forgive Papa for his absence. He should have found a way to be among us, to tell us that she had been his love, too, that he had loved her so and would always love her, that he shared our sorrow.

In my sister's kitchen, we bent over the urn to inspect the ashes. We were hoping not to find any lumps. Using spoons, we carefully divided the contents into little plastic bags, these ashes that couldn't help but remind us of the cigarette butts we'd emptied into garbage bags throughout our childhood. Eight bags which we hid in tin cans full of loose tea leaves in order to get through Senegalese customs. One box per person.

I flew to Dakar in advance of my sister, with my boyfriend and my friends, to scout things out. My sister and I had decided to take separate flights because of the ashes; maybe if one portion of Maman's ashes were confiscated, another would get through. Maman's house, which I was seeing for the first time, resembled a cenotaph. She'd moved there just a short while earlier, and it was still under construction, because the work she'd wanted to have done had been so extravagant that she'd needed more money to continue it, money which we—my sister and I, Papa—had refused to give her. She'd gotten another dog, a detail I'd forgotten until I arrived before her gate on a dirt road. She lived in Yoff, in a working-class neighborhood by the sea, a district to the north of Dakar, on the way to the airport, at the edge of a huge beach with long, rolling swells that tossed up enormous quantities of detritus and, on more than one occasion, a child who had been snatched by the undertow and had perished in the waves. No one would have thought of walking a dog on that beach. Such an animal was obviously unfit for such a setting. Maman had gone completely mad, and the fact that she had chosen to adopt a giant German shepherd, purebred and as tall as a pony, in a city whose climate and landscape were absurdly ill-suited to him, and in the heart of a neighborhood populated by Muslims, who were distressed by the beast, was more proof that she had completely lost it. Maman must have negotiated a lot with her companion for him to have agreed to shelter a dog in their house. As soon as I arrived, he and I agreed: *khalas* the dog. We sent it to a farm in the countryside.

The first morning, I went looking in the kitchen cupboards for coffee. I found a family-size box of Nescafé, the instant coffee I considered undrinkable but which Maman always preferred to the espresso I served her at my house, which she dismissed as an affectation, and to which she made me add cold water. I pulled out a plastic chair to go sit on the terrace, still under construction. I took a sip of coffee, and this time it tasted like Maman's lips. I began to weep. The more I cried, the more I told myself that Maman would have slapped me if she'd seen me in such a state; I could hear her upbraiding me, and as I heard her voice, I cried even more. I couldn't keep the memories from breaking over me in waves. Suddenly I noticed the bell hanging on the exterior wall, under the porch, the bronze bell from Corrèze that she rang when it was time to sit down to lunch or dinner. Oh god, the bell! Corrèze! Only Maman would think of re-creating Corrèze in Dakar. Only Maman. She was impossible. She was irreplaceable.

My sister and her delegation arrived four days after me, after their flight was delayed by several hours, in the dead of night. None of the luggage had been lost, all eight boxes were safe. That's what mattered most. The evening of their arrival, the monsoon dumped its tropical rain, heavy with dust and pollution, onto the tarmac. I was waiting in the car, my head pressed against the window, watching a lake of black ink form all around the terminal. Despite the late hour, the Léopold Sédar Senghor airport was swarming with people. Crowds quickly gathered under the makeshift awnings. I drew little crosses on the fogged window, tears running down my cheeks like the rivulets on the glass. I saw my sister crossing the airport's parking lot, shielded by her handbag in place of an umbrella, her friends in tow, Maman's husband, her widower, leading the way, the water halfway up his calves. She'd scarcely slammed the car door when my sister started yelling at me, as if I were responsible for Maman moving to Dakar, as if I controlled the rainy season. Why the fuck did she come to Africa, my sister demanded. Did you take your Malarone? I'm serious, don't fuck around, all we need now is to go home with malaria! My sister was even more of a hypochondriac than Papa.

We spent the evening at Maman's house, which smelled like wet dog, listening to the sounds of children laughing or crying in the street, the noise of the generator, the humming of the fan overhead, except for when the power went out, and the incessant buzzing of mosquitoes, which kept everyone on edge. My sister had reserved rooms for herself and her friends at the Méridien des Almadies, near where we would scatter Maman's ashes into the sea. During the first years of her time in Dakar, Maman spent her afternoons beside the hotel pool with her Senegalese friends, sipping multicolored cocktails decorated with little paper umbrellas. The Almadies neighborhood was her favorite, not that she would have wanted to live there, the houses were too *toubab*, ritzy and flashy, but she loved the Méridien and its outdoor bar and restaurant, which faced the sea. It was there, on that little length of beach, her husband told us, that she liked to go admire the sunset, there where she wanted her ashes to be scattered. During my first visit, two years earlier, he'd brought me there for a drink. Imitating the tone of a tourist guide, he had said to me: This is the westernmost point of the entire African continent. He'd laughed and added: If you look closely, you might even see New York!

On the appointed day, each of us—regardless of gender—selected one of the printed, brightly colored outfits found in the Senegalese wing of Maman's closet. Her closest local friends had joined us and they knotted scarves on our heads. We proceeded through the streets in our African dress, holding transparent plastic bags showing boxes of Kusmi tea. Djembe players had set up on the beach with their drums. A pirogue pilot was waiting for us. We started to get on the boat, but since it quickly became clear that we couldn't all fit, some of our party volunteered to stay on the shore. One of my friends who would stay behind tore off a bit of her scarf for Maman. There were still too many of us in this canoe. We were soon soaked. The ashes might turn to mud before we could scatter them. About a hundred yards off the shore, we stopped. I would have liked to say a prayer, but my sister and I didn't know how to pray. We only knew how to beg. We looked at one another, and with trembling hands we emptied the boxes, one after the other, from the boat that was now violently pitching back and forth, the wind blowing ashes back at us, where they stuck to our wet eyelashes, faces, hands, but we kept at it, until the boxes were empty. And then I let go of the piece of fabric that my friend had given me, and my sister asked me why I was throwing an old rag into the sea. For no reason, I said to her; I couldn't explain. Then the pilot tried to restart the motor, but it was flooded. We had been tossed well beyond the inlet. The shore was no longer visible. We were surrounded by rocks, the waves were carrying us rapidly toward them. Please, Maman, not that, my sister exclaimed. Now we're all going to die, thanks to her crazy ideas! But the motor started up again. Relieved, we caught our breath, then started to laugh, to giggle like two little girls; without saying it, we knew perfectly well, both of us, that it was yet another one of Maman's nasty jokes. Hey, what's with the long faces! Have a little fun, for fuck's sake. I said that I wanted it to be a party!

We spent the next few days going through her things, changing the title deed on her car, which she had wanted to leave to her husband, with a strike-through, the addition of the words *given to*, and her signature. Maman's bank account was in the red, as had been the case ever since we were old enough to know what money was. In the room that served as her office, we found mounds of little papers on which were scribbled notes that were as obscure as they were evocative: we had both of us seen Maman tirelessly occupied with writing things, using the same felt-tipped, green Pentel pen on the same gridded, orange Rhodia notepad. Among the hundreds of loose sheets of paper on which were scrawled numbers, philosophical musings, incomplete sentences, names, statements, abstract or figurative drawings, we also found photographs of her father whom we didn't know had visited her in Dakar, and postcards from him and people unknown to us. Maman had lived far away from us in this African capital, she had made a life for herself that wasn't ours, that was none of our business. As long as she was well, as long as she seemed to be getting along, we didn't bother her, we didn't ask questions about her daily life or whom she saw: I'm big enough to look after myself, as far as I know! Will you ever stop asking me to justify my every move! Maman is a big girl, she can do as she likes with her ass and her dough with sixty-two years under her belt; even if it was Papa's dough, she'd certainly earned it. She had warned us that she would decide when it was time to go, she had no intention of finishing her life in a wheelchair or senile, no, she would leave with dignity, she would leave us, she would take her leave, like a queen. We combed through her notebooks, we read every word as if searching for a secret message, a different explanation than the one she had offered us in her letter: I've had enough, I'm through. We couldn't accept this. How could a mother say to her daughters that she'd had enough? It was never enough, she had set a bad example, we were just as excessive as she was, we wanted more, and more, and more, we were addicts, we were addicted to her presence. We were ingrates because we were her children, even at thirty and thirty-two years old, we were her baby girls, her darling adored daughters, or her little bitches if she preferred; babies or bitches, we couldn't let her go. My tears would finally bring me back to the other side of the Atlantic, of the Acheron. I was certain, at least, that my sobs would never cease, that I would remain attached to her in grief, no matter where I traveled, grief would never leave me.

In one of Maman's desk drawers, which I opened late at night, I found an old, unused envelope, a new missive from the past. It wasn't sealed, and I raised the flap without thinking of her privacy—I felt the dead had nothing more to hide. Slowly, I pulled out a sheet of ruled paper, with light blue and pink lines. It was folded in half. I opened it. I recognized my schoolgirl script. I couldn't read the words, which all ran together, blurred by my tears. I didn't need to read them, I knew these words by heart, the way people of faith know prayers:

Maman, maman,
You who love me so,
Why without telling me would you go?
Because now I am hurt,
Hurt that I cannot hold you against my heart.
What have I done for you to go,
Go without even a note?
I hope that this was your choice.
But how would I know
Whether you feel joy or sorrow?
Maybe you are starting to grow
Old and sleepless from being alone?
My deepest desire is to express to you
How deeply I love you!

ACKNOWLEDGMENTS

THANK YOU TO MY EDITOR, Valerie Steiker, for her faith in my work; to Nan Graham, for her extraordinary support, and for giving the book its title; to Sarah Goldberg and the wonderful team at Scribner; to Lennie Goodings at Virago; to my agent, Mark Kessler, and Susanna Lea for ushering *Fugitive parce que reine* into the world; to Leslie Camhi for her translation; to my French editor, Maud Simonnot, for her rigor and her sensibility; to my makeshift family: Lauren, Ael, Raphaëla, Camille, Lili; to Frédéric for his presence; and to the inimitable Seven Stories crew, Jill Schoolman, Tania Ketenjian, and Dan Simon.

Thank you to my sister, Elsa, for embracing my project unconditionally.

Three years ago, Jamie Dowd and I opened The Floor, a movement studio and community space in Brooklyn. It has been a haven. I'm indebted to Jamie for her strength and vision.

This novel is the result of my conversations with Ben Lerner.

Tom, George, and Sissi: I love you.

ABOUT THE AUTHOR

Violaine Huisman was born in Paris in 1979 and has lived in New York for twenty years. She ran the Brooklyn Academy of Music's literary series and has organized arts festivals across the city. Originally published by Gallimard as *Fugitive parce que reine*, *The Book of Mother*, her debut novel, was awarded the Prix Françoise Sagan and the Prix Marie Claire, among other prizes.

Leslie Camhi is a New York–based essayist and cultural journalist who writes for *The New York Times*, *Vogue*, and other publications. *The Book of Mother* is her first book-length translation.